DARK DESIRES

EFFIE CAMPBELL

Enjoy diving into this spice-fest with Logan and Valentina

love Effie Campbell

DARK ROMANCE AUTHOR
Effie Campbell

For all the readers who crave a man who's older, hotter and willing to enthusiastically share you with all of his friends as he calls you their best little cock-taker...

This one's for you.

WARNINGS

This book contains spicy content, depictions of death and sexual assault (not between the main characters). There is discussion of grooming and SA from childhood (not the MC's and not depicted). There is violence toward numerous characters as part of the plot, but not toward each other.

It is also written in the UK, and I use British English for spelling. If you are from elsewhere - forgive me! Remember that these are hot Scots and just imagine it in their voices, it makes it all better.

CHAPTER ONE

VALENTINA

Rain battered down onto my head as I punched the code into the door. Smiling as it opened beneath my hands and Muhammed, the doorman, ushered me inside.

'Evening, Miss,' he said, the crinkles surrounding his eyes deepening as he set me with a grin.

'I've lived here for four years. You can call me Valentina.' We had the same conversation periodically, but he was ever the professional.

'Yes, Miss Valentina.'

I shook my head and smiled as I stood dripping rain all over the entryway.

'Busy night?' I asked, taking off my raincoat and folding it over my arm.

'Nothing crazy happening so far. Plenty of time to catch up on my reading.'

'Oh, that reminds me!' I said, pushing my coat under one arm as I rooted through my bag. 'I saw this one in the bookshop earlier and thought you might like it.'

I held out the brown paper package containing the book I picked up for him. He lowered his eyes to the package as we completed our usual dance around it.

'You shouldn't have...' he started.

'It's nothing much, it was in the second hand pile.'

'Well, if it needs a good home.'

'Precisely!'

I smiled as he took the book, eagerly peeping into the package.

'You haven't read it, have you?' I shifted on my feet, my heels making my arches ache after a long day of shopping and doing life admin.

'I haven't! And it's by Greene too. You're a wee star, Miss. Thank you.'

A thread of satisfaction flowed through me at his pleasure. Gifting him a book was a simple thing, but even though he was my doorman with a family of his own, I was a sucker for making people happy, especially older men. Classic case of missing my father growing up, I supposed. I'd never even had the chance to meet him. He put a baby in my mother, then a drunk driver removed him from existence before he even knew I existed.

It's why people thought I cammed. Classic Daddy issues. Maybe it was a part of it, but mostly it was because I loved sex and all things smutty, but didn't want to invite a string of guys into my life who only ever disappointed me. Cam girl me was a fantasy, and I could play with the dangerous without it ever really being harmful to me.

'Right, off you go upstairs and get yourself dry. You'll catch your death if you stand here soaked.' Muhammed walked me to the lift, pressing the button to call it down before ushering me inside.

'You just want me to leave so you can get back to your books,' I said with a false pout.

'Can't blame me. He's about to confront the killer.'

'Well, in that case, I'll leave you to it.' I stepped into the lift and gave him a wave.

A few moments later, the lift pinged on the 5th floor, and the doors opened out onto the small corridor which held four flats. Mine with my roommate Lara, old Mrs Graham's with her rowdy Jack Russell, Ivor, the one owned by an American who had never visited it as far as we knew, that sat at the end of the corridor, and our neighbour, Tim's.

Tim had a knack for needing to put the bins out or collect mail right as I came home. I swore he must spend as much time in the corridor as he did in his flat.

He was sweet, but intense.

Sure enough, he was watering the plants that he kept outside his door as I exited the lift.

'Evening, M'lady.'

Honestly, who says M'lady? What was he, a knight?

'Hi, Tim.'

I stood awkwardly in the corridor as I pulled my key out of my bag.

'Lovely evening for ducks.'

He was only my age as far as I could tell, mid twenties maximum, but he spoke like he was seventy.

I smiled tightly. 'Sure is. Tipping it down out there.'

'Good for the grass.' He chuckled to himself while keeping his eyes fixed on me.

'Yeah,' I replied, toying with the key in my hand as I glanced at my door. We didn't even have grass. My flat was in Glasgow city centre and entirely surrounded by pavement. 'I should go get some dinner. Lara will be waiting.'

He went back to spraying his plants with the tiny spritz bottle with a nod. 'I'll be seeing you.'

Such a freaking weird guy. Nice enough, but talking to him always made me second guess myself.

Letting myself into my flat, I breathed a sigh of relief when I latched the door behind me before hanging up my wet coat and taking off my shoes. Flexing my sore feet against the cold tile was glorious.

'Hey, it's just me,' I called out as I made my way through the spacious flat and into the kitchen, taking a peek into the slow cooker which stood bubbling on the counter. My mother would call it a crime to cook lasagne in there, but it was bloody delicious and ready when I walked in the door. Who can argue with that?

Moments later, Lara popped her head out of her room and grinned. 'Welcome home. Was your little love waiting outside for you?'

'Ugh, don't call him that.'

'It's true though, he practically has those big cartoon heart eyes for you.'

'Shut up.' I nudged her as she walked into the kitchen area, grabbing two glasses and topping them up with a crisp white wine. She put them on the coffee table as I served up the lasagne and sat next to her on the sofa.

It should have been weird that she wore a nurse's outfit, but after living together for two years, and both of us camming from home, there was little we hadn't seen - or heard - from one another. Just another part of the job.

'How's it going tonight? Busy?' I asked between mouthfuls of food as Lara flicked on a reality show she loved. It wasn't my thing, but I could appreciate the toned, buff men and women who loitered around in bikinis.

'Surprisingly busy. You should hop on for a bit after dinner.'

'With my pasta belly? No one wants to see that.'

We looked at each other before laughing. We both knew that the guys rarely gave a darn about a bit of bloat as long as you said the right things and flashed some skin.

'Do you want to tag-team tonight?' Lara asked.

Occasionally we'd team up to get the punters ravenous. It always brought out a few big tippers. But what I actually wanted to do was curl up in bed and finish the scarf I was knitting.

'Not that I don't love you, but I think I'll just pop on for a quick half an hour until I hit my evening goal and then bow out. I don't think I have the energy for more excitement than that tonight.'

'You just hate my vagina. It's okay. I won't take it personally.' Lara's face pulled into a mock cry as I laughed.

'It's as good a vagina as I ever met,' I said with a wink.

'I know you just prefer a big slice of man meat. How can a girl compete with that?'

'You're pretty partial to the special sausage yourself, if I remember correctly.' I raised my eyebrows before waggling them at her.

'It is pretty addictive.'

'Truth,' I agreed, taking a sip of my wine before finishing my food while watching the hotties fumble under a duvet on the TV.

My laptop hummed to life as I sat on my bed in a pink, frilled lingerie set. I'd pulled my dark hair back over one shoulder and put on a full face of makeup, loving going all out even if it was only for a short time. I swore half of my income went on makeup while the other half went on pretty clothes. Well, the amount I allowed myself as spending money, anyway. Growing up with little while related to incredibly wealthy people had left me with a fierce need to have a nest egg. Money was power, and I didn't want to need help from anyone financially. My family's money came with chains, and I wasn't for being tied down. Not like that, at least.

Pulling up the 'Primal Pretties' site, I sat back on my bed and waited as my open chat filled up.

'Evening, beautiful.'

'You've got too many clothes on.'

'Come on, slut, show us your pussy.'

'How's u?'

Message after message popped up, and I typed out replies to most of them, purposefully ignoring the rude ones. I'd learned early on that they were looking for a rise. As long as they were in the chat, I've made some money, so I consoled myself by taking their site credits and utterly ignoring them. The site was for people with kinks that veered toward the more extreme, and it tended to attract a few total weirdos. Not the usual kinky guys and girls, but those who were looking to scare and provoke the women who cammed. I reported them every time and thankfully the female owner of the site took reports seriously. No one should feel unsafe at work, not even in more risque jobs.

I smiled as one of my regulars stood out among the crowd. The guy was super into feet and had probably stumbled onto the wrong site, but happily kept coming back as long as I stretched my legs toward the camera without shoes on. Wriggling my stocking clad toes had him sending a tip that almost filled half of my nightly goal.

'Thank you, Sir,' I said, which sent the guys into a tumble of messages. Sir, Daddy, Master, hell even God. They went crazy for it. So did I, if I was being honest. I'd only had a handful of lacklustre kinky sex experiences, most guys saying they were into choking, or rough sex, but actually just willing to say anything to get their dick wet. Once the pants were off, they all turned into the same little jack rabbits with one goal in mind. Nutting.

At least with the camming they were often willing to fall into the fantasy a bit more, so I could get off at least imagining that it was real. What it would be like to be with someone who actually wanted to drag me over his knee, or punish me with a hard cock in front of his friends for bratting out.

A girl could dream, right?

It's why I mooned over the older guys,. Guys my age - twenty two - were too unsure in themselves to take the lead. I'm sure some, somewhere could, but all the ones I'd tried out were all bluster, no substance.

A request for a private chat popped up after a few minutes and I said goodbye to the open chat as I accepted it. Private chats were where the big bucks were.

'Hi,' I said, reading the screen as I clicked on his profile quickly. Breathplay lover, Dom, Doesn't like brats. Shame. Time for the good girl act. 'How are you?'

'Good. I like you in pink.'

'Thank you....'

'Master, call me Master.'

His video clicked on and showed me a stained t-shirt stretched over a large belly, and a small, hard cock already being tugged furiously.

I sighed as I sat up on my knees, toying with my hair. 'Yes, Master.'

He groaned, and I knew it wouldn't be a very long call, and definitely not one that I'd be able to dip into fantasyland for.

'Get your tits out, girl, and your pussy. I bet you're so wet for me.'

Dry as a flipping desert.

'Oh yes, Master, I'm so wet. I've been waiting for you.'

'Yes, you fucking have.' He fisted his dick and gave it a furious tug.

I removed my bra and dropped it onto the bed, sliding my hands down over my nipples to get them to stand to attention. Then the panties, leaving me in nothing but my frilly pink garter belt and stockings.

'Fuck, I want to bite your little tits,' he said as I ran my fingers past my clit, trying to elicit some sort of fun out of it. Some nights were just duds. And Mr. Stained Tee wasn't doing anything for me.

'Oh, Master, I'd love to feel your teeth on my tits. Would you be ever so rough?'

'I'd fucking destroy that snatch of yours.'

Snatch. Ugh.

'Tell me what you'd do...' I hoped he was a talker, that made it easier. A lot of the guys loved to hear their own voices.

'I'd fuck that dirty little snatch until you begged me to stop.'

I moaned as I pushed two fingers inside myself, arching my back like I was having the best time. Should have grabbed the lube, not nearly wet enough for it.

'Then I'd stuff my cock into that ass and fill it up with cum. I bet you'd cry.'

'I would Master, it hurts so bad being fucked there.'

'But you deserve it for being such a little whore, spreading your legs for anyone who will open their wallet.'

It stung a bit, because it was true. I loved my job, and I didn't feel ashamed about it most of the time. But when guys looked down on me for it, it still hit a spot inside that I couldn't quite shut off completely.

I watched the clock as I put on a fake performance, mewling and moaning in all the right places as his tiny dick reddened in his furious death grip. He was taking longer than I'd bargained for. More money, but he wasn't nearly as fun as some others. Should have waited for the foot guy. He just let me read or knit with my feet close to the camera as he wanked. The easiest nights ever. Or the hot old guy with the deep southern accent from the US. He wasn't much to look at, but his voice was growly and low and it made me tingle.

'Bend over for me, slut, I'm going to fucking cum.'

At last.

I bent over on the bed, spreading wide while fingering myself slowly.

'Come for me,' he said as he let out a whimper.

'Yes Master, thank you,' I said as I went into an over the top cry of pleasure, tensing around my fingers rhythmically in case he was watching close enough to suspect it was fake. 'You're cock feels so gooooood.'

I sat up as my laptop dinged, letting me know he'd ended the chat.

Not even a good night. Arsehole.

I closed the computer and tidied away my lingerie, tipping it into my laundry basket before grabbing a cute nightie covered in paw prints that I wouldn't be seen dead in on camera, and tugging it over my head.

Finally, after tidying up, removing my makeup and brushing my teeth, I climbed into my bed, grabbed my vibrator and finished the job that was sorely left lacking.

I didn't imagine the stained tee guy. In my head I was with a tattooed freak who pinned me to the bed by my throat and whispered dirty, degrading things into my ear. I came hard, crying out into my pillow as my fictional man called me names which I'd never dared utter out loud.

If only he wasn't imaginary.

I cleaned off the toy before tossing it back in my drawer and sighing.

Maybe tomorrow would bring a little more excitement to my chat room.

Unlikely.

Hopefully, the foot guy would at least be back so I could finish my scarf.

CHAPTER TWO

LOGAN

'Just get it done.'

My leather desk chair creaked as I leaned back, watching the door slam behind my men as they left to finish the deal.

How had my father done it all?

He'd had a wife and six kids as well as running the McGowan syndicate, and he'd done it seamlessly. Or so it had always seemed in my eyes.

I was never supposed to be the one to take over. That had befallen me through my eldest brother's death, and while not unheard of for a second kid to end up in the hot seat, I still didn't feel ready for it.

Lately, beneath the stress of my siblings getting themselves in scrape after scrape as they tumbled into relationships and securing my father's business after his death, I was feeling every one of my thirty-eight years weighing down on me. Making it to eighty would be a fucking miracle if my body felt broken already.

Getting up at five every morning to workout before anyone else was up was taking its toll. I'd have to start napping, for god's sake.

My life sucked.

We had ridiculous wealth, needed for nothing, but all I ever did was work bar the occasional dinner with my siblings or friends.

Not to mention my fiancée.

A text message still sat on my screen, waiting to be clicked.

> 'Dinner tonight at seven with the fam--'

I hadn't dared click it, knowing I wouldn't be able to feign ignorance if I had.

It's not that I didn't want to marry Nicole Valetti, but it was her connections I was marrying, not her. She was beautiful, accomplished, intelligent: everything the head of a syndicate needed by his side. She fit.

The fact that we had little in common bar our family associations, and that if rumours were to be believed she was madly in love with her bodyguard, were just hiccups. Over time, we'd be able to iron them out and come to some sort of agreement about what our union would do for us both.

I hoped.

I'd seen the insane passion with which my siblings had been brought to their knees when they found the right person, but they had the space and time to think with their hearts. I needed to use my head.

I needed a new generation of McGowan's, and a decent, understanding wife to have them with. Someone who understood that the next generation mattered most. More than desire. More than love. More than what I wanted.

Expansion into Europe would have the McGowan legacy being more than just money. Our hold in Scotland was strong, and our connections through England were tight. But Europe was next on my list.

And I would take it.

The Valettis were my key.

I opened the text as I stood and ran a hand down my wrinkling shirt. I'd need to change, but I should be able to make dinner if I had my driver blow a few red lights.

The Valetti mansion sat on a sprawling estate in Glencoe, surrounded by acres of heather topped hills, glittering lochs and hundreds of deer. It was no wonder that it enticed Tony Valetti into staying there for more than half of the year.

The main house was vast, even compared to my mansion near Glasgow, and surrounded by intricately styled gardens and a swath of staff flitting around to tend to the Valettis every whim.

My driver dropped me at the door, while two of my men followed me into the home, the butler nodding as I passed.

'Good Evening Mr. McGowan, the family are in the dining room, I'll see you through.'

I returned his nod stiffly before following him through the marble laid hall and down a series of wide halls. There were only four people who lived in the vast estate, from what I understood. Tony and his wife, Anette, my fiancée Nicole, and her stepbrother Hugh. The art on the walls stared back at me as I passed the grand portraits that lined the corridors, and I couldn't imagine living there. Would Nicole move in with me after we wed? I doubted she would be keen on that. Her family seemed to be her life as much as my siblings were mine.

Everyone was eating when I walked into the room, an awkward silence falling over the space.

'Mr. McGowan,' the butler announced as I took a slow breath.

'Lost your watch, Logan?' Tony said, his voice dry as he set down his soup spoon and indicated to an empty chair beside Nicole.

'My apologies. Work held me up.'

'Maybe you need to work on your delegation skills.'

I bristled as he stared at me, reminding myself that he would be my father-in-law when the temptation to shut him up swept over me.

The marriage had been agreed upon between Nicole and me, and her father wasn't happy about it. In most crime families, the head of the family could have overruled the decision, but he was allowing it. Begrudgingly.

Nicole was his only daughter, and heir to his extensive crime organisation. Perhaps she held more sway than I thought.

'I like to be in the swing of it,' I said, taking my seat as a member of staff briskly set a plate of soup down in front of me.

'I hear you are involved in the shipment that just arrived from South America,' Hugh said, changing the subject. 'Sounds like you've got your fingers in a lot of pies.'

'The grapevine's been chatty lately,' I said, ignoring his probing as I made to eat my soup.

Hugh was a smarmy git. I'd known both him and Nicole as acquaintances for years, seeing them at parties and events. Occasionally a job would involve the Valettis in one manner or another. Nicole had always been aloof, but pleasant enough. Hugh was the opposite. Forever trying to insert himself where he didn't belong. As a member of the family who was both older and male, I imagined it stung that his step sister would inherit the business from her father. Hell, I'd half expected that she would have suffered some sort of terrible accident over the years, leaving him to take over. But Tony couldn't stand his lazy, indulgent, entitled ass any more than I could. There wasn't a chance in hell that Tony wouldn't have Hugh strung up by the bollocks if any harm befell his daughter.

'We're going out on the boat tomorrow. You should stay and come with us. A pootle around the loch with champagne, how about it?'

I would rather die.

'Sorry, I've got to get back to the city after dinner.'

Hugh smiled, his mouth gaping like a deranged hyena. It was

unsettling. 'Don't you want to spend some time with my dear sister? You've both got a wedding to plan.'

'There's plenty of time.'

Nicole and her step-mother ate in silence, barely glancing at myself or the others.

'How are you?' I asked, directing my question to Nicole, catching the narrowing of her eyes as she looked up at me.

'Fine. Thank you.'

We need their connections; I told myself internally as my body screamed at me to get the fuck out of the situation.

'Shall we have a dram after dinner, before I head back?'

Her eyes flicked past me to her bodyguard, who loitered at the edge of the room behind Hugh, before she pulled them back to me.

'Sure. Sounds good.' It sounded like I'd asked her to murder a puppy, not have a drink.

With a sigh, I continued to eat. The sooner the dinner was over, the better.

Nicole leant against the balcony barrier as the night sky dipped to an inky black, barely a light visible in the remote surroundings.

'That was painful,' I said, swigging my aged whisky as I sat on an ornate bench seat which was far prettier than it was comfortable.

'It's not normally so strained.'

'So it's just for me, then? Wonderful.'

A small smile turned the corner of her mouth as she watched me. 'My father keeps trying to get me to call off the wedding.'

'You really know how to inflate a guy's ego.'

She laughed, and I smiled. Nicole really was a beautiful woman. All svelte lines and monied grace. But when she let go and laughed it really made her shine. It still did nothing for me in the pants department, though.

'Do you need your ego inflated? You McGowan men never seemed to struggle in that area.'

'All men need our egos to be stroked occasionally.'

'Ain't that the truth,' she said, finally relaxing enough to come sit beside me, still leaving a healthy amount of bench between us.

The gentle slosh of the loch joined the sounds of the night's creatures as we sat sipping our drinks, the cool of the evening settling a moist chill over me.

'We don't have to do this,' I said, swirling the amber liquid that clung to the remnants of ice that littered the bottom of my glass.

'You want to expand your interests. You need me for that. My name.'

'I do. But why did you agree? You don't need me.'

'I'm almost thirty and the pressure to settle and create heirs for my father is crushing. The man I'm seeing isn't an option. I need a man who's acceptable to marry, and who isn't repulsive. That's you.'

Well, it was good to know I wasn't repulsive.

'Andrew, your bodyguard?'

She raised an eyebrow before looking away. 'It doesn't matter who it is. But I need this as much as you do.'

'You need a cover, a face to present to the world.'

Nicole nodded, toying with the stem of her wineglass.

'How are we going to do this? Where will we live? What about kids?'

'Publicly, we need to be a united front. To look every bit smitten with one another. Privately, we lead separate lives. We can get our own place if you wish, but it'll be unlikely that I spend much time there.'

'Kids will complicate it.'

'How much time did your parents spend at home with you growing up? If you were anything like us, your nannies did most of the day-to-day stuff.' Her words held a touch of strain as she spoke about children.

'Is that life the life you want for your kids?' I asked, knowing just how shit it felt to have seen my father as a figurehead for most of my childhood. My mother had been loving, and losing her as a teen had been a tremendous loss, but my sibling group had always been the place I found love growing up.

'It's the done thing.' Nicole straightened up and faced me. 'I'll give you two children, if all goes well, via IVF. We can spend the holidays together with them, and work around our schedules for the remaining time. I imagine we'll board them once they get to school, so it's only for a few years, anyway.'

She spoke about her kids as though they were a stranger's cat. A problem to be solved. It wasn't healthy. But I needed children as much as she did to see our family business continue.

I nodded my assent.

'You're a nice guy Logan, but I just need you to understand that I'm doing this for my family, and for myself. Not for us.'

'There is no us.' Saying it stung. I'd never have an us.

'Precisely.'

She smiled and placed a hand on my arm, squeezing softly. 'I hope that you keep any woman, or man, on the side discreet. Image is everything.'

'Noted.'

She relaxed back against the bench and tipped her face to the night sky.

'I guess we'd better pick a date for the engagement party.'

'Do we need one?' I asked.

'Yes.'

'Fine.'

'Is two weeks on Saturday too soon for you?'

My stomach lurched at the thought of everyone gathered while we put on a show, pretending to love each other.

'Okay. Have your people call my people and get it set up. I'll cover the cost.'

'Good, because my father has refused to pay a penny out on it.' Nicole shrugged.

'He really hates me, doesn't he?'

'Yes. But I'm sure you'll win him over when he sees how you run your organisation. Tenacity and success always impresses him.'

I grinned at her. 'I feel like that was almost a compliment.'

She got to her feet and looked down at me. 'Don't get used to it.'

CHAPTER THREE

VALENTINA

Dough seeped up through my fingers as I pulverised it into submission, waiting for it to take on just the right texture. All around me, mess piled up. Flour dusted the counter top while bowl upon bowl stacked up waiting to be washed. I adored baking, but I wasn't a clean cook.

'Darling, you have to come. She's your cousin.'

My mum's face peered out amongst the baking debris from the screen of my phone.

'She's not really my cousin. Hugh is. You know she doesn't like me. Why would she want me there?'

'Because you're family. It's the done thing.' Mum tutted as I smacked a fist into the dough before stretching it out.

'So they want us there for appearance's sake? No surprises there.'

'I know you've had your differences with them, but maybe this will be a good time to let bygones be bygones.'

I tilted my head at my mother with a raise of my eyebrows. 'There is no way they are going to be suddenly cool with my job. They loved us being the poor relations. They hate that I've made good money without them.'

My mum sighed and ran a hand through her dark hair.

'You know I'm proud of you, sweetheart, but your job isn't one that most people can accept.'

'I don't need their acceptance. I'd be quite happy never having to talk to them again. They are up their own arses all because of their bulging pockets. I don't need their toxicity in my life. I have you. And you're all the family I need.'

Mum's face softened as she watched me roll out the dough into a large square and sprinkle the brown sugar and cinnamon topping over it.

'It's not good for you to isolate yourself from everyone.'

'It is when they are a bunch of twats.'

'Valentina!'

My cheeks heated at my mum's admonishment. 'Sorry, Mum.'

'Please come, love, for me.'

And then I saw it, the real reason she wanted me to go. She needed me. Facing her sister and the others alone would be as painful for her as it was for me. A reminder of everything she didn't have. No husband, no security, no big family surrounding her. All we'd ever had was each other. She and I against the world.

Fuck.

I couldn't leave her to face it alone.

'Fine. I'll come. But the first sign of one of them trying to put me in my place and I'm out.'

Mum's face broke into a smile as her shoulders dropped. 'Thank you, love. Do you need a dress?'

'I'm sure I've got something here that would work. It's going to be fancy, right?' Of course it would be fancy, only the best for my cousin.

'Yes.'

'Do you have anything to wear?'

My mum shifted uncomfortably and shrugged. 'I have the dress I wore to their wedding.'

'That was almost twenty-five years ago. It'll be nothing but moth-balls.'

'It'll be fine. It's not like anyone will be looking at me.'

There was no way on God's green earth I was going to let her go to their posh-ass party in a dress that was older than me. Mum deserved better. She deserved the best.

'Pick me up tomorrow. We'll go shopping. My treat.'

'Oh honey, you can't spend your money on me.'

'Mum, it's the only way you will get me to the party. Plus, it'll be fun. We haven't had a girly day in forever.'

Her face warred between hesitation and delight, and I saw the moment she caved with a smile. 'Well alright, but I'll buy lunch. And keep one of those cinnamon buns for me. They remind me so much of your Grandma.'

The tug I felt took my breath away for a moment. God, I missed my Grandma. She never let my aunt and her family make Mum and me feel like we were lower class. She'd have slapped my uncle upside the head no matter who he was. She did, once.

'I will.'

'You're such a good girl, Valentina.'

I gave her a soft smile as I brushed my hair back from my face with the back of my flour covered hand.

'Bye, Mum, love you,' I said.

'See you tomorrow. Love you, too.'

Then it was just me and my buns.

I wrapped and cut the dough into glorious cinnamon swirls, covering them over with a tea-towel and leaving them to rise. Flicking on some music, I danced around the kitchen, cleaning as I went. One of the most wonderful things about an empty flat was that I could caterwaul to my heart's content without disrupting Lara's camming, or just annoying her with my out of tune voice.

Gathering up the bin bag, I sashayed my way toward the door, grabbing my keys, and slipping on some shoes. I took the stairs as one of my main forms of exercise and tossed the rubbish in the big bin out the back of the apartment block.

I'd almost made it home without bumping into anyone when a shadow crossed my path.

'Miss Valetti, something smells awfully good around here.'

Tim stood against the narrow corridor wall facing me, partially blocking the way back to my flat.

'Oh, hey Tim. I'm baking. That's probably the cinnamon you're smelling.'

Sliding a hand up the wall near my head, he leaned awkwardly on his gangly arm and looked down at me. 'It wasn't the cinnamon.'

I ducked down beneath his arm and walked toward my door, throwing him an apologetic smile. 'Sorry, got to get back to the buns. I wouldn't want to burn them.'

'You'd never burn them,' he said as I unlocked my door and slipped inside. Just before I closed the door, I heard him mutter something that sounded very much like, 'You're perfect.'

Poor guy didn't have a clue.

He saw a sweet girl next door, who he probably thought wanted flowers and walks in the park. I wanted to be pursued and fucked amongst the flowers while someone licked up my tears.

I was absolutely not the innocent girl next door.

If he knew, he'd run a mile like all the others did.

CHAPTER FOUR

LOGAN

Lights danced across my bedroom ceiling as someone approached the mansion, likely Ewen returning from working at his sex club, or a member of our household staff checking in for the night shift. They sent shadows flying over the walls, dancing in the beams of light.

Yet again, sleep evaded me.

It had time and time again since Dad's passing and my promotion to head of the syndicate. I'd tried drinking to sleep, exercising until I nearly passed out, napping. None of it made a difference. More often than not, I laid awake and watched the minutes tick by until it was time to get back up and put my mafia hat back on.

With a groan, I picked up my phone and started flicking through socials, but they had never been my thing. It only took a few minutes to catch up with my siblings on WhatsApp. Reading through their updates was a mixed blessing. Was I happy that Mac, Maeve, and Esther were thriving? Sure. Did it make my life any better? Not really? They were all so sickeningly happy.

Bunch of fucks.

I loved them, but if Esther sent me one more goddamn adorable video of my niece chattering away, I might explode.

I needed a distraction.

Something to knock me out for the night.

I needed a wank.

The porn sites showed reel after reel of sex for the camera, where it was performative rather than real. Fake orgasms and the same script every time. Five seconds of warming the woman up, a brief face fuck and then position after position while they moan in that same fake way before coming on her face every damn time. After ten minutes of finding nothing that sparked an interest, I turned to Reddit. The homemade forums were often full of amateurs, who at least seemed to enjoy themselves.

Thrusting one hand under the covers, I toyed with my dick, waiting for him to figure out that it was time to wake up and join me. Clearly he wasn't getting the memo, as bored with online videos as I was.

Scrolling down, I'd almost given up when a video of a young woman popped up. She was heart-achingly pretty. The sort of face that made you want to take her home to the family, but that also called out to be fucking ruined. Big hazel eyes drew me in. Moist, pink lips that I wanted to drag my dick along while she begged to taste me.

Fuck. I'd only seen her face, and I was rock hard.

I had to click on the video.

It opened up to her sitting on a pristine white bed, all lacey and sweet. She was talking to the camera, but the video that had been reposted had no sound. Damn it. I wanted to hear if she was a honey-sweet as she looked.

She slid a hand under her pyjama shorts and touched herself, and the look of utter want on her face made my balls tighten.

Who was she?

I scrolled through the comments, dismissing the lewd and the jealous, until I found one that named her.

Sweet-CherryxX over at Primal Princesses

My hand stilled against my rigid dick. Primal Princesses? It was probably just a marketing tactic, but that didn't stop tingles from spreading up my arms. The idea that this cute, pristine twenty-something wanted to be pursued, pinned and fucked, hell it hit me right in the ball sack.

I found the site in minutes, watching as it loaded up with pictures of women and men interacting in the most wonderfully depraved manner. A woman pinned in the dirt with two guys inside her. A man tied to a log while a woman rode his face. Cages. Bruises. Tears.

A twang of guilt hit me as it often did with porn - never knowing what was consensual and what was coerced. I knew well enough that not everyone chose to perform. It's why amateur hit my buttons way better.

The site wasn't actually a porn site upon further inspection. It was a cam girl website.

I clicked on the search icon and typed in her name, holding my breath as I waited, hoping to find her.

A profile popped up and there she was.

Sweet Cherry. Twenty-two. Glasgow.

I almost choked when I saw her location. It could be some clever trick from the site to match to your location, but there was a possibility she was within the same city as me. Sitting up in my bed, I grabbed my laptop from my bedside table, needing to see her better than on my phone screen.

Her pretty face lit up my screen as her profile picture smiled coyly at me.

'Oh, Cherry, I have a feeling that sweet smile is a lie.'

Then I saw the green button that said Live Now, and my stomach did a flip. Cherry was online. I could see her in the flesh, right as she was that very minute.

Clicking the button opened up a chat room with a host of users inside. Half of the screen had an empty bed, the same one from the Reddit picture.

'Where are you?' I muttered as I glanced through the open chat.

It was a mixture of men desperately trying to get her attention, and others trying their hardest to debase her as thoroughly as possible.

A box popped up, asking for me to input a username. My fingers hovered over the keyboard. Did I really want to watch some camgirl in a room full of other men with their dicks in their hands? No.

But my resolve weakened when she crawled onto the bed and sat on her knees, sucking on a red lollipop and sending a sunny smile our way.

I'd never been so fucking jealous of candy before.

She leaned forward and started typing on a keyboard, giving me a view right down the frilled, love heart dotted underwear set she wore. She was more slight than my usual type up top, with maybe an A-cup and thickening about the hips and ass, with thighs I'd gladly get lost beneath. The panties dug lightly into the tanned flesh at her hips, and I imagined my fingers gripping her there, seeing them indent into her skin.

I hesitated as I considered a username. My actual name was obviously not going to cut it. It was a primal site, and looking through the other users there were plenty of beast this, and Master-so-and-so that, but she was bringing out a side of me I'd long kept hidden.

ScotsDaddy38

Hardly rocket science, but even typing the Daddy in made my balls twitch. It had been years since I'd last entertained that kink, knowing that the woman I'd likely marry wouldn't be one who deigned to indulge those sorts of kinks.

But Nicole had all but given me permission to play away, as long as it was discreet. A little indulgence for my poor blue balls online was pretty under the radar. Plus, I was only watching in the open chat. Cherry didn't even know I existed.

Pushing down the covers, I put my laptop on the bedside table and did my best to ignore the tirade of messages swapping between the other punters and her.

Music played softly in her room, and I imagined being there, leaning over her and pushing my hands into her long, thick dark hair and dragging her mouth to my own. Tasting that sweet candy on her lips before pressing my dick into her throat to see if the candy would leave a sticky residue around the base.

My hand slid over the engorged tip of my dick, and when she shifted position on the bed, leaning over to grab something and giving me a full view of her round arse, I muffled my groan.

'Cherry, I'd fucking ruin you.' I growled, my balls tensing as she turned back to the camera, twirling the lollipop over her tongue before pressing it in between her lips.

Thrusting into my hand, I focused on her face. The dark lashes would stick to her cheeks when I fucked her so hard I made her cry. She'd give me the sweetest sighs when I closed my hand around her neck, cutting off the air until she came hard beneath me. Sweet Cherry would enjoy it. She had one of those faces which people mistook for innocence, but it wasn't innocence, it was a sweetness which always hid a deeper darkness. I'd seen it before and I didn't doubt that she was on the primal site for a reason. She could cam anywhere and be successful with her looks, but something must have attracted her to there.

Or maybe I was thinking too much into it and it was just better money.

Either way, imagining her squealing beneath my hands was exactly what I needed.

With a groan, I focussed in on her mouth as she toyed with the lolly, picturing those perfect lips sucking down my cum.

Then she spoke. Her voice was soft and with only a gentle Glaswegian lilt.

'Thank you for joining me ScotsDaddy.'

And the daddy on her lips was my undoing. It was all I needed to fill my fist.

The orgasm ripped through me as I rocked my hips, picturing her throat taking every drop.

I fought the temptation to smear my cum over the screen, just to see it marring her face.

'Fuck, Cherry. I needed that,' I said before laying back in the bed, willing myself to go clean up.

I left her on the bedside table as I took a quick shower before crawling back into bed and facing the screen.

And with her laying on her bed, I fell into a deep, decadent, dreamless sleep at last.

CHAPTER FIVE
VALENTINA

'Lara, did you pinch that cute pink set I bought last week?' I shouted through the flat while looking through my wardrobe.

My new, pristine black dress hung in its plastic on the front of the wardrobe door, mocking me with its prim, sleek lines where I preferred ruffles and silk and sweet patterns. My mum had informed me that the party was strictly black tie, so we'd both opted for stylish but sedate knee-length dresses. I tried not to wince at the price tag, begrudging every penny spent on my big-headed family. Mum's delight when seeing herself in her dress soothed my soul a little at least. She was only in her forties, and still every bit as beautiful as she'd always been. I'd always hoped she'd find someone new to cherish her, but after my dad, she'd focused her whole life on me. Maybe I should sign her up to an app...

Lara appeared at my door with a pile of pink lace in her hands. 'Sorry babe, the bodysuit was still drying in the bathroom.'

While we both had plenty of work clothes, we often raided one another's stash for something different for our regulars. Her punters were far more into leather and PVC, where mine seemed to enjoy my overtly feminine style. When I first started camming, I thought I'd have to follow Lara's lead and dress in kinky clothing, but I hated every minute of the hot, sticky, clingy fabrics. Eventually, I fell back into my personal clothes and sets and found way more success when I was leaning into what I enjoyed.

'No worries, I bought that baby blue hot-pants pyjama set. I'll throw them on.' I hung the pink set over the radiator to finish drying as I slipped out of my lounge set and pulled on the PJs.

'Man, your arse looks great in those shorts.'

'Why, thank you,' I said with a smile as I winked at my bestie.

'Seriously, they are going to eat that set right up. Underboob, too. You're going to break their little hearts.'

'Hardly underboob,' I said, brushing out my hair and teasing it at the roots.

'I'd love your tits. Not an ounce of sag. What am I going to do with these beasts?' Lara said, lifting her boobs up with her hands and letting them drop back into place. 'I'll have to get them tightened up before long.'

'No, you won't. The guys are always banging on about them.'

'Is it Footguy tonight?' Lara said, leaning back against my door frame as I reapplied some lip oil.

'Usually. I could really be done with something more exciting, though. He's easy money, as he'll just keep going as long as my feet are near the camera, but it gets so bloody dull. And he rarely tips.'

'At least your vag won't be chafed come morning.'

'It could be done with a good chafing,' I said with a laugh. It wasn't exactly a joke. It had been a while since a cock that wasn't rubber had been anywhere near it.

'I told you I know a few guys I could set you up with. Jeremy is super sweet.' Lara was forever trying to set me up.

'I don't want sweet. I want a guy who will come in and blow me away. A guy who doesn't need instructing or baby steps. Someone who knows what he wants. Knows the right things to say.'

'I think you are holding out for a man who doesn't exist, babe. If he can find your clit and work his tongue, he's already ten steps ahead of most guys.'

'I'll just stick to camming and my wee rubber pals, then.' We cracked up before she left as I fired up my laptop and phone, connecting them to the site so I could use the camera on my laptop but reply with my phone.

Taking stock of the usernames that popped up as I sat on the bed and toyed with my hair, I noticed a few regulars. Foot guy was there, along with the one who liked to tell me how he wanted to fill me with his wee, and the one who sounded eighty but spoke like he'd screw me six ways from Sunday.

There was only one who stood out as different. ScotsDaddy38 was back. I'd tried to talk to him when he'd popped into the chat but hadn't got a message back. Probably another one who popped into the chat and came three minutes later, barely spending a penny. They made up ninety percent of the visitors, but rarely did they come back. They were most likely to be casual perusers who'd forget the site's name as soon as they jizzed.

I pulled up his profile, which was as sparse as they always were. No pictures, no info.

Was he thirty-eight? Older guys always made me weak at the knees.

I fired off a message to him, not really expecting a response as I chatted on and off in the group, sitting and moving in ways that showed off my tiny PJs.

Hi ScotsDaddy! Thanks for joining me. Hope you're enjoying the view. ;)

Minutes later, his icon flashed up on my phone.

'The view's pretty sweet.'

Hmm, playing hard to get... usually guys would react far more to a private message.

'What brings you to my cam chat?'

'Bar the obvious? I'm waiting to see what a sweet little thing like you is doing on a site like this.'

My hackles raised as I looked up into the camera with a frown.

'One of those who thinks all cam girls are sluts, I guess?'

'Quite the opposite. This is a site for people who like primal play. But you don't seem like the kind of girl who's into being chased down and fucked into the ground. Is it just a marketing ploy?'

My fingers hovered over my phone as I bit my lip. Most guys didn't seem to care about what the site depicted, they just wanted to beat the meat with a pretty girl on the other end.

'And are you the kind of guy who's into that?'

I shifted on the bed, leaning closer to the camera as I typed.

He made me wait for his reply, nibbling at my lip as I glanced at the screen.

'I'm the kind of guy who would love to take your breath away, but not with flowers and sweet words.'

'What would you use?' My heart rate picked up.

'What wouldn't I use? sweet Cherry?'

My private messages popped up with a request for a call from Foot Guy, and I hesitated as the invitation hung on my screen. It was the sensible choice. The easy choice.

'I'm getting a call for a private cam session. I should take it.'

'What will he have you do?'

'He likes to just look at my feet while I ignore him.'

'And does that get you wet?'

I couldn't help but smile.

'No. But it pays the bills.'

'If I call you, you can still pay the bills, but you can tell me all about what makes your sweet little cunt drip.' His text sent a jolt right through me.

'Most guys want to tell me about what they want.'

'I'm not most guys. I enjoy inflicting pleasure as much as receiving it. When was the last time someone else made you come?'

I didn't need to look at myself in the picture on my screen to know I was blushing. The heat practically burned from my cheeks.

'That long, huh? Call me.'

I rejected the call from Foot Guy, and rang through to ScotsDaddy, my video disappearing from the group chat.

'All yours,' I said, as he accepted the call.

'Don't make promises you can't keep, Cherry.' Nerves fluttered in my stomach at the sound of his deep, rich voice. He was far better spoken than most of my clients, but there was no doubting the Glaswegian lilt that lightly decorated his words. He was from my city. Flip.

'Don't I get to see you?' I asked, curiosity getting the better of me.

'I'm not putting my face on here.'

'It doesn't have to be your face...' I blinked up at the camera with my best doe-eyed expression.

When he didn't reply, I thought I'd pushed too hard. I shifted on my bed as my mind ran, trying to figure out how to keep him on the line.

'Fine, but no face.'

I grinned as his video blinked into life. He was sitting on a leather armchair with a spacious, high-ceilinged room behind him. Unlike a lot of the dinge-fests I normally saw, it was pristinely neat; the bed made with precision in cloudy white linens. Not a single thing out of place.

The man himself looked equally well turned out. He wore a white shirt, rolled up over thick forearms in a way that made me feel funny between the thighs. A golden Rolex fit snugly across his wrist, his hands relaxed as he waited.

No wedding band.

Jesus, Valentina, why are you checking for a wedding ring? Half of your clients are married, it doesn't matter.

'Nice place,' I said, wishing I could scoot his camera up to see his face. It stopped at chest level and as much as the view of his thick, toned arms was enjoyable, I wished I could see him in his entirety. 'Are you hiding in the bedroom because you have a girlfriend lurking downstairs?'

He drummed his fingers on the arm of his chair, his thighs relaxing open as he laughed.

'You're brattier than I expected, with all your frills and lace. We're not here to talk about me. I want to hear about you. Why are you on a site for primal play, Miss Cherry?'

My throat bobbed as I swallowed, not used to being under scrutiny.

'I hoped that it would be a bit more exciting than a regular cam site.' It was partially the truth, anyway.

'Is that why you cam? For excitement? You're a beautiful woman. I'm sure there are plenty of guys who'd fall over themselves to fulfil whatever fantasies lurk in that pretty head of yours.' His voice had the most delicious timbre to it, low and growly. I hung on every word.

'I do okay.'

'Mmm,' he murmured, leaning forward in his seat and getting so teasingly close to showing me his face. 'I think that maybe sex has been a little bland in real life. Too vanilla. Are you hunting out men who can fulfil your dirty fantasies without opening yourself up to the reality of it?'

Bingo.

Him slicing through my bullshit had me feeling far too exposed. Torn open.

'Is that why you're here?' I asked.

He laughed, and the throaty sound of it had me in a choke hold. 'I guess it is. I've done a lot of the things I crave in the past, but I've got myself in a situation which makes me require discretion. And I stumbled upon you. There's something about you that makes me want to break you open and see what you are hiding beneath the surface.'

'You're supposed to be just looking for a quick wank,' I mumbled. 'What is this a therapy session?'

'No. I'm not someone who you'd find solace in, I'd only go ruining you.'

'So, I want fun that can be done on my terms, safely and from a distance, and you want something discreet. Seems like the perfect situation.' Not to mention his chatting was wracking up quite the sweet payment for me.

'I don't know if my fun will align with yours. How about you get comfortable and tell me all about whatever dirty thoughts plague your mind when you're touching yourself? The ones that you keep hidden beneath those sweet smiles and fuck me eyes. If you're a good girl, I might even let you come for me.'

His words sent thrills shimmying up my spine. I knew I had control, with a click of a button I could close him down. But the thought of his dirty mouth and those thick arms of his was enough to let me play along.

What harm could be in it?

'I'll tell you mine if you tell me yours...'

CHAPTER SIX
LOGAN

God she was a hot little thing. Far too young for me even if I was single, not to mention only indulging me to get the maximum money she could. I didn't care. It was the perfect solution to my Nicole problem.

I needed a safe, discrete solution to my blue balls, and Cherry was a pay-per-minute sexy distraction. She could say all the right words and give me enough interaction to stave off my loneliness for a time. I needed no more than that.

'Tell me, Cherry, what it is these boys who have been disappointing you are missing.'

She sighed sweetly before rolling onto her tummy, her feet kicking up behind her as she watched me through the screen.

'Well, they just have one goal. Get from point A to point B with as little time and effort as possible. They think that bending me over and taking me from behind is kinky. There's never anything exciting, or surprising. Nothing that makes my insides squirm.'

'What's the first thing you remember being excited by? That did make your stomach flip?'

Her cheeks pinked as she let out a laugh. 'You'll think I'm crazy.'

'What's the loss if I do? You can block me on here and never have to talk to me again.'

Her hesitation made me want to drill down into her mind even more. She ran her fingers through her thick, dark hair as she blinked up at me through the screen. What I'd have given to reach in and drag her through the screen and into my lap. To make her confess her dirty little dreams into my ear as I fingered her pretty little cunt.

'Okay. You win. It was in the Lion King... I had the biggest crush on Scar, which sounds insane I know, because he's a cartoon lion. He pinned this little mouse before toying with it and telling it how unfair life was before eating it. And damn if I didn't want to be Scar's little mouse.'

Well, it wasn't exactly what I'd pictured, but prey I could work with.

'You like the idea of being hunted down by someone with bad intentions who will use you for their own desires. Who can pin you down and tell you exactly what they are going to do with you?'

She nodded sweetly while chewing on her bottom lip. I couldn't help but wonder what her lips would taste like. Whether she'd gasp sweetly if I nipped her full lower lip between my own teeth.

Calm down.

It's not going to happen. She's just good at her job.

'And you like them older too? Experienced. Not afraid to fuck you the way you so desperately crave. Boys your age are too nice. Too desperate for a shag. Correct?'

'Yes.'

'You want to be dicked down real good, made to scream, made to cry but in a way that feels safe. That doesn't expose you to the danger that seeking those guys in the real world brings.'

Her eyes widened as she nodded again.

'And, sweet Cherry, do you find that amongst the guys who contact you here?'

'Not yet.' She swallowed hard before looking up at me. 'But I'm hoping that might have changed.'

The way she blinked through those thick lashes at me had me hardening in my trousers.

'Show me, Cherry. Show me how well you can listen and I'll let you come for me.'

'What do you want me to do?'

'Take off those pyjamas and kneel on the bed.'

She did as I asked, her nipples already peaked as she tossed the top aside. I let out an involuntary grunt as she pulled down her shorts, giving me a side view of her well-rounded arse. It would look fucking epic with a series of handprints left on it.

If only.

'Will you touch yourself?' She asked, her voice almost too coy for the current situation.

'Not tonight. Tonight is all about you showing me that this is something you crave. That it's not all words just to push up the bill.'

Her mouth opened as if to argue.

'Don't tell me, Cherry, show me.'

She spread her knees wide on the bed, arching her back and folding her arms behind her.

'Such a pretty position. Too pretty. Put your hands on the bed behind you and arch yourself upward, I want you to put your cunt on display for me. Come, now, closer to the camera so I can get a good look at you.'

I left her holding the position as I drank her in. Her skin was tanned and taut, creasing where her hips met her thighs. She looked fairly short, and carried her weight around her thighs and ass, perfect for putting over my knee. Her tits were small and topped with brown nipples, which I wanted to sink my teeth into.

It was taking all my restraint not to pull my dick out and sate my own desires at the sight of her, hell, the sound of her.

'Cherry, turn around and spread yourself for me. I want to see everything.'

She did as asked, positioning herself at an angle so she could look back at me, giving me a full, glorious view of her visibly wet cunt.

'My, my. Wet already?'

Her cheeks flamed as she nodded.

'Tell me, Cherry. There will be no hiding behind nods and head shakes.'

'I'm soaked... Sir.'

The hesitation in her voice made me want to pull her into my lap all over again.

'Mmm, good girl.'

I saw her cunt clench at my words and grinned.

'I'm going to tell you a little story, Cherry. And while I do, you are going to sink your fingers into yourself until I tell you to stop. Do you understand?'

'Yes.'

'Yes, what?'

'Yes, Sir,' she whimpered.

She slid two fingers into herself, shifting her hips to accommodate them better. My dick throbbed against my trousers, desperate to replace her fingers. If only there wasn't a screen between us.

'Such a dirty little thing, Cherry. A delightful little tease. But it's not teasing you want, is it? You want to be seen. You thrive off showing men your wet cunt, don't you?'

'Yes, Sir,' she panted, grinding her clit into her palm as she fucked herself with her fingers.

'Imagine I had you in front of me, touching yourself while a roomful of people watched you. Focusing in on my voice and following my commands while dozens of eyes were on you.'

Her moan made my dick throb.

'They'd gather around you, watching you fuck yourself and discuss you. Maybe they'd bargain to be the first to sink their dick into your hot little holes. You'd look so pretty airtight. Stuffed full of dick in every hole.'

'God...' she moaned.

'I'd pull you up onto your knees and sit you down over my cock, make you arch and writhe and perform for everyone. Whisper in your ear and point out how hard they all are for you, sweet Cherry. How many gallons of cum they have to spill on you, in you, over you.'

Her fingers thrust quicker, her pussy visibly soaked. Her ass tightened as she whimpered. She was close. Such a dirty little thing.

'Please, can I see your dick?' she begged, her cheeks flushed pink as she continued to touch herself.

I hadn't intended on joining her, but my balls ached to release and my dick rubbed against my clothing. It couldn't hurt...

'Why do you want to see it so badly? I imagine you see plenty of dicks in this job.'

'Because I want to imagine it inside me. To dream of it tonight.'

I let out an involuntary growl at her confession.

'Please? Sir?'

'Turn over and spread your legs, and put another finger in there and I'll let you see.'

She flipped onto her back, sitting upright against the pillows, and spread her thighs wide for me.

'Good girl.' I stood and repositioned my camera to give her a view of my hips and thighs as I unbuckled my belt.

'If I was with you, I'd use my belt to mark up that sweet arse of yours before I fucked you. You'd feel the stripes with every thrust.'

She quivered on the bed as I spoke, her eyes glued to the screen as I slowly undid my zip. When I pulled out my dick, her gasp made me grin.

'Oh, my god... It's... big.'

'It is. And I bet you'd take every inch and still beg for more, wouldn't you?'

She nodded and licked her lips.

I fisted my dick for her, running my hand up the length before focusing on the engorged head.

'Now fuck that cunt for me Cherry, I want to see you come hard for me. Imagine me pinning you beneath my dick and making you scream for everyone. Filling you up to bursting with my cum before letting someone else take my place while I held you against me and told you what a good girl you are.'

Her thighs trembled, and I groaned. I'd barely even begun with her, and my dick was ready to explode.

'And when you'd taken all of their dicks, I'd spread you wide and let their cum drip down onto the floor, then fist your hair and make you clean up the mess you made.'

The dirty image was her undoing. Her whole body quaked as she cried out, her chest flushing pink as she fucked her hand.

I joined her, my balls tightening as I unloaded a fuckload of cum into my fist. My head swam as I focused on her pulsating little cunt. I'd have given half my wealth to have been balls deep inside of her instead of filling my fist.

'Fuck, Cherry. That's it, baby. Keep riding your hand until you've got nothing left to give.'

'Can you show me?' she panted.

'Show you what?'

'Your cum...'

I held out my hand and let her see the glossy, sticky mess I'd made for her.

'I wish I could taste it.' She smiled at me, her eyes half lidded. She was either a fucking supreme actress, or had actually enjoyed herself very much. Her dirty confession made me want to scoop her up and keep her chained at the end of my bed.

'I wish you could too. I'd happily feed it to you for every meal.'

She squirmed and pressed her thighs together, wrapping her arms around her knees as she drew them up to her chest.

'Will you come back?' she asked.

'Do you want me to?'

'Yes, please.'

CHAPTER SEVEN

VALENTINA

'What sort of time do you call this?' Lara said as I trundled into the kitchen. I glanced at the clock and groaned.

'I need coffee...'

I put a pod in the machine and waited for it to spit out some black goodness before bundling in sugar and frothed milk. Lara watched me with a raised brow from the dining table.

'If I didn't know any better, I'd have thought you had been out and doing the walk of shame home,' she said as I shuffled over and sat down next to her.

'Walk of victory - not shame,' I said before taking a sip of the coffee. It was too hot and the top of my mouth burned, but I didn't care. It was hot and sweet and exactly what I needed. 'I met a guy last night.'

'Online?'

'On the cam site.'

Lara rounded on me, shaking her head. 'Nope. No. Nuh-uh. You know better than that.'

'I know,' I groaned, rubbing my hands over my face. 'But he was so freaking hot. Like twelve out of ten. I mean, I didn't see his face, but the rest of him was full marks. God, he has a cock like a baseball ba--'

Lara cut me off. 'Absolutely not. You know how the customers view us. As a commodity. Not a real woman. Undeserving of respect. You'd have to be insane to even consider anything real.'

She was right. One of the first rules we had was to keep it on the site. No phone numbers or email addresses, no Snapchat or TikTok. Definitely no real life.

'I know,' I sighed. 'He was just so perfect.'

'Tell me about him.'

'He's older, like, fifteen years older.'

'V...'

'I know, but you know I love an older guy. He has this deep voice that just does insane things to my insides.' I closed my eyes as I remembered his filthy words as I'd touched myself. 'His arms are thick and veined and he has those long, chunky fingers that just beg to be wrapped around a throat.'

Lara rolled her eyes, but kept quiet as I continued.

'And his cock. Lara, I'm not kidding you when I say it was flipping massive. Like girthy AND long. The sort of cock you see in porn and wonder whether it would leave you walking like a cowboy for days.'

'That sounds unpleasant,' Lara said, screwing up her face.

'It sounds bloody magical.'

'Nah, give me 6 inches and the ability to fuck down hard over splitting me in two any day.'

I laughed and shrugged. 'I'll leave the six inchers for you while I dream about his baseball bat sized cock. And the things he said, it was like he reached into my head and yanked out the fantasies I'd always kept hidden. It was so hot.'

'It's hot because it's not real, babe. You wouldn't want him doing any of that in real life.'

I sipped my coffee while my brain ran. I wanted it. God, I wanted to experience the filthy things he'd spoken about for real. I wanted to be watched, displayed, used.

Lara watched my face intently before reaching out and slipping a hand over mine. 'Just remember that top priority is safety, and if the guys are on the site, there is a reason why. Keep it online. Enjoy it from behind your screen while he's filling your purse up. It's a win-win.'

'Yeah, you're right. Plus, he might just not show back up again.'

It wasn't unusual to have a guy come along a handful of times and then disappear. We were a service, and often they moved onto another one. There was an endless amount of variety on the internet, and no real reason anyone would stick around with my site in particular. I had my regulars, but ScotsDaddy38 didn't seem like the sort to obsess over a cam girl.

We both jumped as the buzzer rang loudly, alerting us to someone at the outer door of the apartment building.

'Are you expecting someone? I asked, and Lara shook her head.

I jogged over to the tannoy and pressed the button. 'Hello?'

'Hi, I'm here from Belle's Floristry. I have a delivery for a Valentina?'

I furrowed my brow as Lara shrugged at me.

'I'll be down in a minute. You can leave them with the doorman, thanks.'

Throwing on a coat to cover my pyjamas, I took the elevator down to the ground floor where Muhammed stood behind his desk, an enormous bouquet of deep red roses perched on top of it.

'Well, Miss Valentina, it seems you have yourself an admirer,' he said with a warm chuckle.

'I'm not expecting anything like this...' I walked over and ran a finger over the large blossoms before finding the card tucked in amongst them.'

Sweetest V

I've missed you.
Don't be a stranger.

Confusion swept through me. Who on earth were they from? I didn't have any exes who pined for me, and never went anywhere enough to have gained an admirer. A shudder cascaded down my spine as I flipped the card over, looking for a name. Nothing.

'All okay, Miss?' Muhammed asked, frowning with concern.

'Yeah,' I said, plastering a smile on my mouth, 'Of course. Thanks for grabbing these for me.'

'My pleasure.'

When I got back into the apartment, Lara's eyes were like saucers.

'Fuck, babe, what a bunch! Must have cost a bomb. Who are they from?'

'I don't know, it didn't say.' I handed over the card and watched as Lara read it. 'I've no idea who could have sent them.'

'You haven't given your address to anyone on the site, have you? Or your number or anything?' Lara asked.

'No, not even my socials. I keep it all off there.'

Lara tapped the card against her hand as she bit her lip in thought. 'Call the florist. They might know who it was.'

I tried. But they were of no use either. It was an online order paid using a paypal address which they couldn't hand out for GDPR purposes.

'Maybe it's someone you know fucking with you. What about your bitch cousin?' Lara pinned the card to the fridge with a magnet before eyeing the flowers. 'Shall we bin them?'

'No, I'll drop them down to Mrs Haggerty. She doesn't get many visitors and I think they'd cheer her right up.' I didn't want them in the flat. Could the flowers be from someone in my family? They weren't my mum's sort of idea at all. And my cousins weren't usually the type to fuck with me, and certainly didn't miss me for it to be genuine.

Whoever they were from, they were the reminder I needed to not let my guard slip online. No matter whether it was a sinfully hot older man with an absolutely filthy mouth or not.

CHAPTER EIGHT

LOGAN

'Dude, you suck today.' My brother, Ewen, punched me lightly on the arm as he passed, picking up his golf club and nudging me out of the way of the tee.

'All okay?' Mac asked.

'Fine,' I grumbled as I pressed my club into my caddy's hand and ran my fingers through my damp hair.

I didn't enjoy golf at the best of times, and neither did my brothers, from what I could tell. Yet we often bashed balls about the course nearest our home. Ewen and I's home. Mac had fallen in love a few months prior and buggered off to live with his girlfriend, Katie, in her house. With my younger two sisters married and settled, it just left Ewen and me rattling around the mansion with the staff.

'I'm getting soaked through with this pissy rain. Can we call it quits already?' I slid my ass into the golf cart and folded my arms over my chest.

'You just want to quit because you're losing to me,' Ewen said with a shit-eating grin.

'I couldn't give a hairy shite who's winning. I don't even like golf.'

'Yeah, you do. It's why we play.' Mac frowned as he walked over to the cart and climbed in.

'No, I don't. It's boring as all hell.'

'So why are we here?' Mac asked.

'Dad liked it. I played with him as it was the only time he'd drop out of his syndicate king persona and be a normal human.' I'd hoped that golfing would make me feel closer to him after the loss, but it just left me feeling more lost and empty than I had before.

'If you don't like it, then fuck this shit,' Ewen said, passing his club back to his caddy before hopping in beside us. 'Let's get back to the clubhouse and hit the sauna.'

The rain picked up as I whipped the little cart through the course and toward the swanky resort building where we held lifetime memberships. Golf aside, it was a pretty sweet place to hang out. It had a five-star restaurant, multiple bars, a swimming pool and sauna, and top tier masseuses. There were also plenty of other people like us there. People who had money, or fame, or dodgy backgrounds. A place where no-one batted an eye at where your wealth came from as long as you were tipping with fifties. In my twenties, it had been a regular place to pick up women, and the occasional guy, for a night of fun. When my eldest brother died and the torch as the eldest son had passed to me, I'd had no choice but to step up and be the man my father needed me to be. No time left for playing. It was all about pulling up my bootstraps and becoming a fitting heir for my father. I'd expected to have years to figure out how to be like him, but his life had been cut short, too.

Then it was all on me.

The steam clouded around me as I relaxed into a wooden bench in the sauna, my skin coated in droplets of sweat as I closed my eyes and shut out the world.

For all of three minutes before my brothers joined me.

'I can see your balls, mate,' Ewen said, launching a towel at my groin.

'Jealous?' I pulled my towel over as he laid on the bench across from me while Mac took the one along the rear wall.

'Nah, I don't need a monster shlong to please women.'

'I don't need it to please them... but they seem to want it bad enough.' My brothers had joked about the size of my dick enough to give me a complex when I was a teen, but soon enough, I learned that plenty of people loved a man to be packing. I'd rarely had any complaints...

'Can we stop talking about dick?' Mac said with a yawn.

'You must be sick of the sight of yours,' Ewen said. 'You and Katie are at it like rabbits.'

'His security made me wait an hour last week outside the gates.' My voice cracked in the dry heat as Ewen added more water to the coals and sent a huge cloud of steam hissing into the space.

Mac grinned at me. 'You don't want to know what we were doing.'

'Correct.'

'Have you tamed that haughty fiancée of yours yet? Mac asked.

'I have no interest in taming her. I told you, it's primarily a business relationship.'

'Bullshit. She's hot, and the sole heir to her father's huge mafia organisation. You need to lock her down properly if you are going to do it.'

Nicole was hot. She looked every bit like she'd walked straight out of a Victoria's Secret catalogue, tall and slender, with a face that men would kill for. But there was just no spark, nothing that made me sit up and pay attention.

'My kids will take over both the Valetti and the McGowan lines. I'm building them a future that Dad would have been proud of. It's what he always wanted. The Velettis have the key to that expansion and I'll do whatever it takes to secure it.'

'Even being a cuckold to her fucking bodyguard,' Mac said.

'That's all rumours.' My shoulders tensed at his accusation. It was true, though. I'd be her cuckold to someone, whether or not it was the bodyguard. 'We have an agreement.'

'What kind of agreement?' Ewen asked.

'We both put on a united front, and make it work as a family for any children. Behind closed doors, we both do whatever we need to, discreetly.'

'All good and well for the fucking, but what about the other stuff?' Mac said, sitting up and looking at me with his intense gaze. 'Who's going to look after you when you're sick? Share a takeout with you while you watch a shit film on a Saturday night? Who will make you feel loved?'

I bristled. 'I don't need all that.'

'You're an idiot.'

'Just because you've got your head lost up your girlfriend's arse doesn't mean we all need that.'

'Talk about Katie like that, and brother or not, I'll lop your big fat balls off.'

Tension knitted through the air for a minute before Ewen let out a peal of laughter.

'You bunch of fannies, quit it. If he wants to be successful but miserable, who are we to tell him otherwise? He wouldn't be the first guy to find his happiness between a mistress's thighs.'

My mind flashed back to the cam girl. Cherry. As it had tended to in the few days since we'd spoken. My dirty little Cherry. She'd only been mine for the duration of our call, but it had felt almost real while she performed for me.

They probably all felt like that. The others. The other lonely guys who beat their meat for her.

I banished her from my head again.

I didn't want her.

Fuck, I wanted her alright.

But I didn't need her.

CHAPTER NINE
VALENTINA

'That's it, Cherry. You don't stop until I tell you to stop.'

I whimpered as I held the vibrator against my already swollen pussy, having already come twice during our session. My thighs trembled as he leaned forward, so close to letting me see his face, but stopping before giving me that pleasure.

'I don't think I can take any more...' I whispered, but already the next wave was building.

'Don't you want to be a good girl for me? I'll take and take my pretty little slut, and you'll keep on giving, won't you?' His voice was thick with lust as his finger ran over the slick head of his cock.

'Yes... I will. Whatever you want.'

'Now spread yourself for me and fuck that little cunt with your fingers until you come all over them.'

I pressed two fingers inside me, stretching myself around them while wishing it was his dick pinning me wide.

'More, Cherry. Two fingers aren't nearly enough to stretch you out for me. When you take all those dicks for me, you'll need to have all of your holes ready and willing. Get them all in there.'

My teeth grazed my lip as I bit back a moan, filling myself to bursting and grinding down on my hand.

'God, you'd look so pretty coated in my cum. I'd fill you until it leaked out of every hole, dripping down your thighs as you walk.'

'Please...'

'You want that don't you, Cherry, to be a dirty little cum rag for a group of men?'

'Fuck, yes.'

ScotsDaddy38 growled in that low way that made my stomach flip and fucked his fist, his balls dancing as he toppled over into a hard orgasm. His torso twitched in the most delicious way, his abs tensing as he jerked into his hand.

'Look at this mess, Cherry. Look what you made me do. Damn, if you were here, I'd make you get on your knees and lick up every drop.'

'Oh god.' His filthy mouth made me hot every time. The decadent things he said came alive in my mind as I toyed with myself for him. 'I'm going to come.'

'Yes, you are, sweet girl. You're going to come hard for me and make a mess of those pristine white sheets of yours.'

Sensation ripped through me as my pussy all but crushed my fingers, my thighs tightening as waves of pleasure cascaded around me. My breath hitched as I fought against the onslaught that dragged me under.

'Yes, baby. That's it... such a good fucking girl.'

As the orgasm subsided, I collapsed back on the bed, sweat coating my skin as my vibrator continued to buzz in my hand against the duvet.

It took a few minutes before I was ready to move. To clean myself up and move my toys ready for cleaning. I pulled on an oversized oodie - possibly the least sexy item of clothing I owned - and sat back down on the bed. He regained his composure too, in a clean pair of grey jogging bottoms, which gave a despicably delightful outline of his impressive cock. Tattoos followed the contours of his stomach and chest, with old Scot's folklore seeming to be the main theme. I wished I could slink around his tight chest like they did.

'I was beginning to think you weren't going to visit again...' I said, tucking my legs under myself as I watched him. Everything but his face. He kept it off camera.

'I was trying not to.'

'Why? Is it how much it costs?'

He laughed and picked up a glass of amber liquid. Whisky most likely. 'No, it's not the cost. You're worth every penny.'

'So what is it?'

He sighed as I lay down, my face closer to the screen as I yawned.

'You're too damn tempting.'

'I'm a cam girl. I'm supposed to be tempting.' I gave him a bratty smile.

'Mmm. But it's not in my plan to obsess over a woman who's far too young for me.'

'What's in your plan?'

'Besides world domination?' he said, sipping his drink. 'I'm getting married.'

There it was. Of course he was. Why else would he be spending his time, and money, on me?

'Oh.'

'You sound disappointed.'

'It's fine. I mean, it's not unusual for clients to be married or in relationships. I'd say it's more unusual for them to be single.' My words came out too quickly, and I took a breath to try to calm myself.

'Were you hoping for something more, Cherry? To take this out into the real world?'

Yes.

'No. It would be far too risky.'

'So nothing changes. I can still watch you fuck yourself and you can listen to me tell you about all the filthy things I'd like to do with you. It's safe for both of us.'

I rolled onto my back and looked up at the ceiling. 'Tell me about her. Is she into this?'

His laughter makes me look back at the screen.

'I wouldn't know.'

'You haven't asked her?'

'Hell. I haven't even kissed her.'

'How can you marry a woman you've never kissed?'

'It's a business arrangement. It's not unusual in my line of work.'

My mind shot to my aunt and her husband. In their syndicates, stuff like arranged marriages still happened. Rarely, but more than in the general population.

'What could be so important in your business that you need to marry someone to get it? Is your business struggling?'

'No. But it could be better. My dad started it, and he had such high aspirations for it. It's my job to take over and make it happen.'

'Do you want to?' He didn't sound at all like it was a passion of his. More like a hindrance.

'I...' he said before cutting himself off. 'It's not always about what you want. Some things are bigger than that.'

'What does your fiancée think of it?'

He sat forward with his elbows on his knees, making me wish I was perched between them.

'She's all for it. It's a mutually beneficial situation.'

'It sounds stupid.'

'It's just complicated.'

'So you have to spend your life pretending to be one person in public and hiding this sexy ass dom side of you online?'

'I'm allowed to do what I like as long as it's discreet and drama free. We both are.'

'But it won't make you happy.'

'No, probably not.'

'Is your dad forcing you to marry her?' I asked.

'No, he's dead. It's why I need to honour the legacy he was building. To make sure it was all worthwhile.'

'Wouldn't he want you to be happy?'

He laughed again. 'Happiness wasn't high on his radar of wants for his kids. What about you? Do you enjoy this being your job?'

I placed my chin on my hand and mulled it over.

'Sometimes. I enjoy being able to make a good living on my own terms. I'm the black sheep in my family and I'd prefer to keep it that way as long as it cuts off any power over me. Plus, I like sex, so being able to come for cash is way better than anything else I'd be qualified for.'

'What's your end goal?'

'Just to be happy. To live the way I want. To find a guy who can put up with my job and still treat me well. Outside of the bedroom, at least.'

I glanced at the clock and winced. We'd been on the private call for over an hour and he'd be wracking up a hell of a bill. 'I should really let you get on...'

'No... keep it on.'

'You want to go again already?' I asked, raising an eyebrow.

'Just keep me company awhile. My house is so damned quiet.'

'It will cost you so much...' Guilt bit into me. But I wanted him to hang around, too.

'Money's not an issue. Happy for you to have it.'

'Okay, but I have knitting that I'm trying to finish for the lady downstairs. Her baby is due any day and I'm so far behind.'

My cheeks heated as he laughed. 'You knit?'

'Yeah, my grandma taught me when I was wee. It's pretty relaxing.'

'You are one sexy little enigma, Miss Cherry. Go knit. I'm going to lie down and read for a bit.'

I gathered up my knitting and picked up the tiny rainbow cardigan I was working on, counting in my head as I sat back against my pillows and relaxed. Occasionally, I'd glance back up at the screen where I could see my cam-man laying on his bed, still just from the chest down. As my needles clacked rhythmically, his breath settled until he slipped into sleep. The soft sound of his breathing was enticing, and I wanted nothing more than to curl up beside him and rest my head on his muscled, tattoo covered chest.

I left the computer on for as long as I could, until my fingers ached and my eyes itched from tiredness.

'Good night, Sir,' I whispered, before clicking off of the site and closing my computer down.

CHAPTER TEN
LOGAN

Nicole flitted from group to group as I trailed along behind her, making conversation with the endless sea of people I didn't know. From family members, to friends and acquaintances, to business associates, our engagement party was proving to be a baptism of fire.

She'd booked the entire swanky city centre hotel for three days, meaning that there was no escape from everyone.

Thank the lord the top floor held two suites so we could give the pretence of sharing our space, but could get away from one another too.

The room was decked out to the nines, dripping with large white florals from every surface. There mustn't be a single white flower left in the whole of Scotland. It definitely gave the impression that we had sought to create. We wanted people to see our union as powerful, rich, and fruitful. With the massive bill I'd paid, it had certainly needed the rich part. Who knew a party could cost so much? I'd been to plenty in my line of work. My father had loved to throw a party to keep up with the mafia joneses, but I'd never been in on the bill for such a grand affair. It was eye-watering even for me.

'Oh, yes, we met a few years ago. You know how it is in this scene. Everyone knows everyone.'

I smiled pleasantly as Nicole chatted to an older woman in the most outrageously over the top fringed dress I'd ever seen. Nicole slipped her hand through my arm and looked up at me with a sunny smile.

Hell, she could act.

In public, you'd never have guessed that there was no substance to our engagement. Nicole was the perfect, attentive, sweet fiancée. I tried to match her energy as best I could.

Mr Valetti sidled up beside us and watched his daughter, his brow furrowed until she set her smile on him. It was like the sun had shone on him after being stuck in the shadows.

'Sweetheart,' he said as the older woman moved on, leaving the three of us in a little clique. 'Are you enjoying your party?'

'It's perfect. How about you?' Nicole leaned in and grazed her father's cheek with a kiss.

'Mm-hmm. Such fun. Can I borrow your man for a moment?'

'Of course you can. I need to grab a drink anyway, gasping after all the chatting. We'll need to have a dance, Logan, before the Tatler photographer goes.'

'No problem, come grab me when you're ready.'

Dancing with a beautiful woman should bring me something other than dread, but it felt like I was putting on a performance. Being watched. Judged. It made me feel sick.

'I've been watching you. The way you took over and have managed to not have your syndicate crumble from the upheaval of your father's death. It's pretty impressive.'

I stared at my future father-in-law, his tone far changed from the last time I'd seen him.

'Thanks, I intend to make him proud, Tony.'

'I always wanted a son. Not that I don't adore my daughter, but to carry on after I go.' Hugh turned to watch Nicole as she laughed with another guest.

'You have Hugh...' I said.

'Hugh is... well. It's not the same. He's not mine. While I don't mind him, he's not the son I wanted. While the syndicate will pass to Nicole, I'm hoping that you will be the perfect match to help her keep it going. She's a good girl, strong and smart, but I don't think she has the ruthless streak that she'll need.'

Watching the way she acted out our ruse so seamlessly had me doubting that.

'I intend to help support you both with whatever you need for success.'

'And you won't hurt her?'

I hesitated as my mind flicked to my sweet Cherry. Marrying one woman while obsessing over another could only bring pain for someone. But I had her permission, and Nicole was into someone else.

'I'll do my best by her. You have my word.'

Tony clapped me on the shoulder and nodded. 'I know you will. You're a good boy. I can tell.'

I swallowed as another expectation joined the others on my shoulders. What's one more person to please when I already had a lifetime's worth of them there?

Grabbing a drink from a passing waiter, I made my way over to where my siblings and their entourages gathered.

Esther had declined the invite, letting me know she'd only make the trip over from Spain for the wedding, and that she very much disapproved of the whole thing, but the others were all there.

Katie and Mac were whispering at the table, with Katie blushing a deep pink at whatever my youngest brother was saying to her. My brother Ewen was talking animatedly with our brother-in-law Cameron, while my sister Maeve was chatting to the two teens she and Cameron had rescued and adopted.

'Enjoying your engagement party?' Ewen said, grinning at me as he chinked his glass to my own.

'Yeah.'

'You sound about as thrilled as these two looked about coming.' Maeve said, pointing a thumb at Grace and Elias, who looked furious at being dragged out of their bedrooms and into the real world. Man, teens were weird. We'd spent our teen years doing whatever we could to slip out from under the watch of dad's men and get up to all sorts. I don't think I could convince the teenagers to misbehave even if I paid them.

'It's just been a long night.' I said, knocking back my champagne and setting the glass down. 'Thanks for coming. I appreciate you all being here.'

'She's pretty hot, but I still think you're an idiot,' Mac added and Katie nodded at his side in agreement.

'Join the long, long list of people who keep telling me how stupid I am.'

'We don't think you're stupid. We just don't think you need to put Dad's plans ahead of your own life. You only get one. We just want you to pursue happiness. We have enough wealth to last a handful of lifetimes. You don't need to hunt out any more.' Maeve gave me a sympathetic smile as she leaned into Cam, who looped his arm around her waist while looking at her like she was made from solid gold.

'I don't need life lessons guys. I'm doing good.'

A member of Tony's staff tapped me lightly on the elbow as I spoke, and I turned to him as he muttered under his breath. 'Miss Valetti is ready to have your formal dance when you're ready.'

I nodded and cleared my throat. 'My fiancée needs me, but drink up and enjoy the party.'

Making my way through the packed room took longer than I could have imagined possible, between being stopped by guests to swap pleasantries and dodging round the many tables with their staggering floral displays.

Finally, I spotted Nicole's sleek figure through the crowd and made toward her and the small group of people she chatted with.

'Hey, here's my man at last,' Nicole said in a light, lilting voice as I joined them.

'Logan, meet my aunt Lucille, and my cousin Valentina.'

I held out my hand to her aunt as my eyes took in the figure next to her.

My breath punched out of me as I looked into the face of my very own sweet Cherry. Cherry was Nicole's cousin? I felt like my brain exploded into a thousand pieces and rendered my mouth useless.

'Lovely to meet you, Logan,' Lucille said, furrowing her brow at my dumbstruck face.

Cherry... Valentina narrowed her eyes at me for a moment, not having seen my face, before her eyes flicked down to my hand that still gripped her mother's. They roved over my watch, and the tattoos across my knuckles, before flicking back to my face and widening.

I opened my mouth, trying to find words, but seeing her in person at my fucking engagement party left me floundering. She was even prettier in person, in a knee-length black gown with a deep slit and her dark hair pulled back into a chic ponytail. Her cheeks pinked up in the same way they did when she came. I ignored the thickening in my groin at the thought.

'Logan,' she said smoothly, holding out her hand as I took it. 'A pleasure to meet you.'

It was like she electrocuted me with the brief touch of my hand, sending shocks through my system and frazzling it entirely.

'You too.' I stuttered out before Nicole linked her arm through mine.

'Sorry to love you and leave you, but we've got the magazine's photographers waiting to capture a dance between us. You know how it is.' Nicole levelled an icy stare at Valentina before smiling at Lucille. 'So lovely of you both to have come... we'll need to get a little picture of the family together.'

Then she was dragging me into the middle of the dance floor as the band struck up a romantic tune.

'Logan, why are you being so weird?' Nicole whispered into my ear as she pulled me close. 'We need this to look like we are madly in love, remember?'

'Yeah, sorry. It's been a long night.' I pressed my hand tightly around Nicole's waist and pulled her flush against me as she rested her cheek against mine. My body may have been on the dancefloor, but my gaze solely remained on my sweet Cherry. Nicole's fucking cousin. Fuck my life. It should have solidified how bad a plan it was to do anything other than cut contact immediately, but I couldn't take my eyes off of her.

She was pretty online, sweet and curvaceous, a luscious little treat. In person, she stole my very breath away. I wanted nothing more than to stalk across the room, throw her over my shoulder, and find a quiet place to absolutely ruin her.

Cameras flashed around us as people smiled and swooned, Nicole and I making the perfect mafia offspring pairing. Visually, at least.

Couples joined us on the dancefloor mid dance, and I lost sight of Valentina through the throng, only picking up glimpses occasionally as we danced. Then I spotted Hugh beside her, his fingers gripping into her arm as he whispered into her ear. The hairs on my neck stood up as I watched her glare at him and snatch her arm from his. When she walked off, he followed.

He's her cousin.

It's probably nothing.

The end of the song seemed to take hours to come. As soon as it did, I kissed Nicole on the cheek before following in the direction Valentina and Hugh had gone.

It was the last thing I should have done.

But I had no choice.

I needed to talk to her.

CHAPTER ELEVEN
VALENTINA

Holy bloody fucknuggets.

ScotsDaddy38 was Nicole's fiancé. She's the fake relationship he told me about.

Fuck, fuck, fuck.

I watched as Nicole led him to the dancefloor, wrapping herself up in him as she looked every bit smitten for the cameras.

His eyes found me repeatedly as they danced and I couldn't look away. Finally, I could see his face and unfortunately it was pressed against my cousin's cheek. His hair was dark and swept back from his eyes with grey beginning to pepper the area near his temples. And his eyes. God his eyes! They'd been that icy grey-blue and full of an intensity that made me want to drop to my knees and worship him right there and then.

My filthy mouthed camera man was going to marry my cousin. And I was fucking furious.

Yet again, life left me with nothing while she got everything. And worst of all, she didn't even want what she had.

'Valentina.' Hugh sidled up beside me as my mother left to grab us drinks. 'I'd say it's a pleasure to see you here, but we both know I'd be lying.'

'Bugger off, Hugh.'

'Tsk, tsk. You know better than to talk to your superiors like that. While I know you make a living off of that dirty little mouth of yours, there's no need to be crass here.'

I glowered at my older cousin. 'I may be a cam girl, but at least I have a purpose. What's your purpose in your family, Hugh? Nicole inherits everything and takes over the syndicate. Where does that leave you? Begging your sister for handouts for the rest of your life?'

Hugh grabbed my upper arm as I winced, digging his fingers into my skin. 'Shut your mouth, you dirty little whore. I know my place. Nicole needs me by her side, supporting her with the business. No-one needs you. No-one wants you. Just a stupid little girl with daddy issues who likes to show her cunt to strangers.'

Fury bubbled in my chest as I yanked my arm out of his grip. 'At least people want to see mine and I don't have to trick people into touching me. And you think I have daddy issues? My dad died. Yours chose the bottom of a bottle over you.'

It was cruel, but Hugh deserved my ire.

'You little bitch,' he whispered as I turned and walked toward the ladies' room. Anger too often brought tears, and I had no intention of giving him the satisfaction of seeing mine.

I'd almost made it down the corridor and into the ladies' when a hand grabbed me and slammed me into an alcove.

Hugh glared at me as he forced my back against the wall.

'You think you can come in here acting like betty big bollocks and get away with it? You are a piece of shit, and the family only tolerates you for your mum's sake.'

'Get off of me.' I kicked out at him, not quite a match for his strength.

'I wonder how many people in there have found your little website and tossed themselves off to you whoring yourself out? How many of them know exactly what you are hiding beneath this dress?'

Hugh used his other hand to touch my waist, fingering the silky material as he licked at his thin lips. 'Maybe I should look for myself? It's only fair.'

'I'd prefer to be me than you any day.' I laughed almost manically as I fought his grip. 'Nicole is going to marry Logan, and he'll fill that position as the man they need. He's from a wealthy mafia family, he's been running his own syndicate, he's steady and solid and Nicole might not love him yet, but give it time and she'll see him for who he is. He'll be the son your step-father always wanted, and then what will you do? Try to beg and scrounge for scraps? At least people want my body. You'll have nothing to offer anyone.'

If Hugh's glare could have killed me, it would have. He looked ready to blow a gasket.

'What's going on here?' A voice said, and I breathed a sigh of relief as Hugh dropped his grip on me and stepped backward.

'Ah, Logan, nothing. Just helping my cousin with a little issue.'

I couldn't meet his eyes as I felt his gaze burning into me.

'I don't think she needs any more of your help. I think it would be best if you returned to the party.'

Hugh's mouth opened as though he was ready to argue, but then he thought better of it before spitting out, 'I'll catch up with you another time, Valentina.'

When he left, I closed my eyes and leant my head back against the wall, the fire leaving me.

'You okay, Cherry?' My screen-name on his lips in person was a delight.

'I'm fine.'

'You don't look fine. Did he hurt you?'

'No.'

Then his fingers were on my chin, tilting my face to look up at him. When I did, I fell in love a little more. Up close, he was everything I could have wanted. Full lips, intense eyes and that kind of stern, stoic expression that made me wet.

'I didn't know...' he said.

'It's okay. I didn't either. It's nice to put a name and face to you, though.'

His touch felt like fire searing across my jaw as my heart rate picked up. I wanted nothing more than to wrap my arms around his neck and taste him.

'I guess I should call you Valentina.'

'I guess I shouldn't call you Daddy.'

His expression darkened as he bit his lower lip. 'Fuck, you can't call me that.'

His reaction made me want to call him it all the more. 'Why? Will you spank me if I do?'

I felt the tremble in his fingers as he wavered. 'I can't. God, I fucking want to, but I can't. You're too young. I'm engaged to your cousin. It wasn't supposed to be real.'

It hurt. Another rejection. Another win for Nicole.

'There's only a sixteen year gap, it's not that big...'

'I'm engaged to your cousin.'

'But you don't love her. And she doesn't love you. She gave you permission...'

'Permission to be discreet. I don't think it would extend to fucking her family members.'

I was sick of always being second best. Sick of never having what I wanted, always wearing the hand-me-downs from my cousin. Swallowing hard, I stepped forward, sliding a hand up his chest and around the back of his neck.

'You know it could be so good though, don't you? The fire. You must feel it. The dirty things you told me, let's make them real. Pin me down, spread me open, make me scream a thousand 'please daddies' into your ear.'

His fingers found my neck as he held me back, sending a thrill shooting through me as his hand tightened around my throat.

'Cherry, I'd fucking destroy you.'

'Destroy me, Daddy.'

He choked back a growl as he neared me, his breath tickling over my lips as I tipped my head back to welcome him.

'No.'

I blinked my eyes open as he walked backward, holding his hands up, removing the delicious pressure from my throat.

'No?'

'I can't do this. I'm not that guy.'

'Logan, please...'

'Valentina, this isn't going to happen. Pretend that tonight was the first time we ever met. I'm done.'

I watched as he walked away, his shoulders bunched while I stewed.

The hell it was done.

I'd show him.

Somehow.

CHAPTER TWELVE

LOGAN

It was late by the time I got back to my room and every single part of me ached. The city glittered outside of the hotel suite windows and I could hear Nicole moving about in the apartment next to me on our exclusive floor.

It was an insight into what our marriage would be, she and I living different lives while presenting a joyous union to the rest of the world.

The suite was spacious and luxurious, with its sleek furnishings and chrome. And it was empty. Cold. Lonely.

For the thousandth time that night, my mind went back to Valentina, and her exploding into my real world unexpectedly. Our camming was supposed to be a bit of fun, a harmless deviance away from my actual problems.

Then there she was, all delicious curves and fuck me eyes, begging me to take her. It had taken every fucking inch of my resolve not to fuck her right there on the spot. Especially when she'd called me Daddy. That word on her lips was hellish perfection. I wanted to hear her whimper it beneath me and scream it from the rooftops as I bent her to my desires.

But I couldn't

It was too messy.

And she was too young. A twenty-two-year-old was one thing for playing with online, but to actually toy with her in real life would be wrong.

But fuck, had she felt good beneath my fingers. The way she wet her lips and looked up at me like a little doe waiting to be devoured would stay with me for an eternity.

In my head.

In my dreams.

Definitely not in person.

A knock at my door broke me out of my train of thought. I looked through the peephole to see my future father-in-law and two of his heavies in the corridor.

With a sigh, I opened the door and welcomed them inside.

'How can I help you, Tony?'

'A drink would be a good start.'

I poured us both a heavy measure of whisky from the suite bar before sitting at the table in front of the floor to ceiling window.

'I want to send you on an assignment. See it as your first job as part of the Valetti family.'

I sat forward and eyed Tony sceptically. He'd gone from unwelcoming to sending me out to work for him in a remarkably quick turn around. 'I'm not officially a part of your family yet, Tony.'

'I need you to show me you'll be a good fit. That I can trust you to look after my Nicole and my business going forward. I'm not naïve enough to believe that you and her can keep things mostly separate. It's not how life works.'

'Nicole is intent on marrying me, whether you see me as a good fit or otherwise.'

Tony grinned and swirled the amber liquid in his glass. 'But I know that what you really want is access to my connections. For that, it's me you need to sweeten up.'

I sat back and ran a hand over my face, my eyes burning with exhaustion as I mulled over his words. His connections were what I was agreeing to the union for, and he knew it. He had me by the fucking balls and there was little I could do to get around it.

'What's the job?'

'Don't worry, nothing too grisly. I need you to get chummy with Alfie Rosenhall at his estate up north. Rosenhall Estate. You'll have heard of it.'

Not only had I heard of it, I'd been there numerous times. Never for business, always for pleasure.

'I've heard of it.'

'Good, well, you'll know that Alfie runs it. He's been a tricky wee bugger to get hold of and he's due me a significant payment for our last deal still. I don't want to go in guns blazing and kill the little fucker, but I want him to get the message.'

'You want me to go extract a payment for you? It's a little below my paygrade.'

'Mmm, you've met him. You know what he's like. Charm works better than offensive, and unfortunately I have little charm to give.' Tony slid an envelope across the table. 'Some spending money and your invitation to attend.'

Rosenhall was a playground for sexual deviants. Hardly the place you sent your future son-in-law.

'What about Nicole? Do you think she'll like her dad sending me to a sex soaked paradise?' I left the envelope where it sat, holding off on agreeing to anything.

'My boy, I'm not stupid enough to think she'd give a rat's ass about where you're sticking your cock. See it as a wedding gift from me to you. A last romp amongst a bevy of women before you settle down. We all know the two of you aren't a love match.' He downed the rest of his drink before standing. 'I know the rumours about my daughter and her bodyguard well enough, Logan.'

'Yet, you let it go on?'

Tony gave a wan smile before shrugging. 'All I want is for her to be happy. I'll do whatever it takes to see my baby girl smile.'

An hour later, after I'd had time for a scalding shower and a burger from room service, I lay in bed and listened to the city din below.

Cars zipped along the road, fewer as the night sank into the early hours. Drunken groups of young folk yelled and laughed as they tumbled out of bars along the busy street, while the occasional siren wailed from afar.

It wasn't long before I noticed another noise, a rhythmic knocking coming from the wall which connected my suite to Nicole's.

And a moan.

Multiple moans.

I groaned as I pulled a pillow over my head. The last thing I needed was to listen to my future wife getting it on with her man.

The pillow couldn't drown out the racket that built next door, the moans increasing until they reached a crescendo.

So much for discretion.

Well, two could play that game.

It looked like a trip to Rosenhall was exactly what I needed.

I'd rid myself of my blue balls and thrust Valentina out of my head, knowing that my abstinence of late was likely the driver for my need for her.

CHAPTER THIRTEEN
VALENTINA

There he was.

After four days with no sign of him, Logan's username popped up in my cam room. My fingers hovered over the keys as I decided whether it was a good idea to message him when he'd been pretty clear in his rejection.

> Hey.

I waited for a response, the jumping of the three little dots. Anything.
Nothing.

> Look, I'm sorry for how things went down the other night.

Silence.

> Please don't ignore me.

Anger flushed through me at his continued silence.

> You wouldn't be here if you didn't want to talk.

At last, the dots in the chat box danced.
I frowned as his message popped up.

> We can't do this.

> Why?

> You know why. I'm engaged to your cousin.

> And she's shagging another man. Why do you care what she thinks?

> It doesn't matter.

If he wasn't on the other side of a screen, I'd have gladly socked him one. Such a total pillock.

> You want me. I can tell. The things you said, the way you reacted. It was real. Will Nicole give you those things you crave? Will she get on her knees for you, Logan? Will she call you Daddy as she takes--

> Listen, V, you're a good-looking girl, and we had some hot moments, but it would never work. Even if I wasn't marrying your cousin. You are too young for me.

> That's a crock of shit and you know it. I'm not trying to marry you. I just want to experience the things you whispered about in the dead of night. I'm not asking for you to fall in love with me.

His dots bounced on and off for minutes before he finally messaged me back.

I'm only here to delete this account. It's done, V. Sorry.

Before I had the chance to reply, his username disappeared without a trace. Gone.

I let out an angry groan as I slapped my laptop shut and threw myself back on the bed. Yet again, Nicole had won. Like she always had. Perfect mafia princess versus the black sheep. It was no contest for a guy like Logan. How could I have thought any different?

The bridal shop was awash with glitter and tulle and I'd have loved it if I were in any other company. Watching Nicole try on dresses was the furthest thing humanly possible from my idea of fun.

'Can I go?' I whispered to my mum as we waited for Nicole to grace us with another perfect dress, which she'd um and ah over before rejecting.

She was fucking glorious in every single one, and I'd never hated her more.

I sat sandwiched between my aunt and my mother as Nicole's bevvy of bridesmaids took the other couch in the luxurious bridal shop. Nicole had secured the entire store for trying on her dress. A single changing room wasn't nearly exclusive enough. With the swooning sales assistants filling up everyone's champagne every few minutes, we were all halfway to being smashed at three in the afternoon on a Tuesday.

Nicole appeared in a dress that was more see-through than could surely be deemed acceptable in front of your own mother. And looked bloody fantastic.

No wonder Logan chose her.

She was pretty, rich, and well versed in the decorum required for their sort of circles. Everything I wasn't. I didn't do bad, but I wasn't what anyone would consider svelte or with the model good looks Nicole had.

Was I jealous? Abso-fucking-lutely. And that just made me all the angrier. I shouldn't care.

'Ooh,' came the collective gasp as Nicole ascended the mirror-surrounded white podium and moved this way and that.

'Oh sweety, I think that one's the best so far,' my aunt said, bursting into another round of tears at the sight of her step-daughter in a wedding dress.

'Calm down, Anette,' Nicole laughed as she spoke, 'I think Dad would have a heart attack if he had to walk me down the aisle in this one.'

'You can totally pull it off,' said one of Nicole's friends.

'What do you think, Valentina?'

I almost choked on my champagne as Nicole called me out. 'I think you look great.'

'Hmm, probably not the right one.' I worked hard to not roll my eyes as she dismissed my comment. 'This looks more like something one of those slutty girls at the resort Daddy's sending Logan to would wear.'

My ears perked up at that. What resort? I hadn't heard from him since he deleted his account on Primal Princesses.

'Is that the sex one?' Nicole's friend said, 'What's it called again?'

'Rose Hall, or something.'

My mum and aunt dipped out of the conversation, going to the far corner of the store to sift through rack upon rack of white dresses.

'Aren't you worried about him being there?' Another friend chipped in.

Nicole let out a sweet laugh and shook her head. 'No, of course not. Logan's not like that. He's only going for business. He's very loyal.'

It took everything in me not to laugh out loud. She was busy getting it on with her bodyguard every night and talking about her fiancé as if she actually gave a darn about him. She had no idea the things Logan was into, the dirty things he'd growled at me before he knew who I really was. The things I was so desperate to hear him say again.

I pulled out my phone and typed Rose Hall into the notes.

It looked like I had some research to do.

Later that night, Lara and I sat curled up on the sofa, eating a mountain of Chinese food, and scouring the internet for any sign of a hedonistic escape in the highlands.

'Are you sure it exists, and she wasn't just having you on?' Lara asked, pushing her iPad away with a sigh. 'We've been searching for hours and are still no closer to finding an answer.'

'It's got to exist. Why would she say it otherwise? She doesn't know that he and I... well you know.'

'That you flicked the bean online for your cousin's fiancé and are stalking him?' Lara was less than impressed with the turn of events after I got back from the party and filled her in.

'Well, yeah. That. Stop being judgy and help me find it. She said he goes for ten days on Wednesday and I need to try to find a way in.'

'Do you think he'll just fall in love with you when you show up there? He sounded pretty definitive about his no.' Lara scooped a load of chow mein into her mouth as she eyed me sceptically.

'I'm not looking for love. I want to experience what he was offering, just for a day or two. Then I'll get it out of my system and come home. Just a fling. Nicole never needs to know.'

'It's a terrible idea, babe,' Lara said after swallowing down her noodles and taking a swig of the awful blue alcopop she favoured.

'I know. But your twenties are a time for terrible choices, right?' I winked as I went back to my deep dive through Reddit threads, following half mentions and skirting language. It was a whole warren of rabbit holes to fall down, but the place that seemed most promising.

'Do you want a top up?' Lara asked as she stood and stretched.

'Yeah, please.'

Then I saw it. A thread buried in some random Reddit community that mentioned having been 'prey' at Rosenhall Estate. Rosenhall, not Rose Hall! Adjusting my search brought me a little closer, with the occasional mention here and there. But nothing concrete.

Lara handed me my drink while looking over my shoulder. 'Found something?'

'Yeah, a mention of being prey at Rosenhall Estate. Nicole got the name wrong. But nothing else is coming up.'

'Prey?' Lara asked, raising a brow. 'That sounds like a perfect reason to go no further.'

Or a perfect reason to have damp knickers...

'Lara,,,'

She held up her hands and sighed. 'Okay, but if you get yourself killed, it's your own damn fault.'

'So what should I do?'

'Message her. The woman who said she'd been there. She must know how to access it.'

A grin swept over my face as I pulled up the profile, seeing nothing particularly untoward about it. Most of her posts were in the romance reader communities or the BDSM ones.

I took a deep breath and penned her a message.

Much to my surprise, she answered almost immediately.

> I'm not supposed to share the details, but if you can go, you HAVE to go. It's amazing. Intense and overwhelming, but there is nothing else like it. Even better, you get paid to go! If you enter the auction, you get half of whatever you go for on top of the daily fee. Click the link HERE and it'll take you to the sign up forms. Don't mention that I sent you though, otherwise I won't be able to go back.

My fingers trembled as I thanked her and clicked the URL.

CHAPTER FOURTEEN
LOGAN

My car pulled into the estate, the driver inching up the gravel driveway, which extended for over a mile.

I should have been excited. Over a week in a lust filled paradise, with only a few business agreements to complete. My cock twitched at the very thought of it, but I shook my head. My father-in-law to be was counting on me to represent him, and falling into a pit of depravity wasn't the way to go.

However badly I needed it.

Dark green towering pines lined the drive up to the house, with the forest extending thickly around the estate. The building came into view in a towering castle-like structure made from a rainbow of orange, pink and grey granite. I'd been in my fair share of beautiful, historic Scottish buildings, but Rosehall Estate always took my breath away.

The car pulled to a stop, with my driver coming round to open my door for me. Three staff members arrived within moments, carrying my luggage inside while the aged butler greeted me.

'Mr McGowan, it's a pleasure to welcome you back to Rosenhall. We hope you have a delightful stay.'

'Thank you, Grieves. It's a joy to be back. Is Alfie around?' The sooner I sorted out business, the sooner I could get out of there.

'Mr. Rosenhall had to pop down to London for a spot of business. He'll be back in a day or two, but has asked me to see that you long for nothing in his absence.'

I ground my back teeth together as I followed the butler into the cavernous entry hall, decked out in rich old wood and deep, sumptuous fabrics.

Alfie had always been a sneaky little fuck, even when we were in boarding school together some twenty years ago. When he'd grown up and inherited his father's cartel and his decadent highland playground, Alfie had very much focused on the latter. He was a terrible syndicate boss, but not an unlikeable one. He'd have lost limbs by that point had he not held a particular charm and a hedonistic paradise to smooth over any issues.

Getting into the estate as a player was extremely difficult and happened in only a few ways: you were invited, or you threw huge money at Alfie. Money he then used to pay off the debts, he dodged like the money he owed Tony.

"Mr. Rosehall has put you in one of the east wing suites. He remembers how you prefer the, uh, amenities there.'

Grieves was being polite. He knew as well as I did that those suites in particular had multiple points fitted for restraining sweet little subs, as well as a built in cage at the foot of the bed. No luxury was lost at Rosenhall Estate. They fit the rooms with all the mod cons you might need for the stay, as well as glistening bathrooms with dropped jacuzzi baths and showers big enough for multiple playmates. The rooms themselves maintained the original character of the building, with thick rugs under foot, covering ancient wooden floorboards. They boasted high ceilings and immense windows which looked out over the hills and lochs as the Scottish landscape stretched out of view. The beds were enormous, four posted monsters, ready for all manner of sordid deeds.

There wasn't much that didn't go on there.

You could fuck in the dining room in front of bemused guests, or whip your sub up the stairwell. You could bend over and take a cock in the forest or on the front steps if you pleased. There were dedicated playrooms, but most evenings everyone gathered in the grand old banquet hall around its multiple fireplaces and let their wildest fantasies come true.

But I was there for business, not pleasure.

It was harder to keep my mind out of the gutter as we reached the top of the stunning staircase and it opened out into the upper hall. Wooden posts held up decorative wooden arches, and to each post was affixed a male or female plaything, their hands secured above their heads to rings in the post. As naked as the day they were born, and some even oiled to gleaming in the soft interior lighting.

They were the ones who were being punished, albeit lightly, for minor infractions. People would toy with them as they passed when going to and from their rooms, often getting them right to the point of orgasming before walking away and leaving them desperate. Even more deliciously, they could see the others who were secured around them but not reach them. A wet cunt and insanely hard cock only a metre or two from one another, but with no way to satisfy themselves. It really was a stroke of genius, as Alfie had pointed out, because when they were untied and led downstairs on an evening, they were game for just about anything to satisfy those urges.

One woman with the most luscious red hair whimpered as I passed, letting out a soft 'Please, Sir?'

I turned to face her, grinning as she positively arched in excitement.

'Yes? What do you want?'

I knew exactly what she wanted, but it was always far more delightful to make them say it.

'Please play with me?'

The request had me halfway too hard at the pure need in her voice. I stepped in close and told myself to calm down when the intake of breath that lifted her exposed tits made me react. 'What sort of games do you like?'

'Whatever you need. Whatever you'll give me?'

A tempting offer for sure, but when I looked down into her pretty little face, it was all wrong. Her hair wasn't dark and gleaming, and her lips weren't stained with cherry fucking lollipops. Her eyes were the wrong shade of hazel and she lacked the curves of the particular cam girl who I couldn't get out of my mind.

'Maybe later, sweetheart,' I said, unable to help my grin at her crestfallen expression.

An indulgence or two would be impossible to avoid. Hell, Alfie would see it as an affront to his hospitality, but perhaps I'd find myself a curvy little brunette who I could fuck from behind and call Cherry.

It was close enough...

CHAPTER FIFTEEN

VALENTINA

A handful of other women and I stood awkwardly in the ancient study. I should have spoken to them, but my stomach kept somersaulting and threatening to make me vomit all over the fancy old rug I stood on.

Serious doubts about my plan kept flying through my head.

What had I been thinking? Filling out the forms had been such a turn on, that I'd barely stopped to think from the moment I'd submitted them until I'd stepped off of the train in Inverness and into a luxury car with blacked-out windows and full cream leather interior. Sitting in the back of the car as we headed further and further from civilisation had brought the doubts sweeping down over me.

I fidgeted with the buttons on my coat, too hot to be wearing it but also too unsure to remove it. The mansion was warm. It must have cost them a fortune to heat it with its vast windows and high ceilings.

Warm enough for the playthings - as they called us - to be wearing very little.

An older man walked into the room with two women following

him. They wore an outfit - if you could call the scrap of material that - made from a deep red linen material. It looked like two long strips of material that draped over the shoulders and affixed around the waist with another strip of material that formed a belt. It fell to their knees at the front and back, but only covered the necessities. Other than the areas where the belt looped about their waists, their full side profile lay exposed with no underwear or bra to be seen. I was desperate to be seen in the sultry outfit as I was to hide. There's no doubting it left the playthings exposed and easily accessible, and it had me wet just looking at the two women wearing it.

'Good Afternoon, ladies, a pleasure to meet you all. I am Grieves, and I am your point of contact for running the household during your stay. If you find any issues with your accommodation or amenities, let me know.'

Grieves smiled warmly at me before continuing. 'You have all chosen to join us here at Rosenhall for the next few days, and I am delighted to welcome you. You will have gone over most of your rules and limits when you filled out your forms, so I'll just go over the necessary with you. You should have handed in your STD test results upon entry and your confirmation of birth control use, too. If you've yet to do so, please put them on the desk. If you have chosen to be a part of the hunt on Tuesday morning you will wear one of these metal collars during your time here. At the auction on Monday night, someone will bid for you and will win two days and nights with you in their company alone. They will be able to do whatever they wish with you as long as they respect the limits you gave in your contract. I encourage you to remind playmates of your limits prior to play. If you are wearing a collar, there is a no-penetration rule until after the auction.'

I nearly choked upon hearing the sweet old man talking about penetration.

'You may be touched and played with orally or digitally, and you may have your mouth used however your playmates see fit, but you must defer from vaginal or anal sex until after the auction. There must be a little sweetener for our buyers. The players know they must respect this rule and know any collared plaything is out of bounds regarding those acts. If you consent to joining in the auction and hunt, you will be paid half of the sale price directly, so it is worth your while to garner interest over the week. If you successfully avoid being caught by your buyer during the hunt, you will receive the full sale price.'

There was muttering from some of the other women. I had no intention of trying to avoid capture, as I fully intended to seduce Logan into purchasing the right to hunt me.

'Whether they catch you or not, you will still be their plaything for the full two days thereafter. At any point you can use the safe word 'cease' and all play must stop immediately. You may use it if there is someone you do not wish to play with touching you, or if someone pushes your limits past those you have stated you are comfortable with. It will not be held against you, but excessive use may have us evaluating whether this experience is right for you. You may leave the experience at any time if it doesn't match up to your expectations, you will still be paid for the days you complete.'

I shifted from foot to foot as I continued to fiddle with my buttons, glancing from the women who waited with me to Grieves.

'Now you may strip, and those who have expressed interest in the auction will be locked into their collars.'

'Strip?' I asked, 'Now?'

'Yes, my dear. You will not be allowed any clothing other than what we provide during your stay. You will hand over all clothing to our safekeeping until leaving day. The girls here will help you with your linens.'

There was an awkward few moments as everyone looked around, before one woman dropped her bag and took out a pile of clothes, handing them over to one of the red-clad women who put them in a box and marked her name on it. Samirah. Before I had moved, she stripped down to nothing and added those clothes, too. I swallowed hard as others stripped.

I may have been perfectly comfortable naked in front of strangers on a webcam, but in a room full of them, and women no less, it was completely alien.

Taking a breath to steady my nerves, I removed my coat and folded it neatly before stripping off my clothing and shoes. My cheeks flamed as I tried to ignore the many eyes around me, gathering up my carefully selected wardrobe of clothing and putting them into a box.

One of the women wrote my name on the top before bringing me a set of the rich red linens, draping them over my shoulders and fixing them snugly with the belt.

In my deepest fantasies, when I'd delved into them to indulge myself, having my possessions removed and being given something so revealing to wear was a huge turn on. And as Grieves walked up to me with a smile and an open metal collar, I was wet. Even though I didn't find the man attractive. The whole situation had me on tenterhooks, and my thighs were slick as he circled my throat in silver and locked it shut with a small key.

'Good girl,' he whispered in my ear as he patted my shoulder before moving on.

Hell, if I couldn't make Logan want me, at least I would experience things I'd only ever dreamed of.

With only my bag of toiletries and my phone, keys, and purse, Grieves led us through the mansion toward our lodgings. Every time we passed a guest, their eyes burned into me, with a delightful mix of desire and shame mingling in my stomach. They openly watched and assessed us in a way that would be frowned upon in polite society. That triggered something feral deep inside me. I looked for Logan as we passed through the house, but didn't see him. Grieves led us up a large, ornate staircase, and my eyes nearly fell out of my head when I saw multiple women and men tied naked to posts at the top. A man knelt in front of one woman, his mouth on her as she shuddered and cried out, not caring who saw. Maybe enjoying being seen. The woman attached to the post next to her begged the man to let her play, and the desperation in her voice made me widen my eyes. I would never beg like that. Even if I wanted to.

Eventually I was shown to a neat, well presented little room with a private bathroom. It wasn't as luxurious as the rest of the mansion seemed to be, but perfectly adequate. I imagined it to be former servants' quarters.

When I closed the door and looked in the mirror at the flushed cheeked, red clad image of myself, I closed my eyes.

What on earth was I doing?

What if Logan wasn't here?

Or worse, what if I couldn't make him want me?

CHAPTER SIXTEEN

LOGAN

'A little more whisky, Sir?' a blonde asked me, hovering by my chair with a decanter in hand.

'Please,' I said, holding my glass out as she topped it up.

'Is there anything else you need?' Her eyes glittered as she spoke.

'Not right now, but thank you.'

The night was wearing on, and all around the room I could hear soft moans and pained cries. It hadn't quite descended into a full on orgy, yet, but I had no doubt it would.

The girl left, and I resumed my idle chat with the other fully clothed guests who sat on the ring of chesterfield sofas gathered around one of the mantle pieces. The fire crackled noisily as the amount of moans increased on my periphery, and my dick thickened in my trousers.

A gong sounded from the far left and I turned to watch as a group of new playthings were led up to the central dais in the large room. Like everyone else, my eyes stole over the neatly displayed human toys, the women in the over the shoulder red linens and the men in ones which fell from their waist belts alone to cover their crotches. One of them blushed beneath the venetian masks they wore, for their first night on show, as his linens tented impressively. Evidently, he was excited to be there.

Passing my eyes over the other new recruits, they caught on a brunette near the end. Her hair was pulled into a high ponytail, showing off the metal collar that graced her neck. Fuck. The collars were a particular turn on for me. I loved to touch the collar while a plaything sucked my dick, threatening to fuck them before the auction to see them fight the war between desire and wanting to obey the rules. Not only that, but she looked a bit like my sweet Cherry from what I could see. The same curves displayed faultlessly in the red clothing, or lack thereof.

She would do nicely for a distraction, a bit of fun to get her out of my system.

Grieves spoke out in a bellowing voice. 'Ladies and gentlemen, we have some lovely new playthings joining us for the next few days. Remember to respect their safe word, and their limits, and to show them a good time. They will wear their masks for tonight to let them explore with that bit of privacy before joining the main ranks of recruits tomorrow. They are also not eligible for punishment tonight, pleasure only.'

As if punishment and pleasure couldn't be the same damn thing.

I kept an eye on the curvy brunette as she stepped down from the dais and made her way through the room, stopping to stare at a few scenes as she passed them.

Pressure against my leg had me looking down to see the blonde from earlier resting on her knees by my calf. She smiled up at me and I let her be, enjoying the warm body pressing into mine. My eyes returned to the brunette as she made her way closer before stopping beside me and looking down at me. With those same hazel eyes. Those eyes were impossible to forget.

Anger bubbled up in my chest at the sight of her. Anger and lust. Valentina was there, in Rosenhall, dressed up like a little sex slave and wearing a glinting metal collar around her neck.

I reached up from my seat and thrust my fingers into the base of her ponytail, pulling her head to my mouth as I whispered in her ear.

'What the fuck are you doing here?'

Her breath was hot as she gasped at my tight grip. 'I'm going to show you that you should fuck me, Daddy.'

'Stop that. I'm not—It's not going to happen.'

'You couldn't keep your eyes off of me. I saw you.' Her voice was a throaty whisper that made me swallow hard. I wanted nothing more than to pin her down right there and agree to her request. 'Don't you like it, Logan? Look at me. I'm dressed like this for you. I'm wearing this collar for you. I'm entering the auction for you.'

Fuck. The auction. She couldn't be...

'No,' I said, catching her eyes and shaking my head. 'You are going home. Right now.'

'I'm staying. I may have come here for you, but I'm not leaving without someone fucking me like I deserve, and if that's not you, I'm sure I'll find someone willing.'

My mouth went dry. She followed me to Rosenhall. Despite me saying no. I should have been appalled, or worried, but my dick was rock hard. She wanted me badly and that was fucking hot.

'So, are you going to let me get to my knees and take care of that?' she said, licking at her lips.

It took everything in me to shake my head no. 'You are too young and I'm marrying your cousin. I can't do it.'

She pouted, her face pulling into a bratty expression.

'Shame...'

I let go of her head as she stood and smoothed down her linens. Before I'd taken a full breath, she'd moved to the two men sitting across from me and knelt at their feet, murmuring to them as they sat up and looked at her.

Jealousy boiled in my stomach when one reached out and ran a thumb over her lips before she sucked it into her mouth. The little bitch was going to taunt me.

The blonde placed a hand on my thigh, toying gently with the seam of my trousers. I ignored her touch as I kept watching my Cherry.

She stood and lowered herself onto one of the men's laps, spreading her legs to either side of his thighs and I all but trembled with barely concealed annoyance. I tried to talk myself out of it. I didn't want her. Why shouldn't she have some fun? She'd probably discover that she hated the games we spoke about when it was real. It would be the driver she needed to go home and get out of my life.

When the older of the two men whispered in her ear, letting his hands rove over her skin, it took everything I had not to stomp over and rip her away from them.

I couldn't reject her and expect to possess her at the same time. And despite myself, the sight of her tilting her head as his fingers grazed her throat had me hot.

When he pulled at the belt holding her scraps of fabric in place and exposed her slick pink cunt to the room, I wanted to fall to my knees and join them in worshipping her.

'Please, Sir?' the pretty blonde said, glancing at my dick and practically writhing against me.

'Go on,' I said, needing something, anything to stop me marching over there and ruining everything by sticking my dick in her off limits cunt.

She unzipped my trousers and released my cock, practically panting as she wrapped a hand about my engorged girth. I'd never been so fucking hard.

My eyes rolled when she set her mouth over the tip and swirled her tongue around the head.

My Cherry had noticed too, and she bit her lip as she saw the blonde taste me. Electricity sparked between us as we both sought our pleasure with others.

The man behind her slid his hand over her throat and gripped her tightly, whispering in her ear as the other man slid two fingers into her. My balls tightened as hard as my shoulders did. Seeing her displayed in front of me with another man tasting her sweet pussy while I wanted to devour her was as hot as it was enraging. Our eyes met as she whimpered, arching her cunt toward him as he continued to stroke her. A familiar pink flush fell over her chest as she writhed in their arms and I needed more. More of the blonde's mouth.

I looked down into her eyes and ran a hand over her jaw as she took my cock like a good little slut.

'I need to fuck your face, sweetheart. You ready?'

'Please, Sir.' Her voice held a whine that hit me right in the balls. I needed to unload in a tight, wet throat. Hers would do.

And Cherry would get to see that I wasn't going to back down.

I wouldn't give in to her.

I'd make her leave, one way or another.

CHAPTER SEVENTEEN
VALENTINA

My whole body trembled as I lay spread across one man's lap while another thrust his fingers inside me. It was the dirtiest, most erotic thing I'd ever done, and in a room full of people, no less.

I felt their looks, their desire seeping out toward me as I became an amusement for them. It was better than I'd ever imagined. I only wished that Logan was the man touching me.

He stood, and for a half a moment I thought he was going to leave. That I'd driven him mad with jealousy. Instead, he fisted the blonde girl's hair and pulled her up higher on her knees and forced her mouth onto his dick.

My stomach flipped with envy. His beautiful, big dick disappeared into her mouth as she tried to swallow the behemoth down fully.

I wanted to stab her.

To walk over there and pull her off of him and tell her he was mine.

But I didn't.

'Taste me,' I moaned to the man between my thighs, crying out as his mouth fit over my clit and his tongue made me buck against him.

'Yes, baby, you take his tongue. You love this, don't you?'

'I do...' I whispered, keeping my eyes on Logan as the girl worked hard to take all of him. She couldn't. I didn't think it was physically possible.

But I didn't tell them that what I loved most was Logan's tortured glare as he watched someone else taste me. He wasn't fooling me in the slightest. He might fight his urges, but I knew they were simmering there.

The man behind me slid his hands over my nipples and pinched them roughly, making me cry out as I arched while the other used his hands to pin my hips down hard.

'God, I wish I could fuck you. You're so responsive. You'd take both of us, wouldn't you?'

I didn't want their cocks. I only wanted Logan's. Well, maybe Logan's and a few more in addition, but I needed him. I practically salivated at the sight of his enormous dick covered in the other girl's spit and tears.

My body clenched around the man's fingers as their combined attention drove my body to new heights. My eyelids dipped as the wave approached, but I never took my gaze off Logan, who glared right back at me.

Then the wave hit as I cried out, the man twisting my nipples hard as his friend thrust a third finger inside me and rode out my orgasm with his tongue.

I saw it hit Logan, he couldn't mask the erotic rage which swept over him as he slammed the blonde back into the couch and held her with both hands as he buried his dick in her mouth, holding himself in her throat as he came hard all the while staring at me and my writhing body. She fought for breath as he gripped her tight, fucking her face hard until he'd given her every drop.

Every drop that should have been mine.

He released the woman, before pulling her up into his lap and brushing the tears and saliva off of her face, whispering to her and ignoring me entirely.

'Thank you,' I said to the gentlemen as I remained awkwardly spread over his thighs.

'Gerome, knees,' the older man said to the younger one, who'd barely wiped his face clean from my wetness.

He dropped to his knees and sucked the man's cock while I still sat over his lap. Gerome's nose bumped into my clit with every bob of his head as I watched him expertly swallow down his friend's — or lover's — dick.

Logan still ignored me completely, taking softly to the woman curled up in his lap. I was green with envy.

I gasped when the man behind me slid his fingers inside me.

'You're a sweet little thing,' he said as he wetted his fingers. 'I might bid on you at the auction. Have Gerome fuck your pussy while I whip him to go faster.'

I bit my lip as he thrust harder inside me while Gerome picked up speed on his cock.

'The only problem I see, sweet girl, is that if you stared any harder at Logan McGowan, he'd combust.'

I snapped out of my glare and turned my head toward him.

'I don't know what you mean...'

'That's the first time you've looked away from him since you came into the room. Now I'm partial to fucking with the McGowans, and I might well bid on you just to rile him up. If his glares are anything to go by, then you two are hot for each other. Is it all a game?'

'No. He doesn't want me.'

The man laughed in my ear and twisted his fingers inside me, gasping as Gerome swallowed him to the balls. 'He wants you, my dear, which makes me want you even more. One slip of my dick and I could ruin it all for you. Your wet little cunt is an inch away from my cock, one slip and that collar would be off.'

I sat upright and turned, looking at the man with a furrowed brow. 'You'd be kicked out.'

'It'd be worth it to see Logan squirm.'

He slid his fingers out of me and thrust them in my mouth, the taste of me sweeping over my tongue. He pinned my tongue down harshly as he held me tight to him, bucking his hips as he came hard in Gerome's mouth.

'Next time you try to use me in your games, your cunt will get my load, whether or not you like it. Be careful who you play with. You're not dealing with dumb university students here.'

I stood up and righted my clothing, his threat making me go from blissed-out to full of concern. My legs trembled as the blood rushed back into them. With a last glance at Logan, only to find him gone and the blonde gently sleeping on the sofa, I made for my room.

Maybe I'd bitten off more than I could chew in my bid to make Logan jealous.

Why had it been such a turn on to be watched by him while someone else pleasured him? I should have been mad, or repulsed, but even with the man's warning, it still had surpassed my dreams.

If only I could get Logan to crave me.

CHAPTER EIGHTEEN
LOGAN

'I just need you to get Tony's money squared away for me so I can go home,' I said, running a hand through my hair as the infamous mafia playboy grinned.

'Why so eager to leave? Is my playground not to your liking these days? You used to love it here...'

'I've got things to do back home. Business doesn't wait.'

'Ah yes, now that you are the head honcho of the McGowan clan. Tell me, why are you running errands for Tony? A little below you these days.'

'I'm marrying Nicole.'

Alfie burst into a merry laugh, slapping his knee as though I'd told him a cracker of a joke.

'Oh, that's too good, Logan. Marrying Nicole. No wonder you're here. She's all tied up already, mate, we all know that.'

I ground my jaw as I cleared my throat. He wasn't wrong.

'Listen, just pay the man. I know you are good for it.'

'But then I'll miss out on so much of your company. It's been ages since you last visited me. You'll stay for the hunt, at least.'

I caught sight of movement outside of the window and saw the very reason I needed to get out standing in the garden. Watching someone else taste her had been a delicious torture, and I'd fucked the other girl's poor throat raw. Not that she hadn't wanted that, but still.

She was walking through the rose garden which sat to the south of the main house, stopping to touch a flower or two gently, sometimes sniffing them. Her feet were bare against the grass and she wore another of those maddening linens. I clenched my fist as I imagined marching out there and putting her in her place for following me to Rosenhall. I'd bend her over my knee and...

No.

Absolutely fucking not.

'Can you remove her?' I blurted out.

Alfie raised an eyebrow before following my gaze. 'Remove her? Why?'

'Because I don't want her here.'

'Do tell. I'm not one for chucking out perfectly delicious morsels. You know that.'

I sighed and leaned against the back of the polished antique leather sofa. 'She's Nicole's cousin, and she's trying very hard to make me stray.'

Alfie laughed again while watching Valentina. 'You've got yourself a little stalker? How delightful.'

'Alfie. Please?'

'Oh, but this is far too fun to send her home. You must like her too, for it to be bothering you. Otherwise you'd just give her that monster cock of yours and get her fixation over with.'

'I'm not convinced that would make her stop.'

'Has she done anything to hurt you or threaten you?'

'Well, no. But she's followed me here. Last night she let two guys finger her and go down on her right in front of me.'

'If you don't want her, then why is that a problem? She should be able to explore her fantasies.'

'She kept her eyes on me the entire time. She was goading me.'

My insides still felt tangled between desire, jealousy, and annoyance.

Alfie stood and made his way over to the window, watching Valentina thoughtfully.

'I'll make you a deal, Logan. You stay the rest of the time while she's here and I'll pay Tony on your last day in full. No games. You'll have your deal to bring back to your father-in-law, and I'll have a fun distraction for a week. You know how I love a game.'

Closing my eyes, I took a breath before letting it out slowly. Fucking Alfie and his fucking games. He'd always been a trickster, thriving off of others' discomfort. It had just rarely been directed my way.

'Fine,' I said after a few moments. 'But it won't be a game. She's not going to get to me.'

With Alfie's laughter still ringing out behind me, I headed for my room.

By early afternoon, I'd had all of my room that I could take, even with a suite there was little to do other than watch daytime telly. And no-one needs that for more than a few hours.

With a rumbling stomach, I headed past the tied up whimpering playthings and down the stairs to seek out something to eat. The manor was fully staffed and each mealtime offered a plethora of fine dining, but between the official meals food could be ordered to suit in the whisky room.

I walked in, much relieved to find only a handful of other guests, giving them a nod as I took up position on one of the barstools that lined the long bar's side. Behind the barman stood a floor to ceiling wooden shelf structure which held bottle after bottle of whisky. There were those from the surrounding distilleries, as well as bottles from around the globe. There were newer bottles right up to dust coated antique ones that would cost an eye watering amount, even for me.

'What can I get you, Sir?' the man asked, setting out a heavy crystal glass and fixing me with a friendly smile.

'Whatever you have open. Nothing younger than twenty-five, please.'

'It's a shame you are so strict about age,' a sweet feminine voice said. 'I bet I'd taste better than the whisky would...'

I turned to see the little she-devil herself standing beside me, toying with the hem of her linens in a way that made me want to snatch them off.

God dammit.

'Valentina,' I said coolly, turning my eyes back to my drink. Should I just ignore her and hope she buggers off?

'Logan,' she said right back, leaning one arm on the bar and looking from my drink to my mouth as I took a sip.

'It's not going to work. This badgering. I'm engaged.'

'Yet, here you are in one of the seven deadly sin's poster places. Don't tell me you planned to keep your penis in your pants the whole week?'

'As you saw last night, I very much do not intend that. I intend to keep it out of your pants for the entire week.'

She bit her lower lip and blinked up at me. 'I'm not wearing any...'

And there it was, a lightening bolt to my fucking traitorous dick.

'Valentina,' I said, warning in my voice.

'Yes?'

'Go away.'

'No.'

She was bratting, and it took every ounce of willpower I possessed not to throw her over the bar and let rip on her perfectly round arse. But that was exactly what she wanted.

'You don't love her. She doesn't love you. I'm not looking to break you guys up or steal you away. I just want a chance to experience the things we spoke about. No-one else has ever hit so close to what I crave and it's not fair that it's wasted on Nicole. She doesn't even want you.'

Her words were like prickly barbs as they hit me.

She was right. Nicole didn't want me. And I didn't particularly want her, in the traditional sense. But I gave my word.

'I don't think you know what you are getting yourself into. You've followed me here after what? A few video calls. That's insane. You're just young and reckless and getting into shit you can't handle.'

'I can handle it,' she bit back, her hazel eyes flaring. 'I think you were just talking out of your arse and are like all the other men who claim to fulfil fantasies but are just damp squibs in bed.'

Within seconds, I had her hair fisted in my hand and forced her to her knees beside my stool as she yelped. 'Watch your words, Cherry. No-one likes a brat.'

'Make me.'

Goosebumps stormed up my arms at her defiant words as I looked down into her glittering eyes. My little cherry had *bite*.

'You think you want this? Open your mouth, you little whore. That's it, spread those lips like Daddy is about to feed you his cock.' She licked her lips before spreading them wide, her tongue behind her teeth. Fucking delicious. 'You'd look so pretty with that dirty mouth spread around my dick, wouldn't you?'

Her pupils dilated as I spoke, my fingers still clasping her head back. 'It's a shame my cock isn't for you.'

Lifting my glass with my other hand, I took a swig, holding the fiery liquid in my mouth. Valentina's eyes widened as I stood above her, holding her firm, and let the whisky drizzle from my mouth to hers. I expected her to wince, or spit it out, or at least look horrified, but she practically humped her heels as she swallowed the whisky down.

'That's all you're going to get from me. I'm going to go around here and give my cum to every other plaything while you watch.'

I was rock hard against my trousers already.

'I'll crawl around after you and lick it from their thighs.'

Mother-fucking shit bollocks.

This damn girl.

I let go of her hair and stood back from her.

'This can't happen.'

'Please?' she said, licking whisky from her lips.

'Never.'

When I made it back to my room, I tore the shower door open and got in, fisting my cock roughly as I pictured her on her knees before me, drinking down my cum instead of my whisky. Guilt flooded me as I came with her name on my lips.

Worst of all, I was still bloody starving.

CHAPTER NINETEEN

VALENTINA

I stared at Logan from my seat in the hallway, watching as he laughed with the other diners at the mammoth mahogany dining table. Waiters served them up a mouth-watering meal as they drank wine and talked business.

Some playthings sat next to their playmates' feet, being fed titbits directly from their fingers. A furious jealousy swept through me as I watched them. As I wished that I was knelt with my cheek against Logan's thigh as he fed me cubes of steak. I'd lick the juices off of his fingers until he couldn't handle it anymore and pulled me under the table to suck his fat cock until he filled my mouth in front of everyone.

But no.

He'd done nothing but ignore me for two solid days since spitting his whisky into my mouth. His resolve had wavered, only briefly, but enough that it had made him vulnerable. Then he'd battened down the hatches and shut me out completely.

I'd barely seen him in the public spaces in the house, and whenever I had, he'd simply turned the other way and pretended I didn't exist.

I was sick of it.

It was time to make him see me.

The waiter had just finished serving him up a plate of delicious looking tiramisu, which looked as heavenly as it smelled. Logan scooped up a spoonful and put it in his mouth, his eyes closing momentarily as he savoured it. There I was, jealous of a fucking dessert.

I stormed into the room before anyone could intercept me, standing beside him. Eyes settled on me. All but his.

'Logan, stop ignoring me.'

He simply took another spoonful and continued to pretend I didn't exist.

'Logan. Please?'

He turned to the man on his left and smiled at him before continuing whatever conversation they'd been having.

Fire surged in my veins as I took a sharp breath.

Fine. Let's play.

I placed one foot on the edge of his chair, pulling my linens to the side, and pivoted myself up onto the table. Gasps sounded from around the table as I sat my arse down fully on his plate of dessert.

'Ignore this,' I challenged, squirming at the cold, creaminess invading my nether regions. God, I hoped I didn't get a yeast infection.

For a moment, I thought he'd continue to look away from me, until he deliberately put his spoon down on the table.

Within a breath, his hand was on my throat as he pulled me forward, the dessert squelching between my thighs.

'You are such a fucking brat,' he said, his breath hot against my cheek as I winced at his tight grip restricting my air. 'Why won't you let this go? There are dozens of men here who would fuck you the way you want. You should indulge yourself in them instead of following me like a lost fucking puppy.'

'I want you.' The words were barely a whisper with his fingers digging into the side of my neck, but I saw the way his pupils dilated and smiled. 'You want me too.'

We stayed there for a few moments; him eyeing my face while holding me still by the throat, while around us people went back to eating their desserts like it was all perfectly normal. Would he send me out of the room? Would he throw me over his shoulder and take me somewhere to ravish me? Would he bend me over the table and claim me right there?

'You have been nothing but trouble since the moment you walked into my life. An entitled little brat. And brats need to know when their behaviour isn't okay.'

He lifted me off the table, cream and coffee soaked biscuit stuck to my naked arse, and with one swift movement bent me over his lap, with my face toward the other diners. Snatching up my hands, he gathered them against the small of my back with one large hand and held me tight.

'Are you sorry, sweet Cherry?' he said, his voice tight as I squirmed against his lap.

'No.'

'You will be.'

He slid my linens to the side, exposing my ass to the room. I kept my legs firmly closed for the only scrap of modesty I could.

The first hard slap of his hand against my arse sent cream splattering around us, the sting shooting through my body as I yelped and writhed.

It wasn't a play spanking like the ones I'd wheedled past lovers into giving me. It was quick and fiery and sent blistering pain through me.

'Oh, my god. Ouch,' I cried as the next slap came.

'Maybe you'll realise that you are playing a game you can't handle, little girl.'

'Maybe... you'll realise... I'm old enough... to know what I want.' Whimpers and yelps punctuated my words as he kept reddening my arse with his solid palm.

'Even now you're being a brat.'

'Even now, you're being a pussy.'

The hand holding my wrists released and slid up into my hair, tightening close to the roots and pulling me up toward him so that my back arched even further. 'What did you say?'

'I said, you're a pussy. Hiding behind this shitty fake marriage and your dad's death. Living a half life because you're too much of a wimp to take what you want.'

His body stiffened beneath me and I thought I'd gone too far. That he'd push me off his lap and leave me there.

'You're playing with fire, Cherry, and you're going to get burned.'

'Incinerate me then.'

He let out a growl that had my already soaking pussy flooding. I didn't think it was possible for him to spank me harder, but he did, letting slaps rain down until my tears flowed freely.

'Look at them,' he said, pulling my head up to see the diners and playthings watching. 'They see you for what you are, a desperate little slut who will do whatever it takes to get her cunt filled. That's what you want, isn't it? For me to pull you onto my dick and stretch you out in front of everyone.'

'Yes,' I moaned.

'Tell them.'

'I want to be fucked in front of everyone. I want everyone to see what a slut I am. I need it.'

'Except you can't be fucked, can you?' He let go of my hair as his fingers gripped the thin metal collar which sat low on my neck. 'This means you are off limits. This means you've got my dick so fucking hard and there's nowhere for me to stuff it.'

'My mouth. I could use my mouth.'

'You don't deserve that, sweet Cherry. You need to earn my cock by learning how to behave. How to obey. Good girls get treats. If you were a good girl, I'd slide my fingers inside that tight little snatch of yours and make you squeal for all the dinner guests. I bet you'd sing me a sweet song with how desperate you are.'

'Please... I want that.'

His fingers slid briefly between my thighs, gathering up the wetness that coated me there.

'So bloody wet, aren't you?' He pulled my head up by my hair and thrust his fingers into my mouth, letting me taste myself amongst the cream and coffee. It should have repulsed me, but I licked and sucked at his fingers eagerly as he groaned.

His hard dick dug into my side and I pressed myself against it, eager to get him to abandon the wall he still put up between us.

Another series of spanks soon had me writhing for a different purpose. My arse burned as the spanks echoed in the tall dining hall, my cries reverberating with them around the room. I glanced up to see one of the women sucking a man's cock beneath the table while fingering herself. Another had pulled his playtoy up into his lap and seated her on his cock as they watched us, not fucking, just pinning her there around him. He clasped her about the waist as she fought the urge to ride him.

I'd never been so horny in all my life.

I wanted his dick so fucking badly that my tears fell harder.

Before I knew it, I was sliding to the floor as Logan unbuckled his belt. I got to my knees, ready to worship that thick cock of his. Confusion swept through me when he fisted my hair in one hand and started masturbating with the other.

'Please, can I suck it?' I asked, the swollen tip of his cock so close, but just out of reach. 'Please, Daddy?'

The moan he let out went straight between my legs.

'You don't deserve my cum. You need to behave before I'll fill that throat of yours.'

'I need it so bad.' The whine in my voice made me cringe, but I couldn't help it. I'd never wanted a man so badly in my entire life. I wanted Logan. I wanted his rough hands and huge cock. I wanted his dirty words and his ardent kisses. I wanted him to smile at me before making me cry. I wanted it all. It was just lust. I knew it, but I wanted to get what I wanted for a change. He was holding out for a woman who didn't give two fucks about him.

'You need it, don't you, my little slut? I'll make you a deal. If you can eat it all up, I'll think about letting you have more.'

Logan slid a hand over my face, gathering my tears and using them to stroke his dick faster. It was thick and veiny, far larger than anything I'd taken, human or rubber, before. I held out my tongue as his balls bunched and his fingers tightened in my hair. The others watched him too, eyes on his impressive cock as he groaned low.

'You look fucking hot there on your knees with tears on your face and a red raw arse. A beautiful little whore. I'd love to paint your pretty face with my cum, but you need to show me how far you'll go for me. How low you'll sink, hoping I'll pull you back up.' His words were tight, spoken through his teeth as he held off his orgasm.

Then he turned toward the table and came hard, ropes of cum landing on the plate of squashed tiramisu, the thick, white liquid merging with the cream and pooling.

My eyes flicked back to him as he grinned.

'Dessert time, Valentina.'

I swallowed hard as he placed the plate on the floor before gathering my hair up into a fist and pushing me down toward the creamy mess. My stomach turned at the ruined pudding. I didn't mind swallowing cum straight from the source, by eating it as a meal was a whole different level.

Logan crouched down beside me and met my eyes. 'You don't have to do it. No-one will force you. You can use your safe word and I'll let you go. We can forget all about this.'

My eyes roved over his face, the stubble covered jaw up to his piercing blue eyes. He made my stomach flip in the best way possible. A little cum wasn't going to make me miss out on something I wanted so badly.

'I want to,' I whispered as his eyes fluttered closed and his teeth caught his lower lip.

'Fuck, V. You're killing me.'

He held my hair up while I lowered myself to the floor, crouching like a dog at its bowl. My stomach heaved as I dived in, licking and biting at the salty, creamy plate of pudding. It was dirty and disgusting, and I was wetter than ever.

'Look at you, my sweet girl, eating up Daddy's cum like a good girl. You're doing so fucking well. On your knees with a fiery rump and everyone watching you eat like a dog. Is this what you wanted?'

I nodded, though my cheeks burned at both ends. It was exactly what I wanted. The filthy acts and the even filthier words to go along with them.

It didn't taste so bad once I got past the idea, and the filthiness of the act far outweighed any grossness. I lapped it until the plate was clean, my breath coming in pants as I drove myself mad with lust beneath his gaze.

'Atta girl, isn't it so much better when you can listen to instructions? I should get you a bowl of my cream every morning for you to lap at like a pet. You'd make such a pretty pet. But for now, I need you to have some reflection time to think about what you'd just done for me.'

'Please, I'm so horny.' My tears renewed afresh as he pulled me to my feet and picked me up in his solid arms. I sighed against his chest, disappointed that he still wasn't fucking me, but glad for the ounce of closeness that his carrying me afforded.

'I know you are.'

'Please, can I just come?'

'No, brat. You can't. Not until I say so.'

Even that was hot. His claiming of my orgasms. His telling me no made me just as wet as his telling me yes.

I was a knotted jumble of emotions.

Then he took me upstairs and fixed me to one of the pillars.

'No... please.'

'Do you want to use your safeword, Valentina?'

I shook my head. I didn't want him to stop. I just needed more.

'Good girl,' he said, leaning down after he fixed my arms above my head. For a moment, I thought he'd kiss me, his breath whispering over my lips as his eyes met mine. 'It's fucking hot to see you struggle against it, to see you accept wanting this. But I still belong to your cousin. I'm trying to figure this out in my head. Whether I can play with you here and still go back to my life with a free conscience. It's not that I don't ache for you, because I do. I just don't know if I can fuck my fiancé's cousin without ruining my own moral code.'

'I won't tell...'

'I'd still know.'

And then he left me there, attached to the pillar, as he sat on the couch across the hall from me.

Watching.

CHAPTER TWENTY

LOGAN

I clenched and unclenched my fist against my thigh as I watched Valentina cycle through a range of emotions.

At first she found it hot, being attached to the post like the few others who were equally situated throughout the hall. Eventually the ache started in her arms and feet as she held her position, cycling between stretching her shapely calves and sagging against the cuffs that held her up.

Her chin would lift as people passed by her, amused at her tear-stained face and cream stained linens. The occasional man or woman would caress her cheek as they passed, or graze a hand over her exposed sides. None stopped to interact with her with me glaring.

I couldn't help it.

She made me furious. And delighted. And enraged. And so fucking horny that I'd wanted to pin her over the table and fuck her in front of everyone while telling them all that she was mine.

Insane.

We barely even knew one another.

Valentina was young and horny and thinking with her pussy rather than her brain. Her relentless pursuit of me brought out a side that I'd long kept hidden. A side of me I only let out to play on rare occasions. For a day. With a stranger. Not with my fiancé's bloody cousin. She'd stroked my ego and been just as eager to stroke my cock, and that was an addictive high. Being desired above all else is one of life's great pleasures. It was like crack. I wanted more.

Eventually I stood, grinning at the intake of breath that lifted her chest as I approached. When she blinked up at me through her mascara smudged lashes, I had to fight hard not to open my trousers and split her open with my dick.

'Sweet Cherry. Is it as fun playing when it's like this? When you are a little ornament on display for everyone else, but no-one is touching you the way you need?'

She closed her eyes and leaned her head back against the wooden pillar behind her.

'Or do you need more, my slutty wee brat?'

'I need more. Please, Logan?'

My name on her tongue gave me goosebumps.

'If you ask nicely, I'll touch you where you need it.'

'Please, can you touch me? I want you so bad.'

'Mmm,' I said as I pulled out my knife, her eyes opening at the sound of the blade flicking outward. They widened as she watched the sleek metal dance between my fingers. With one slash at the ribbon that held the material to her waist, it fell to the floor and pooled at her feet. Yanking the remaining two pieces of material, I hauled them from her body and tossed them aside before running my blade up her thighs. The way she trembled had me hard.

'Some games can be dangerous, little brat. Do you still want to play?'

'Yes. It'll always be yes.'

I followed her curves with the tip of the blade, keeping the pressure light enough to avoid cutting her, but hard enough so the threat felt imminent. When the metal grazed the mound of flesh immediately above her clit, she whimpered.

'Stay still, pretty girl. Wouldn't want to slice it right off, would we?'

She shook her head and swallowed hard as I slid the blade down over her wetness to the right of her labia. Her whole body trembled as I ran the tip over her clit ever so steadily, her lips opening as she inhaled.

'Is it maddening? The light, sharp touch? You want it harder, but harder would leave you with a lacerated cunt, and nobody needs that.'

I repeated the stroke repeatedly, from side to side and back over her clit as she fought the urge to grind down on the blade. Right where I wanted her, on the edge between danger and desire.

When I pulled my knife away and swivelled it so the blade lay secure against my palm while the hilt pressed against her wetness, she cried out. I lifted one of her legs and balanced it over my other arm before sliding the hilt of the knife into her. Her whole body reacted as she tried to move backwards, to remove the knife's hilt from being sunk in her cunt.

'Do you want me to go sit down and watch you some more?'

'No-- God no. Please...'

'Stop bringing god into this, he's nowhere to be seen right now, baby girl. Now grind that wet cunt against my knife, Valentina.'

Some of the other strung up playthings watched her rapturously, rubbing their thighs together as they envied my slut.

Not mine...

The knife dug into my hand as she moved her hips, gently at first, as she summoned the courage to act on her lust. But soon enough, the pressure building between her thighs won out over any logic or modesty, as it always did. I was convinced the human brain became more and more shut off the closer to orgasm someone was.

'You are so beautiful when you're desperate, Valentina. Such a far cry from that polished woman I saw at the party. Here you are with cream stained thighs and my cum in your belly, fucking my knife as though your life depended on it.'

I wanted to kiss her so badly, to swallow down her cries as she came for me. But she was being punished for being a brat, so instead, I pulled the knife free right as I felt her thighs quake, and sat back down.

'No. Logan. Come back.'

My laughter filled the space as she bucked against the pillar, squeezing her thighs and cursing me. 'Brat's need to be taught a lesson. And you've been such a fucking brat.'

'God damn it. Don't be such a twat.' At first, anger filled her voice, before she gave in and whined. 'Please. Please don't leave me like this. I'm sorry. I'll be good.'

And I did the same twice more to the same effect. Each time, she'd be reluctant at first, until the sensations overcame the mistrust. The third time I removed the knife before she'd come, she cried such pretty tears for me I almost gave in and put my cock inside her. Losing my spot at Rosenhall wasn't an option though, and I knew Valentina would enjoy being hunted by whoever bought her, and would enjoy the freedom her collar's price would give her.

'What's this,' Alfie said as he came up the stairs, seeing Valentina crying, with her thighs slick and me sat watching her. 'My, my, what a little snack.'

He gave me a small nod before approaching Valentina, which I returned, giving him my permission to approach.

'Such a pretty little thing, but so very messy.'

'Miss Valentina was being a brat.'

'Tsk, tsk,' Alfie said as he reached up and ran a thumb over Valentina's lips. Her eyes flicked to my face, and I grinned. 'Brats are such a nuisance. Shame this brat is so very dirty. Perhaps I could aid you in cleaning her up?'

'Hose her down or use your tongue?' I said.

'My tongue? Well now, there's an idea. But I'm not sure she'd want my tongue on that sweet cunt, would she?' Alfie spoke to her, tipping her chin upwards and meeting her eyes.

'Please?'

'Oh, but she asks so sweetly. Shall I bring her over?'

I nodded my assent as he reached up and released her cuffs, pushing her to her knees.

'Crawl, little darling,' he said, following her and watching as her ass wiggled with each movement.

'I've been being so very mean and teasing poor Valentina to the edge with my blade in her little fuck hole.'

'He didn't let you come?' Alfie said as Valentina reached my feet and knelt up to look at me.

'No,' she whispered, her cheeks burning.

Leaning forward, I tipped her jaw with my palm and asked, 'Do you want him to play?'

'Won't it make you jealous?' she asked.

'No, I like to share. And you haven't earned my tongue yet.'

'I'd like you both...' she breathed.

'Climb up into Daddy's lap and spread your thighs for him, then.'

Her arse was still hot as she placed it in my lap, my cock nestling in the cleft of her ass. God, I wished there wasn't material between us. I'd have loved nothing more than stretching her ass out over my dick while Alfie ate her.

'Show him, Cherry. Use your hands and spread your dirty little holes for him.'

She trembled in my arms as she slung her legs over my spread thighs and reached down to splay herself for his inspection.

Alfie knelt between her thighs and took more than a minute examining her to increase her discomfort. We'd played with various girls before, but never shared one. His love of oral, on men and women, was infamous. I'd seen many people brought to a pile of incoherent flesh at the expense of his mouth.

'Do you feel my dick against your ass, Cherry? Do you feel what you do to me? You've got Daddy all hard again and with nowhere to put my dick. Such a naughty girl.'

'Sorry,' Valentina whispered. 'Daddy I'm so--'

Her voice cut off as Alfie leaned forward and licked his way up her slit before sucking her clit into his mouth.

'Steady there,' I said as she bucked hard against me, almost vaulting fully off my lap. Digging my fingers into her hips, I pulled her tight back to my groin.

I watched over her shoulder, her face buried into my neck as Alfie worked his magic. She wouldn't take long with the intense build up. I reached into my pocket and pulled out my knife, again palming the blade as I worked the hilt into her. Alfie licked her all over, from her thighs to her ass to her sweet little tits. Taunting her just as I had.

When he finally gave in and focussed all his attention on her cunt while I fucked her with my knife, she dug her fingernails into me and cried out. A fierce shake stole over her entire body as she cried out my name, grasping at my thighs as her pussy clenched the knife wildly.

'That's it, Cherry, come for Daddy. Such a hot little fuck.'

As I pulled my knife from her soaked slit, Alfie fingered my zip and raised his eyebrows. 'May I?'

I stalled before wiping the knife on my trouser leg and thrusting it back into my packet. Valentina lay panting against my chest, and as much as I wanted to take her, having her watch someone else give me pleasure, to feel them bring me off, would be such a sweet torment.

'Go on then.'

Alfie reached under Valentina's ass and freed my hard dick, pulling it down so it sat snugly against her hot, wet slit. Knowing I couldn't slide into it despite how close I was, was particularly devastating.

Valentina shifted her head as she watched Alfie lick his way up my length, sucking the head of my cock into his mouth expertly.

Fuck, he really was good.

'I want your cock,' she said.

'I know. But you can't have it.'

'I could suck it.'

'I enjoy you wanting it so bad and having to watch someone else have it. Just like I want to taste you so fucking bad, but watched Alfie taste you first. There is a delight in the pain, sweet Cherry. Do you see how he slides down, taking more and more of my thick cock into his throat? It feels so fucking good.'

'I want it.'

'I know. And if you learn how to behave yourself, you might get it.'

Alfie pulled his mouth off of my cock and lowered it onto Valentina, teasing her with his tongue as he stroked my dick against her wet cunt. The head of it sat right below her clit with the way she laid back on my lap, and he let his tongue rove from her to me and back again.

It was sinfully delightful to watch. Even more so when Valentina started whimpering and writhing against me. I thrust my hips, only Alfie's fingers stopping me from sliding into Valentina's wet cunt.

I groaned when Alfie took me back into his throat for a few minutes, reaching down and fucking Valentina with my fingers while he focused on me. Her pussy clenched down on them, so fucking tight.

'That's it baby, you take my fingers, I think you can take another.' I slid a third into her as she buried her face in my neck, her teeth grazing my throat. 'You'll need to learn to take them all for me if you're going to fit on my dick.'

Alfie watched us while swallowing me down, and I grinned at him before moaning, 'fuck.'

I reached up and thrust my wet fingers into Valentina's mouth as Alfie made me cum, pulling off of me at the last minute so the hot streams of cum landed all over Valentina's pussy. It was the hardest fucking orgasm I'd ever had. I fucked her mouth, spreading her wetness all over her lips and tongue as she gagged on my fingers.

'Oh dear, it looks like I've made another mess,' Alfie said as Valentina looked down, practically vibrating at the sight of her pussy dripping with my cum.

'Oh my god,' she moaned as she reached down and touched herself before bringing her fingers to her mouth.

Fuck, had I ever underestimated her.

'That's my mess,' Alfie said before leaning down and running his tongue over her.

I pressed my hand around Valentina's throat and held her tight to me as Alfie licked up every drop; the cum wetting his chin as Valentina ground harder against me. My cock was only half hard after my orgasm, but I slid it up against her tight pussy and grazed it, maddening us both with being so close but not inside.

'Logan,' she whimpered. 'He's going to make me come again.'

'Go on, fuck his face, princess.'

I pressed tighter against her throat as Alfie sucked her clit into her mouth and she clenched her folds around my dick, always wanting more. Her breaths came in shallow little bursts as her face pinked before the mix of Alfie's filthy tongue, the nearness of my dick, and the restriction of her breath sent her over the edge.

She came hard against Alfie's face, reaching down and threading her fingers into his hair as she bucked against him. Her cries filled the hallway as the other playthings looked on with utter envy. And all the while, her sweet little cunt tried its best to suck me inside of her in the most frustratingly hot way.

Eventually, she slackened her grip and let Alfie go, who grinned up at us.

'Such magnificent fun,' he said as he wiped his face on his sleeve. 'I knew you would be.'

'Thank you, Alfie,' I said, wanting nothing more than to wrap Valentina up and steal her away to my suite. To wash her and feed her and then fuck her until I had to go home.

'Thank you...' Valentina sighed, not even trying to cover herself back up.

'I'll take the young lady to the spa,' Alfie said, holding up a hand as I went to refuse. 'I think you could both do with a little time after that. Plus, they have the most wonderful masseuses there who can bring her back around gently after we've got her cleaned up.'

The spa wasn't a normal spa; it was designed specifically to look after people after heavy play, to give them time in a soothing, calm environment away from playmates. The massages and services there were almost as legendary as Alfie's tongue.

I wanted to argue, but as my post nut clarity bounced back in, I relented.

She wasn't my pet.

I'd given her what she wanted.

Alfie was right. She needed time away from me to process it.

'Fine. But make sure she's okay.'

I pulled Valentina to her feet as I stood, taking off my shirt and wrapping it around her. 'I want to come with you.'

'You can't. Not if you want to be in the auction. No-one will believe I had you in my suite without violating the rules.'

'I don't care about the auction.'

'You might later. Now's not the time for hasty decisions. Go with Alfie. I trust him.'

'He just licked your cum from my... well, you know. What's saying he won't fuck me?'

'He makes half the auction fee,' I said with a grin.

With a sigh, she went with him.

When they were out of sight, I sat down hard on the sofa and rubbed at my eyes.

What had I got myself into?

Because there was no doubting it, Valentina was perfect.

And I wanted her to be mine.

CHAPTER TWENTY ONE
VALENTINA

My brain could barely get one foot in front of the other correctly as Alfie led me down the stairs and away from Logan. All I wanted was to run back to him and curl up in his lap, craving more and more of his attention.

'Come on, give me your arm,' Alfie said, gripping me lightly at the wrist as we made our way through the towering, wood panelled halls. It was like him getting both myself and Logan off hadn't affected him at all.

'Didn't you want to come?' I asked, sneaking a glance at his face. He had that handsome, boyish charm going on, not as rugged and dominant as Logan, but almost a prettier, sharper look to him.

'I enjoy giving pleasure. I don't need an orgasm every time I want to get involved.'

'Man, I live for orgasms.'

'I used to, but living here means orgasms on tap, if I want them. They've become less of a requirement. Plus, it's hot to dip into a scenario without demanding something in return. It's hot to be used solely for someone else's pleasure.'

'Are you bi? A switch?'

'Feeling very brazen for a young lady who's just been on one of the punishment pillars.'

'Sorry,' I said, my cheeks burning as we walked.

'It's all right. I don't know. I just enjoy experiences. If I find someone attractive, it doesn't really matter what's between their thighs. It's hedonism, darling. Again, I wouldn't say I'm a switch either. It depends on who I'm playing with. Usually I prefer a dominant role, but I've been wanting to get my mouth on that dick of Logan's for years. I'll happily take the bottom role for a guy like him.'

A little ember of jealousy flared inside me, and I stiffened against his fingers. He just let out a merry chuckle.

'Don't worry, darling, I don't want to keep him. But you've got to admit that dick is quite something.'

I couldn't deny that.

'Is sharing partners normal here?'

'Some couples come just to play in public, but most come to have experiences that will blow their minds.'

We arrived at the door to the spa, and Alfie ushered me inside.

'Two baths please, Marguerite.'

A dainty woman blushed at Alfie before going off to organise the baths. Much to my surprise, when she led me there ten minutes later, the baths were side by side in the same room.

'Oh, I didn't think we'd be bathing together...'

'Shush and get your naked, sticky arse in there before I dunk you.'

The bath looked inviting. The top was littered with coloured petals, and steam rose softly into the air. The baths were rectangular and made from a dark, grey stone, spaced around a foot from one another with a full glass window on the wall at the foot of them. It looked out over the surrounding woodland as the hill the house was on sloped away.

'Don't worry, no one can see us. The windows are one way,' Alfie said.

I ditched Logan's shirt and slid into the bath, groaning as the hot water welcomed me. 'God, that's good.'

Looking over at Alfie, I almost choked on my tongue. He stood buck naked, with his dick still half hard. A full row of piercings littered the underside from balls to tip.

'Take a picture,' he said with a wink. 'It'll last longer.'

'Sorry. I've just never seen that kind of piercings.'

'I'm told they feel particularly magical during doggy.'

He climbed into his bath and leaned his head back with his eyes closed.

I followed suit, resting against the gentle slope of the inner walls of the bath, letting the highly scented bath water soak into me.

We stayed that way for a while, my mind regurgitating everything that had happened with Logan. It had all been a whirlwind after I made the choice to sit on his pudding, and I wasn't sure where it left us.

He'd been content enough to let another man taste me, but he'd also riled me up with the handle of his knife repeatedly. Was I just a fun distraction? Did I want anything more than that? I'd come to Rosenhall to gain an experience like the one I'd just had, but it just left me needing more.

Was it just the heady, intoxicating sexual acts finally being in person and not in my head, or was it really about Logan?

It was stupid pursuing him when he was set to marry Nicole, but I couldn't help it. I had to know if the delicious dirty words he'd breathed through my laptop were all talk or coming from a place of genuine desire.

I slid further into the bath water until it sat just under my nose as a smattering of rain hit the large window. I'd never had a threesome. I still wasn't one hundred percent sure I could say I had, and now I'd been toyed with by multiple people twice in the few days I'd been at Rosenhall. It awoke a fire that seemed to grow with each interaction. Multiple hands and mouths just hit differently. I couldn't imagine how much more thrilling it would get with cocks involved too. I squeezed my thighs together beneath the water before stealing a glance at Alfie, who caught my eye.

'You know he's getting married, right?' Alfie said.

I bit my lower lip before nodding. 'I do.'

'And yet you pursue him, anyway? He's not the type to play away, well, not outside these walls, and even then, not once he's married, I don't think.'

'He's marrying my cousin.'

Alfie grinned before pulling himself upright and leaning his arms on the side wall of his tub to face me.

'I know he is, you little devil.'

Swallowing hard, I tried not to react.

'So why, little demon, do you insist on chasing him?'

'I can't help it. She doesn't even want him. They are not at all compatible.'

'And you think he's compatible with you? Do you long to be a mafia wife, to send him out every day knowing he might not come back? Filling his mansion with mafia spawn to continue his father's bloodline?'

His words were like a smack to the face. I didn't want any of that. I wanted to keep earning my own money, to stay away from the mafia life I'd worked so hard to distance myself from. While I may want a child far, far, into the future, I didn't want one just to damn them to a violent, blood-soaked life.

'I'm just sick of always being second best. The kid who got the hand-me-downs and the pity. The one who couldn't afford a pony and didn't have a father. The one dragged to the parties to see my cousins get everything while my mum and I struggled. She doesn't deserve him.'

'No, she doesn't. But it's what he wants.'

'Do you think it is? Deep down?'

'He's not really one for spilling his heart, took me long enough to let me drain his snake.'

'Ew, Alfie.'

'Sorry,' he said, not looking sorry in the slightest, 'I meant to churn his cream. To batter his sausage—'

'Stop,' I laughed, splashing my water at him to stop his terrible innuendos. 'So gross.'

'It wasn't, though. Aren't you craving a taste?'

'Yes,' I admitted.

'Then let's get him buying you at the auction.'

'Why do you care?'

'I don't, but it's ever so fun to play, don't you think?'

Alfie stood suddenly, water dripping from his toned body as I took another glance at his metal, laddered cock. He leaned forward and patted my cheek.

'Don't worry, little demon, I'm sure you'll have time to try it before you go home. If Logan doesn't bid for you, I might have you myself.'

My cheeks burned long after he left the room.

CHAPTER TWENTY TWO

LOGAN

Auction day had arrived.

What the hell was I going to do?

I had two choices: buy her, or don't.

And neither seemed good.

Would buying her give her the wrong idea? Make her even more determined to continue her infatuation with me. Or would it give us a few days of delicious hedonistic play together that we can always have to look back on secretly?

If I didn't buy her, someone else would. All the playthings always sold, and there had been multiple people watching her over the past few days. Toying with her. Craving her. How could I sit back knowing someone else would give her the experience she wanted so much? Sit there knowing someone else was pursuing her, fucking her tight little cunt, when I wanted her so badly.

I went from room to room hunting for her.

I hadn't seen her since Alfie took her away the night before, not since she'd come so prettily against my dick, and I needed to lay eyes on her. It was like a compulsion that drove my feet forward. Would she even want to see me? What if I'd pushed her too far between my knife and letting Alfie get involved?

My pulse picked up, as I still couldn't see her. Those same linens everywhere fucked with my head, making me think it was her repeatedly, only to be left in the lurch.

Fuck, what if she'd gone home?

The hairs on the back of my neck stood up as I grew more agitated.

She'll probably just be in her room, or at the spa.

Alfie lounged on a sofa in the library, and I sat down opposite him, trying to act like I wasn't going out of mind over Valentina.

'Good morning, sunshine,' Alfie said. 'You look awfully sullen for a man who got his dick sucked so well last night.'

'No-one likes a bragger.' He wasn't wrong. He took my dick like a champ.

'Mmm. I bet your sweet little plaything won't be able to swallow a third of the monster that lives in your pants. I'm sure you'll give her points for enthusiasm, though. The young ones are always so keen.'

'Was she okay after last night?'

'She kept eyeing my dick in the bath like a horny little goblin, so I'm going to say she's fine.' Alfie saw me narrow my eyes and raised a hand. 'Don't worry, we only had baths. I wouldn't fuck her when I know you like her.'

'It's not that I like her.'

'Bullshit. Your little heart's all twisted up already. I've known you for years, Logan, and I've never seen you look at anyone the way you look at her.'

'It's just lust.'

'Sure it is, and I'm the king of England.'

'You're related to him, so that's not as far off as you make it out to be.'

'Two times removed, my friend. As common as muck.'

'Do you know where she is? I want to make sure she's okay after last night.' Not that I needed to lay eyes on her before they fell out of the bloody sockets.

'Sure, I just loaned her a coat to go into the rose garden. It's nippy out this morning. Let's hope it warms up a little for the hunt tomorrow.'

'Are you going to bid this year?'

'If you don't snap up that fine little fire bomb, then I might.' Alfie met my eyes and let me know he was serious. He wouldn't try to take Valentina from me, but if I discarded her, he'd happily scoop her up. The thought of her running from him through the woods, being caught and pinned beneath him as he fulfilled that fantasy for her, made me want to tear my friend's dick off.

'Noted,' I said, rising to look at the garden through the window. The roses would wilt soon, with autumn quickly drawing in. Scanning the well-manicured lawns and pristine cut bushes, I spotted Valentina sitting on a bench, her legs tucked up into Alfie's coat as she pulled it tight around her.

Alfie joined me, leaning his back against the wall and keeping his eyes on me.

'You're going to get yourself in trouble over this one.'

'Already balls deep in it. But after this week, I'm going back to my life and going to pretend like it never happened.'

'And what about her?'

'She's young. She'll have fun. All she wants is someone to try some fantasies out with. It could never be anything more than a tumble in the sheets.'

'I don't think she'll let you go that easily. She's got that look they get. Stars in their eyes and hearts dancing about her pretty little cunt. She likes you.'

'She barely even knows me. It's just an infatuation. She needs someone her age, who is looking for what she wants,' I said.

'And what, pray tell, do you think she is looking for?'

'Experimenting, fun, experiences. I'm not there anymore. I'm looking to settle down, to move on to the next page and fulfil my duties.'

'To your dead arsehole of a father...' I scowled at Alfie and he held up his hands. 'It's true. The only thing he cared about was being bigger than Harold Thompson, and look where that ended for them both. Six feet under.'

'You took over from your dad,' I pointed out, watching as Valentina tipped her face up to the morning sun.

'Yeah, but I leave the bullshit serious stuff to other people. I focus on my first love.'

'Well, I don't have a decadent sex castle to keep me otherwise occupied.'

'You've got a twenty-two-year-old practically begging for your cock, your own little sex demon, if I read her right. Who needs an entire castle full?'

'You do.'

'I do,' Alfie said with a laugh. 'What are you so afraid of? Go play with your shiny new toy.'

I'm afraid she's going to blow my world to pieces.

Valentina looked up at me as I approached, the morning chill seeping around me as I smiled.

'Morning.'

'Good morning,' she said, pulling the sleeves of her coat down over her fingers and wrapping her arms tighter around her.

'I'm sorry about last night,' I said. She narrowed her eyes and my stomach tightened.

'Why are you sorry? Was I not pleasing enough?' There was a hard edge to her voice that filled my chest with warning.

'You were fucking magnificent, pretty girl. I'm sorry because I shouldn't have crossed that boundary with you.'

'I'm pretty sure I offered myself up on a plate, literally.'

I sat down on the bench beside her and rubbed my hand over my face.

'We just can't be a thing. You need someone your own age who can explore everything with you. I'm not the right guy for that. I'm at a different point in my life and I need different things.'

She took a slow, steady breath before speaking pointedly to me.

'I was asking for you to fuck me, Logan. Not to marry me and fill me with your little mafia babies. I want you to chase me through the woods, catch me, and fill me with your cock so hard I cry. I'm not asking for roses and chocolates. I'm asking to get to experience dirty, harsh, primal fucking with someone who is safe. Who isn't going to hurt me outside of the limits of the game. Someone who wants me to leave sated, knowing that he gave me what I wanted, and took what he wanted in return. I know what I want, so stop putting these notions of more into my mouth. There's only one thing I want you to slip between my lips and it's not your stupid ideas about me.'

Silence stretched between us as she held my gaze, fire burning in those hazel eyes. Still, I didn't want to be leading her down a path she could not follow.

'I can give you the money for the auction. You can take it and go home and no-one will ever know. Most girls go for thirty to fifty thousand, and get half. I could have the fifty in your account by the time you packed your bags. You don't need to do this.'

'I don't want your money, Logan. I told you I have my own. I'm offering myself up to you and you keep rejecting me, yet last night you were burning for me. Is it me? Don't you want me?'

'Fuck, no, Valentina. I've wanted to get my hands on you since the minute you popped up on my laptop. You've been on my mind, you've invaded my dreams, I've thought about pinning you down and claiming you more times than I can fucking count. I want you crying and begging and squirming beneath me while I show everyone that you're my toy to break. I want to fucking possess you, baby girl, and that is why it's such a terrible idea. If I didn't want you, it would be all the easier to play.'

She licked her lower lip before getting to her knees on the bench and reaching out to caress my lower jaw. Inching closer, her breath was warm against my cold cheeks.

'Then buy me, Daddy, because if you don't, I'll be screaming someone else's name tomorrow morning.'

I tilted my face, my lips grazing her neck as she let out a whimper before standing up.

'See you later, Logan,' she said, as she turned and left me, picking her way through the wet grass and stony paths barefoot.

My erection and I sat a while longer, deciding what to do about the pile of trouble that I'd let into my life.

He was all for finding any way possible to get back between her thighs, but every part of my brain told me no.

A tale as old as time.

Cock vs brain.

CHAPTER TWENTY THREE

VALENTINA

'I'll toy with you for a little while to garner some reactions. It'll drive up the excitement and thus the bidding. Remember, you can still use your safe word if you are uncomfortable at any point.' Alfie walked back and forth amongst the ten of us going through with the auction for the chance to hunt us. He smiled at me, looking far more devilish than reassuring.

The noise from the great hall was making my stomach churn. It was one thing to have played here and there during the few days I'd been in the castle, and a whole other to be put, naked, on the podium and be made to perform for everyone.

My plan was to find Logan in the crowd and focus solely on him. To let the rest of the crowd fall by the wayside and beg him with my eyes to buy me. To chase me. To take me.

It had to be him.

The fire behind me crackled, making me jump. The heat caressed at my calves and behind as I waited for my turn to be displayed.

Alfie disappeared repeatedly, one plaything at a time. Cheers and laughter and yells arose behind the doors, muffled by the time they reached me.

What if no-one bid on me?

The thought made me want to heave. I'd die of embarrassment.

Finally, at the very end, after waiting in the side room for more than an hour, it was my turn.

Alfie took me gently by the fingers and ran his other hand down the side of my face.

'Don't worry, little demon, I'll make them fight for a chance at you.'

'Is Logan there?' I asked, ashamed at the desperation in my voice.

'Yes, near the back by the biggest fireplace, he'll see everything. Make him sweat, sweetheart.'

'What will you do to me?'

He gave one of his throaty chuckles and shook his head. 'Now that would spoil all the fun, wouldn't it? You'll be a delight, darling, don't worry.'

'What if he doesn't bid?'

'Then I'll have you myself.'

He didn't give me a chance to respond before tugging me forward and leading me into the hall.

Men and women sat and stood around the room, every available chair taken. They dressed in gowns and suits, ready to party into the night to celebrate their wins. Playthings scattered at their feet, or in their laps, ready to console those who would fail to win a chance to join the hunt.

My breath felt restricted as eyes bored into me, so much attention focused on me at once. The hairs on the back of my neck prickled in warning, telling me to run. I hesitated as we reached the stairs that led to the raised stage in the centre of the room. Too many people. It was one thing to be on camera to hundreds of user names, faceless people who were nothing but numbers at the top of the screen. It was entirely different having all those bodies there physically. Whispers whipped around me, movements dragging my eyes from one side to the other.

'Come, little demon, find him and focus on him. It's all for

Logan,' Alfie whispered in my ear before gently pushing me up the stairs ahead of him. 'There, you see him?'

Alfie directed me to face toward the far wall, where I scanned the sea of faces until at last I spotted him. His eyes met mine across the hall and I swallowed hard, pulling from that well of resolve that I had way down inside. I needed to have him fulfil those deepest, darkest desires that I'd kept hidden for so long. Just for a few days. Just once. Before he became hers.

I straightened my back, lifting my chin as Alfie stalked around me.

'Here we have our final offering for the night, and what a little delight she is. This will be the first time that she's taken part in the hunt, a virgin to it, if you will. She shows so much potential though, I think the person who wins her chase will be in for a fun time. She squeals ever so pretty, and that's without a cock inside her.'

My cheeks burned as he spoke, murmurs arising from beneath me as Alfie moved behind me, reaching around and twisting one of my nipples roughly. I yelped, and he laughed, along with a titter of appreciation from the audience. Logan watched on with no reaction at all.

Alfie's hand slid up to my throat, encircling my collar before applying some pressure, making me tip my head back into his shoulder as he pulled me flush to him. The rough feel of his clothes on my naked skin made my lack of clothing even more obvious.

'Look how she arches her arse into me, always searching for something hard to be spread over.' He slid his hand down between my thighs as I trembled against him, my eyes on Logan the entire time.

I wanted him to burn for me. To need to have me.

Alfie ran his fingers between my legs, gathering up the wetness that had already escaped me. When he held his wet fingers up to the light, I could have died. Even as embarrassment gripped at me, it was swiftly followed with a hot need. I enjoyed being a spectacle. Hell, I was getting incredibly horny the longer my stage show went on.

Alfie placed his other hand on my shoulder and forced me to my knees. He remained behind me, but fisted my hair in his hand before thrusting his wet fingers deep into my throat. I gagged almost immediately, coughing up spit that dripped down over my tits. Tears pricked my eyes as he slid his finger in further, holding them there against my tongue as I heaved and choked.

'I can't say she'll take a cock in the mouth well, but I'm sure she'll be eager to learn.'

He removed his fingers and wiped them down over my chest as I panted. Then he pulled me to my feet, his grip tight in my hair as he bent me over, kicking my feet wide so that my pussy and ass were on full display.

'Is she tight?' Someone shouted.

I moaned as he slid two fingers inside me, bringing a cheer from the crowd. 'She'd milk a cock well, that's for sure.'

He twisted his fingers inside me, making me weak at the knees. I couldn't see Logan from my bent position. He'd have a full view of his friend's fingers inside me.

A slap on my ass made me yelp, dancing onto one foot before trying to wriggle out of his grip. Two more landed in quick succession, making me dizzy. Overwhelm was coming for me as the sounds and view around the room swarmed over me.

Alfie twisted me back against his chest, facing me toward Logan. 'Just find him, sweetheart. Almost over.'

The worst part was that I didn't want it to stop. Even though my limits were being pushed, my thighs were slick. The rough treatment and mean words only drove me to want it more.

'Shall we start the bidding at twenty thousand?'

I almost choked when a multitude of hands hit the air. Logan didn't flinch.

'Remember to breathe,' Alfie whispered in between a barrage of numbers.

Forty thousand.

Fifty thousand.

Eighty thousand.

One hundred thousand.

My knees buckled, and Alfie held me up against him with a tight arm against my waist. Who in their right mind would pay a hundred thousand pounds to hunt me down and fuck me?

Yet, still, Logan hadn't joined in.

The numbers kept climbing until there was only one bidder left. The man from my first night who wanted to make Logan mad.

'Not him,' I whispered.

'A little selfishly, I'm going to bid myself,' Alfie said, his dick hard against my ass. 'One hundred and fifty from me.'

Sweat gathered at the back of my neck as he and the other man went head to head until eventually, at the giddy height of two hundred and fifty thousand, Alfie backed out.

'Sorry kid,' he said into my ear, 'but my accountant will kill me.'

Tears pricked my eyes as I watched Logan look down at his shoes.

'Going once at two-fifty to Mr. Edwards.'

My pulse thundered in my neck.

'Going twice.'

I couldn't breathe. I'd done it all for Logan, and he still didn't want me.

'S--'

Alfie was cut off by a loud voice from the other side of the room.

'One million.'

Gasps sounded as I opened my eyes, blinking through the tears as Logan walked forward. 'One million pounds.'

Alfie whistled low next to my ear.

'Edwards? Any raise?'

The man shook his head, scowling at Logan. The room spun as adrenaline washed through me.

'Sold to Mr. McGowan, for one million pounds.'

Alfie swept his arms under my thighs as I swayed. Walking down the stairs as a series of loud cheers rocked the room.

He sat me down on a couch, shooing away the occupants as Logan came to stand in front of me.

'You won,' I said.

'I did.'

'What now?'

'I'm sending you to bed. You'll need your sleep.'

'Why?'

'Because first thing tomorrow I'm going to destroy you.' Logan spoke through gritted teeth, his jaw tight. I slid my eyes to his groin where his monster dick was straining in his trousers almost to his stomach.

'You'll have to catch me first.'

Because despite how badly I wanted him, I didn't want it to be easy for him.

CHAPTER TWENTY FOUR

LOGAN

Early morning mists filtered through the dense woodland as I shifted from one foot to the other. The first gunshot echoed loudly from nearby, signalling it was time for the playthings to run.

Agitation filled my veins as I waited for our signal so I could seek my prey.

'She's going to be one expensive fuck, my friend. I hope she's worth it.' Alfie waited near me, leaning against a tree and tossing an apple up and down.

'She'd be worth triple.'

'And you thought you'd be able to resist her sweet little cunt? You are balls deep into her already.'

'It's just for a few days, then we'll go our separate ways and it'll all be like some mad fever dream,' I said with more conviction that I felt.

'Depends if you can catch her. I don't think she'll give it up easily.'

'She's been trying to get me to fuck her for days.'

'But now she knows you want to. That changes everything. Little demon's going to run you ragged.'

It should have concerned me that Alfie was so familiar with Valentina, but despite the bluster, he was a good guy deep down. He'd have absolutely paid to hunt her down had I chosen not to, but he'd never step on the toes of a friend and knew well when to back off.

A loud crack thundered right through me, the noise sending birds soaring into the sky.

It's time, sweet Cherry. I'm coming to get you.

Myself and the other hunters took off at a steady pace, ripping through the woods to catch sight of our prey. I'd been to Rosenhall enough times to know my way back to the house fairly well, and I hoped Valentina would find her course more slowly, eroding her head start.

Hopping over fallen branches and scanning the woods for a flash of red linens, I made my way through the tangle of trees.

There was a flash of red to my far right, but the hair was blonde instead of dark brown, so I ignored it and kept moving.

Where are you Valentina?

A few minutes further on, I stumbled upon a woman pinned to a tree as her captor fucked her ruthlessly; the bark scoring her tits and stomach. Blood rushed straight between my thighs, my dick filling as I stalked through the woods.

Soon enough, another flash of red caught my eye as I was getting far too close to the mansion for comfort. This time, a full, dark head of hair and a voluptuous ass made me stumble.

Got you.

Valentina looked back over her shoulder, her eyes widening as I changed course and went tearing after her. A pure, animalistic need coursed through my body, urging my legs to carry me faster toward her.

All my misgivings and guilt fell away as I gained on her, knowing without a doubt that pinning her down and taking her was something I was born to do. Like fate had led me to that very moment and promised me her.

Branches caught against my clothing as my boots crashed through the undergrowth, snagging in my hair and drawing blood from my cheek.

I didn't care.

As I gained on her, her panting breath was like a siren call. I wanted her to be panting beneath me, stretched over me as I claimed her as my own.

For today.

Only today.

The walls of the manor peeked out from the trees ahead and I worked my legs faster. If she made it back into the house, I lost.

There wasn't a chance in hell I was letting that happen.

As we made it to the edge of the rose garden that led to the house, cheers and boos erupted from the waiting crowd.

Fuck. She was fast.

But so close.

Her linens flew up behind her as she ran, giving me a mouth-watering view of her ass. I was going to pin her down and fuck every hole before I was done with her. If not that day, then before I left Rosenhall.

Stretching my hand out as we neared the house, I wound my fingers into her hair, hauling her hard as she let out a scream. We both tumbled to the floor as cheers rose around me.

I had her.

She fought like a hellion. If she could escape my grasp and get to the house before I penetrated her, she'd still win.

Nails scored my neck as she flailed, and I reached between us, tearing the linens from her body.

'I'm going to fuck you until you beg me to stop, Valentina. You're going to leak from every damn hole by the time I'm done with you.'

Her breath was hot against my neck as I used my thigh to push her knees apart.

'No,' she moaned into my skin as I pinned her beneath me, my cock straining between us.

'Use your safe word if you want it to stop. Your no means nothing,' I growled in her ear as I nipped at her jaw with my teeth while she thrashed, surrounded by the excited crowd and Alfie's delicate rose bushes.

'Please, it's too big,' she said as I opened my trousers and pulled my cock free, placing it against her hot, little cunt.

'You should have thought about that before goading me. You are going to take my dick whether or not you like it and if you cry, I'll lick your fucking tears up before fucking you harder.'

Her body trembled as I aligned myself with her, pushing the head of my dick against her tight, wet hole. I savoured it for a few seconds, knowing that once I breached it, all bets were off.

Her body tensed as I forced the tip into her before she fought. I wrapped my arms around her shoulders and neck as I thrust hard, forcing her body to accept me. She cried out as she writhed, my dick spreading her wide as I kept inching into her. I fought hard to avoid dumping my cum into her too early. It had been so long since coming that to be inside her was ecstasy.

'It's too much,' she whimpered as I tightened my grip around her and thrust her into the grass.

I bit down hard on her shoulder as I pushed my dick home, fully enveloping myself in her tight, wet heat.

She was like a fucking vice. Valentina cried out as my teeth sunk into her flesh, leaving a deep mark on her skin.

'You're my little slut now, do you hear me? Everybody is watching me fuck your pretty cunt. They all see you for exactly what you want to be.'

She tipped her face away from them as I pulled out before thrusting back into her.

Fuck, she felt good. Too fucking good.

CHAPTER TWENTY FIVE
VALENTINA

I tried to fight him off, despite knowing I was exactly where I belonged.

Logan had forced himself into me, and the pain of stretching to accommodate him was glorious. Knowing he'd wanted me badly enough to take me there, in front of everyone, was intoxicating.

The cold grass wet my back, and his teeth against my throat made me cry out as I struggled in his arms, but the heat of his cock made my insides melt with every wonderful thrust.

Logan wrapped a hand into my hair, pulling it tightly and making me wince as he forced my face back to the crowd. 'Let them see you, Cherry. Let them see how badly you needed Daddy's cock.'

They watched us eagerly, so many eyes seeing Logan claim me for the first time. Then he fucked me, his hips crashing into my own as an animalistic force took over him. He was all teeth and growling against me as he speared me with his dick, wringing pathetic whimpers from me with each thrust. The way he tipped his hips had him grinding against my clit with every thrust, making me squirm and arch against him.

Tears flowed down my cheeks as I stopped fighting him and

accepted my position beneath him, pressing myself up into him to meet each stroke. I'd dreamt about being taken like that for as long as I remembered, and it was everything I'd dreamed it to be.

'That's it, sweetheart. Cry all your sweet tears for me. They make Daddy so fucking hard. You're going to make me come inside you, aren't you?'

'Yes, Daddy,' I moaned, and it was like my words sent him wild.

Heat built as he fucked me without mercy, driving my body into the ground while running his hand over my tears before thrusting his fingers into my mouth.

'It's too big,' I gasped as he pressed harder, my words mumbling against his fingers.

'It's the perfect fit, pretty girl. Within a few days, you'll be an expert at taking it in every fucking hole.'

Logan groaned before coming hard as I whimpered, biting into my shoulder as he filled me with cum to the deafening roar of our onlookers. My tears came all the harder, because I needed more.

'Good girl,' he groaned in my ear. 'Such a good girl.'

'Thank you, Daddy,' I whimpered against his neck, licking the sweat from his skin.

My disappointment was short-lived when I realised he wasn't done with me.

Before I'd even come back to myself, Logan was picking me up and tying rope around my hands, hoisting them high into a tree and hitching them to a branch.

My body stretched out until I was forced to stand on tip-toes, everything feeling perilously on display.

Logan fastened his trousers as he stalked around me, his eyes still filled with heat as he watched his cum drip down my thighs.

'Oh, Valentina. Look what you've done,' he said, running a hand over my jawline before wiping away the tears that still stained my cheeks. 'I've gone and made such a mess of my pretty girl.'

He crashed his mouth against mine, his tongue darting between my lips as he tipped my head for better access. I moaned into him as he stole our first kiss, snatching it from me in a moment of fierce heat. I'd been so focused on his cock I'd almost forgotten how glorious kissing could be. His tongue explored my mouth with expert strokes, making me strain to take more of his kisses. When he broke it off, I growled angrily at him.

He smirked before coming up behind me and letting his hands rove over my body. Everywhere he touched ignited with heat. From my neck, to my thighs, over my ass and cupping my small tits, he took his time to examine every inch, working me up to a panting, needy mess.

'Please make me cum?' I begged as he pinched a nipple hard, my whole body writhing as I tried to hold myself up on my toes. 'I need it so bad.'

'I know you do,' Logan said into my ear before licking up the side of my neck, 'But I don't know if you deserve it.'

'I took your cock...'

'You did. But you have been nothing but a brat since the moment we met. And now you've put me in the position of wanting something I can't have.'

'What?'

'You, Valentina. I'm going to need to leave here and forget all about being inside your perfect little cunt. How am I supposed to do that?'

'I'm sorry,' I murmured as he nipped at my neck before sliding his fingers down into my cum-soaked pussy.

'This is how you should always be. Full of my cum and on display so that the entire world can see what a delightful little slut you are.'

'Yes,' I whispered as his fingers sank into me, making my legs turn to jelly.

His fingers thrust slowly in and out of me as he stood behind me, nipping and kissing at my neck, driving me crazy. He kept me right on the edge of orgasm, slowing every time I got close.

'Look at them, Valentina. This is the you they will remember as. They don't know another person exists. When they go home and think about the slutty little brat strung up in a tree and fucked into the grass, that's the only you that will exist to them. This is the you I'll remember too. My desperate little brat who'd do anything to cum on my fingers. Today, that is all you are.'

His words were dirty and wrong, and as much as I wanted to argue that I was so much more than that, in that moment, his slut was all I craved to be. The idea of people going home and thinking of me that way made my body ache for release.

'Please, let me come? Please?'

My calves burned where I stood on tiptoe, and Logan's hearty chuckle made me cry. I could already feel how hard he'd grown again against my back as he delighted in torturing me.

'Lick Daddy's cum off of my fingers and I'll clean you with my tongue,' he said throatily into my ear.

When he brought his fingers to my mouth, soaked in both me and him, I licked and sucked, swallowing everything I could. My face heated at my desperation as our onlookers watched, their faces a mixture of delight and jealousy. One man pulled out his dick and thrust it into his playthings mouth as he watched us. I didn't care. It only heightened the intensity of it all.

'Such a good girl. Look at you eating up my cum. Maybe I'll have to feed you it for all your meals until we go home. I'd bet you'd drink it right from my cock like the best little cock-sucker, wouldn't you?'

'Yes, Daddy.'

'Fuck, when you call me that, it does unhinged things inside of me, Valentina. Do you know how long I've waited to hear that name on such a pretty pair of lips?'

He didn't wait for an answer. He moved in front of me and dropped to his knees, hoisting my thighs over his shoulders and pressing me against his face with his hands on my ass.

The rope held my arms firm above me as he slid his tongue against me, not caring that his cum dripped from me as he devoured my pussy.

Every slide of his tongue made me arch against him, my breath catching as he drove me to the edge quickly and messily. There was no finesse in the act. It was pure, unbridled hedonism that crashed through us.

Pressure mounted between my thighs as he fixed his mouth over my clit, sucking and licking hard as I cried out. The rope burned against my wrists as I thrashed against him. Everything in the universe focused on that one point where his mouth met my flesh.

I came hard against his face, bucking and panting as he continued to lash me with his tongue. The orgasm peaked, bringing fresh tears sliding down my cheeks, and as I slumped against him, my arms hanging in the rope, he kept going.

'I can't,' I whispered as his tongue slid inside me, teasing me through the overwhelm as I tried to wriggle away from his tongue.

He looked up from between my thighs, those blue eyes almost a dark grey in the morning light. 'You've got little choice.'

I fought against the sensations, arching away from him with little success as he pinned me to his face and continued to lavish me with his tongue.

'You are going to get ready to come for me, little love, so that when I stand up and fill you with my cock, you're ready to scream for the crowd. You are going to come hard on my dick, Valentina, so I can feel that tight little cunt strangling it. Only then will I be done with you. For now.' He bit my thigh after he spoke, sending waves of pain to mingle with the pleasure he wrought within me.

I thought I might black out from the overload of thoughts and touch. My brain could barely process the fact that dozens of people were watching Logan use me. They listened to my gasps, whimpers and pleading and saw me as entertainment. Shivers of want ran through me at the thought. It felt so wrong to want to be enjoyed with an audience, but it took me to a higher plane.

'Logan...' I moaned as he held me tight to his mouth as he worked me back up to the brink.

I cried out when he let go of me, cold washing over my wetness as he stood and captured my mouth for another heady kiss. His lips tasted of both of us before he bit my lower lip, making me whimper.

'Are you ready for me, sweet Cherry?'

'I need you bad, Daddy.'

'Yes, you do. You've needed my cock since the minute I laid eyes on you. Needed to be tortured and tamed on it in front of everyone.'

He moved behind me, turning me to face straight into the crowd of people, their gazes burning into me as he unbuckled his trousers before hitching me up by the thighs, spreading me wide for everyone to see.

'Look at them, pretty girl. They see everything you have. You have nothing left to hide. I spread your cunt for them, wet and dripping with need. They all know who you are, Valentina. They are going to watch as you take Daddy's cock and come all over it like a good girl.'

His muscled forearms were veiny as he held me up in his arms, my knees over his elbows and my arms still attached to the tree above us.

Then he was there, his fat cock pressing against me. I bit my lip as he forced me down on top of it, looking down to watch as my swollen pussy lips split wide for him. It was such an explicit view that it had me quivering in his arms. He reached up with his hands and wrapped them around my throat, pulling my knees high and wide, and compressing my torso as he held me down onto his cock. I cried out as he filled me, by far the biggest cock I'd ever had.

'You can take it, sweet Cherry. You'll take it for me, won't you?'

'Yes, Daddy,' I whimpered as he pressed me down as far as I could go. Still a large amount of his cock remained outside of me.

'Don't worry, you can take it all, baby.'

The thought made my knees weak.

The pressure inside me was intense, a ring of fire burning where I stretched around him. It was the most glorious feeling. Painful, but dizzyingly addictive.

Logan fucked me harder, my stomach shifting with each stroke as I watched him take me.

When he slid one hand down, dropping a leg to the floor so he could touch me, I lost myself. Tremors shook my entire body as I quaked beneath his touch.

'Come for me, my dirty little slut,' he growled in my ear. 'Come on Daddy's cock, so I can fill you up again.'

My orgasm swept through me as he circled my clit, and he rode it out with hard thrusts until I collapsed back against him, my screams echoing throughout the garden. His hand went to my throat, cutting off my air as he chased his own orgasm, filling me again and again with his massive dick.

'Such a fucking delightful little brat.'

'I'm going to fucking destroy you, Valentina.'

'How am I ever going to let you go?'

He punctuated his thrusts with dirty words that made my already hazy mind swirl.

As he let out a groan, dropping my other leg and capturing me around the waist while he fucked me hard, I gasped.

'Keep me, Daddy,' I whispered, as he moaned his orgasm into my hair.

CHAPTER TWENTY SIX
LOGAN

I tossed Valentina down on my bed when we reached my suite, her naked body flopping on top of the pristine white covers.

'I think I need a nap,' she groaned, curling herself into the duvet and trying to pull it over her. Grass stains marked her knees, and her feet were filthy from running through the woods, small cuts abrading her skin here and there. Not to mention the mess I'd contributed. Between her thighs. Twice.

'You are having a bath.'

Her moan brought a grin to my lips as I made my way to the bathroom, turning the taps on the overly large sunken tub. Tipping an excessive amount of bubble bath into it, I waited for it to fill. Large fluffy towels already waited on the heated towel rail, and there was plenty of luxurious, scented shampoo and conditioner provided.

'Come on,' I said, going back to the bed and plucking Valentina out of it.

'God, you're so bossy.' Valentina didn't fight me as I carried her toward the bath, dragging her fingers over my collarbone instead.

We walked past the mirror as we entered the bathroom, and her eyes widened.

'What did you do to my neck?' Her throat and shoulders still showed the red circles where I'd claimed her with my teeth.

'I don't remember you complaining,' I said, dumping her into the bathwater before stripping my clothing off. She squealed as her ass hit the bottom of the tub, but then leaned back as her eyes rolled.

'Oh my god... your room is insane. Who did you shag to get a room like this? Actually, I guess I know the answer to that.'

'I'm not in this room because of who I've slept with, it's because of who my family is. Perks of the job, some might say.'

'Don't you hate your job?'

'No.'

Kind of. Sometimes.

'Bullshit.'

'If you keep that up, I'll find something to fill that mouth with.' Her eyes focussed on my cock as I dropped my trousers over a chair.

'I'm too tired,' she said, 'even if that thing fits in my mouth.'

Sinking into the water felt fantastic, the warmth soothing over my chilled skin. The tub was big, but I still pulled her legs over mine, so that her feet sat on either side of my hips. The intimacy should have felt more awkward than it did, but she fit just right.

'Was the auction and hunt what you imagined it would be?'

Her cheeks flushed as she smiled at me. 'Looking for compliments, Mr. McGowan?'

'Yes. Fill my head with your pretty words.'

'It was overwhelming. And intense. And amazing. Everything I'd always imagined sex could be. I've no idea how I'll go back to lacklustre sex with the guys I always end up with.'

My stomach lurched at the thought of her going back to sex with anyone else. I had no right to be upset by it. We weren't in a relationship of any kind. I didn't own any part of her.

I was going back to my fiancée.

Of course she'd move on.

'Was it worth losing out on the extra money for?'

'Now you really are fishing for compliments,' she said, splashing some water at me playfully. I captured one of her feet and pulled it up in front of me, washing the tiny cuts as she tipped her head back with a groan.

'Why are you being so sweet?' she asked as I let my hands work her calf muscles, knowing they'd ache from being strung up on tiptoes.

'Because it's all part of it. You take from your submissive, but you always give back more than you take.'

'Am I your submissive?'

'For the next few days, if you want to be. It's the rules of the auction, but I won't hold you to them if you've changed your mind.'

'What do you want?' Valentina fixed me with a curious look as my fingers grazed the back of her knee.

What did I want? What I should do was clear: back off and stay away from my fiancée's cousin. But what I wanted was to indulge myself in Valentina. To get drunk on her like a teen being left in a liquor store overnight. Imbibe myself with her until we were both drunk on pleasure.

'You,' I answered, letting that selfish part of me—that I kept stuffed down inside—have some leverage. 'Now turn around so I can wash your hair.'

Valentina squirmed and moaned so prettily while I scrubbed my fingers against her scalp that I was halfway to hard by the time we got out of the tub. We dried ourselves off while I stole glances at her, hardly able to believe that she was really there in my room, in the flesh.

She eyed my cock hungrily as I threw an oversize t-shirt at her before climbing into the bed. 'My eyes are up here, you wee devil.'

'I'm well aware... It wasn't your eyes I was looking at.'

'Get your arse in this bed before you make me slap it red raw again.'

'Promises,' she said through a yawn.

I pulled her tight against my chest, her damp hair smelling of the sweet shampoo as I nuzzled in against her.

With an arch of her back, she nestled my cock against her arse cheeks, both comforting and infuriating me.

'Go to sleep,' I said, grasping her waist in my arm beneath the duvet and holding her still.

'It's the middle of the day...'

'And we've got a long few days of partying ahead. Shut your mouth before I find a gag for it.'

Her giggle made me melt.

CHAPTER TWENTY SEVEN

VALENTINA

Disorientation muddled my mind when I woke up with a thick arm about my waist and the setting sun throwing an orange glow over my face.

I shifted in the bed, turning to see Logan fast asleep beside me, his face softer than I was used to seeing it.

Sliding out from under him, I rolled out of his massive bed and stretched before looking for my linens. They were nowhere to be seen, still out in the garden where he'd torn them off, most likely.

The t-shirt he'd let me borrow sat high on my thighs, barely covering my ass where my hips flared out most. It would have to do until I got to my room.

Logan stirred when I unlatched the door and I held my breath. As wonderful as it had been to snuggle up and fall asleep with him, I knew I needed to guard my heart. As fun as it was getting to live out my fantasies, I had to keep reminding myself it was just sex. Nothing more. A few days of explicit fun before we went our separate ways.

Until I had to pretend I barely knew him at their wedding.

The thought was already a donkey punch to the chest.

Back in my room, I sat on the bed and pulled out my phone, bringing up Lara's number and waiting as it rang.

'How's it going?' she said as she answered. 'Have you landed your prey yet?'

'Maybe....'

'Holy shit, V, for real?'

'Yeah. He bid for me at the auction.'

'Wait, he paid for you?'

'Kind of. But it wasn't about the money. He paid to win the chance to hunt me down.'

'Did he catch you?'

I flopped back on the bed and grinned. 'You could say that.'

'Ahhhh! Was it amazing? Or was he a big fat disappointment?'

'Something was big and fat, but it was in no way disappointing.'

'Oh, my god. Like how big?'

'Big enough that it made me cry.'

'Is that good?'

I laughed. 'Yes, it's good.'

'A package came for you. A big padded envelope. I've popped it in your room.'

I wasn't expecting anything. Had I ordered something and forgotten?

'Can you open it?'

'Yeah, of course.'

I listened as she put the phone down, hearing her feet padding through our flat and a rustle as she came back. 'I'll put you on video, two seconds.'

Her face popped up at the kitchen counter as she held up the envelope. I shrugged, still none the wiser about it. Lara tore at the paper edge of the envelope before tipping out its contents.

'What is it?' I asked.

'Fuck.'

The hairs on the back of my neck rose. 'What?'

'It's screenshots. Of you.'

Lara held one up. A picture of me on my bed in one of my lingerie sets, with the word SLUT scrawled across the page. My stomach clenched as I took in page after page of pictures and slurs.

'Oh, my god...'

'It means whoever sent these knows where you live. It's postmarked, so they didn't hand deliver it at least. Hopefully not someone local.'

'Christ. What am I going to do?'

'Have you pissed anyone off lately?'

'Footguy has been incessant in his messages, but other than that, I don't think so.'

'They all look like they are from open chat. Nothing too explicit is happening. Although a regular would have to be an idiot to include their own chat, I guess.'

I closed my eyes and took a slow breath. Why on earth couldn't good things happen to me? I'd finally got the sex I'd been dreaming about for years, and it's followed up with a nutter sending me photos of my cam videos.

'What should I do with them?' Lara asked, sifting through them.

'Is there a note or anything?'

'Nope.'

'Just put them in my bedside table for now. I'll have a look when I get home. Maybe tell Muhammad to be on the lookout in case anyone who isn't usually around tries to get in.'

I didn't want Lara in harm's way because of me. Whoever sent the mail mustn't know we live together, seeing as they didn't send her the screenshots of herself.

'Did Logan have your address?'

'No. I don't think so. He's not the kind of guy to send stuff like that.'

'Are you sure?' Lara raised a brow and crossed her arms. 'I need you to be sure.'

'I'm the one who pursued him, remember?'

'Who else could it be?'

Anyone who had enough knowledge to hack the site, I guessed. My payment details included my address...

'I don't know. I'll be home in a few days and can get in touch with the site owners, see if it's been hacked or anything.'

'Okay. Just be careful.'

'You, too.' I said.

CHAPTER TWENTY EIGHT

LOGAN

A knock at my door woke me up. It took me a few minutes to figure out where I was before I noticed Valentina had disappeared. The bathroom and adjoining rooms were empty. I pulled on some boxer shorts and a clean tee on the way to the door.

There she stood, weighed down by a heavy metal tray and looking shyer than I'd seen her.

'Good evening.' she said, shifting from one hip to another.

'So you didn't decide to leg it back to Glasgow after all?'

'You wish...'

'No, I don't.' I took the tray from her hands and walked it over to the table, which sat near the window. Removing the silver lids revealed a plethora of meats, fruits, cheeses and crackers.

'You missed dinner, and I didn't want you going hungry,' Valentina said, hovering near the door.

'Come here, sit.'

When she pulled out the other chair, I shook my head. 'Not there, on your knees beside me.'

The way she captured her bottom lip between her teeth made me want to forgo eating altogether.

She knelt beside me, her body resting against the side of my leg as she looked up at me with those hazel eyes.

I ate, loading meat and cheese onto crackers, smiling at having her there beside me. It was one thing to be fucking her in front of everyone, but something far more delicate to share in the quiet moments, when it was for no-one but us.

'Tell me about yourself,' I said.

'What do you want to know?' Her head tilted as she spoke, dark hair falling over her shoulder.

'Anything.'

'Well, I live with my best friend. I love to bake. I got the bug from my grandma when I was little. She used to watch me when my mum worked. I miss her. She also taught me to knit - but you already know I knit as you saw me that one time on camera. I'm an only child. My dad died when I was young and Mum never met anyone else so it's always just been us. Since Grandma died anyway.' Valentina paused before lowering her eyes away from me as she apologised. 'Sorry, I've been told I talk too much. I didn't mean for that to be quite the dump it was.'

I ran a thumb across her lower lip and smiled at her. 'Don't apologise. I enjoy listening to you. What do you like to bake?'

'Cakes, pastries, buns, anything really. My cinnamon buns are killer though, everyone says so. I could make you some...' Her voice died off as we both knew that there was no after Rosenhall for her to make me anything.

'Don't worry, I'll take your word for it. Are you hungry?'

'A little.'

I opened an orange and separated the segments, feeding her a piece.

'It's odd,' she said after eating the segment. 'I shouldn't enjoy being finger fed like a pet, but I do.'

'There are lots of things we feel like we shouldn't enjoy, but as long as it isn't hurting anyone, where is the harm?'

'Do you see me as less than for wanting to be beside you like this?'

'No, Valentina. You're a fucking wonder. Few people discover their likes at a young age, and even fewer see them realised. It's no wonder you are a success at your job with that level of determination. I was hooked from the moment I spotted you.'

She laughed and rested her head on my thigh. 'You sure made me work hard to win you over for a man who was hooked.'

'You know why that is. What we're doing here is... it's not cheating, but it wouldn't be well received.'

'No-one will ever know.'

I popped another piece of orange in her mouth before slicing up a mango, feeding her the dripping fruit as she licked it from my fingers.

God fucking, damn. She was sinfully hot.

Pushing the tray aside, I scooped her up and sat her on the table in front of me. Dragging the red linen aside, I licked the drops of fruit juice that had fallen onto her chest.

'Logan,' she whispered, running her fingers up into my hair as I licked up the side of her neck, kissing at the red marks which still marred her skin.

'Do you want me to get ready to go downstairs? To have you paraded in front of everyone?'

'I think I'm too tired.'

Thank god. As much as I wanted to do filthy things to her in the hedonistic pleasure house that Rosenhall was, I was in no mood to share her just yet.

'And I'm still a bit sore.'

I furrowed my brows, pulling back to look at her face. 'Sore where?'

'Where you stretched me open.'

Guilt bit into me as I pulled her to me, grazing my lips over hers as she sighed happily. 'How about I kiss it better for you? Show you that Daddy can be as gentle as I am rough.'

I didn't wait for an answer as I tipped her back on the table, spreading her thighs wide as I flipped her linen covering out of the way. She did still look swollen and red where I'd ravaged her. It made me hard almost instantly.

'You have such a pretty pussy, Valentina. All out on display for me, just begging to be licked.'

I kissed her softly between the thighs, grinning as she squirmed.

'What's wrong, sweetheart? Am I being too gentle?'

'Yes. Please. It's ticklish.'

'You need to understand that no matter how much you beg once you're all wet and bothered, you'll get nothing inside you until tomorrow night. Only my tongue.'

I slid my tongue the length of her, pleased when her fingers gripped around the edge of the table.

'Such a perfect little slut, spread on the table like a feast. Perhaps I should do this with you tomorrow night. Turn you into a buffet for anyone who needs a taste.' I spoke between licks, taking my time to torture her with pleasure.

'I can taste how wet you're getting already.'

She writhed beneath my mouth as I pressed my hands into her hips, wrapping my arms around her thighs from beneath.

'Oh god...' she moaned, her fingers moving into my hair and tugging.

'God's not here, baby girl. If you need a name in that mouth, use mine.'

'Daddy... don't stop.'

I latched my mouth onto her clit and used my tongue to make her tremble.

'Fuck,' she whimpered, bucking her hips. 'Please, I think I could take your cock. I want to.'

'No,' I said before continuing my feast.

'Please? I need you.'

Her words broke something inside of me. How long had it been since someone needed me? Even if it were only desperate words from a horny mouth. Within a few more strokes of my tongue, she came, her pussy clenching around nothing as I worked her clit.

'Good girl,' I said as I kissed her inner thigh, trailing my lips over the silvery lines there. 'You're going to be desperate for cock by the time tomorrow night comes around. But for now, I'm taking you back to bed, and you're going to lie in my lap while I stroke your hair and we watch whatever shit is on the telly.'

'But your cock is still hard. I could take care of it for you?'

My shorts were tenting, but I had enough willpower that I could wait a little longer. 'Soon enough, Valentina. For now, we both need some rest.'

And as much as I hated to admit it, having her wrapped up in my lap, moaning softly as I ran my fingers through her hair, was the best part of the day for me. Better than hunting her. Better than fucking her.

The realisation sent red flags popping up throughout my entire body. But I pushed each aside, determined to enjoy her while I could.

CHAPTER TWENTY NINE

VALENTINA

'Ready, Cherry?' Logan asked as I knelt in the corridor outside the great hall.

'I think so.' My stomach was tight, in knots with nerves. We'd stayed cooped up in one another's beds since the auction, and after going down on me on the table, Logan had edged me again and again. I'd spent twenty-four hours begging for his cock, or his mouth, or fingers, but each time he's taken me to the edge before snatching me back from it.

I was about feral with need.

'It'll be worth all the torture when you finally get Daddy's cock inside you. Not long now...'

Logan tightened his grip on the leash, which attached my metal collar to his fist. The chink as the chain hit the collar sent me into a tizzy every time it moved. Every single second of my time with Logan had me in a lust-induced haze.

'Come,' he said, tugging me forward on my hands and knees. Metal cuffs dug into my wrists and ankles as I crawled through the tall doors and into the heaving room. They were all I wore. Eyes roved over my naked body as I crawled behind Logan's firm footsteps.

'Such a pretty thing,' someone said as I passed, while another man murmured his agreement.

My cheeks heated as their comments washed over me.

All around me, scenes of decadence unfolded. Playthings being toyed with and fucked for all to see. One naked male was even being used as a footstool for a couple of women while they kissed and moaned above him. I spotted a woman up ahead, sucking one man while another fucked her with slow, sure strokes from behind. My pussy clenched at the sight. I wanted Logan so badly. Needed him to spread me over him again. Her mouth dropped open in bliss as her body shook, an orgasm thrumming through her.

Logan led me to a couch where Alfie sat enjoying a drink near the fireplace.

'Ah, look who's resurfaced. All fucked out?' Alfie said, smiling down at me as I knelt between Logan's legs and his.

'No,' I said, only a little whine slipping into my voice.

Logan laughed and sat back as a waitress came and took his order.

'I've kept her waiting. She's desperate for some cock, aren't you, sweetheart?'

I shifted against my heels as I nodded.

'Maybe you'd like to show Alfie just how good a girl you can be?' Logan slid up next to his friend as the waitress brought his whisky over. 'Up for a little game, Alfie?'

'Oh, always. I'm sure she'll be delighted to show me how badly she needs it.'

'Take our cocks out, Valentina.'

The two of them sat close enough that their hips touched, Logan stretching an arm over the back of the sofa behind Alfie as I knelt forward and unbuttoned their trousers with shaking fingers.

'Remember, you can say cease and it will all stop if it gets too much,' Logan said.

'It won't.'

'So confident...'

I pulled his cock out of his pants, licking my lips at the sheer size of it up close. How the heck I was going to get it in my mouth, I didn't know. Alfie grinned as I undid his buttons and slid my hand into his trousers, pulling out his heavily pierced cock. Side by side with Logan's, they were a sight to behold. Had I died and gone to heaven?

'Go on. Show us what you can do with that hot little mouth and maybe I'll convince Alfie to help you take both of us at once.'

Even the thought of them both had me soaked.

Eager to prove myself, I knelt up, taking a cock in each hand as I ran my fingers up the shafts and over the heads. They felt so incredibly different. Logan was so thick and heavy, his cock veiny and monstrous, where Alfie wasn't as girthy, but long and studded with metal.

I stroked them both in the same rhythm, watching as they enjoyed me. Alfie closed his eyes and leaned back against Logan's arm while Logan kept his eyes on me, his breath hitching as I leaned forward and ran my tongue around his tip.

'That's it, darling, show us what a good little cock-sucker you can be. Show me what uses that smart mouth has.'

I slid my mouth over his cock, feeling the stretch of my skin at the sides as I tried to work him into my mouth, all the while keeping my hands moving on both of them.

'Come now, little demon,' Alfie said, his voice gruff as he reached down and slid his fingers into my hair. 'You can fit more in there than that.'

He guided my face down onto Logan's cock as I tried my best to take it. My stomach heaved as he put pressure on my scalp, holding me firm as Logan's cock nudged at the back of my mouth.

I gasped for air as he pulled my head up, watching the saliva stream from my mouth.

'Mmm,' he groaned as he pulled my mouth to his dick.

The piercings felt alien against my tongue as I bathed his cock with it. 'Atta girl, you show Logan you know how to take a cock and he'll give you another go.'

I was aware of eyes on me as people watched me suck on Alfie's cock, sliding my lips and tongue over it with fervour.

'God, she might not take it deep, but fuck, she knows how to use that tongue,' Alfie said to Logan, arching his hips up to slide further into my mouth.

'Oh, she can take it. I'm sure of it.'

Logan grasped the back of my neck and pushed me lower on my knees so that I was looking up at them with Alfie's pierced dick in my mouth.

'You want to be a good girl for Daddy, don't you?'

I nodded, tonguing at the head of Alfie's cock, metal beneath my tongue.

'Then take it deep, baby girl.'

Logan held me firm while Alfie pushed into my mouth, bucking his hips to fuck my face.

'That's it Valentina. You look so pretty with his dick in your mouth.'

I coughed as Alfie's cock breached my throat, my eyes filling with tears as I tried to breathe through the convulsions of my stomach.

'Such a good girl. Swallowing down Daddy's friend for him. Give it to her Alfie, make her work that dick like a good little slut.'

Alfie groaned as he thrust into my mouth, my body fighting my efforts to stay still and accept his dick.

'Fuck, Logan, you need to get in there. Our little demon is perfect.'

He pulled out of my mouth as I choked hard, my tears mingling with the strings of saliva that joined his pierced dick to my lips.

'Daddy's turn,' Logan said before filling my mouth with him.

If Alfie had been a struggle, Logan's cock was near impossible. Every time he thrust it to the back of my mouth, my whole body heaved, threatening to upend my dinner. I wanted to please him so badly that I licked and sucked whenever he pulled back.

'Such a messy little slut,' Logan chuckled as he wiped a hand down through my tears and spit. He gave me a reprieve from trying to fit him in my throat, pulling my lips and tongue onto both of their dicks at once.

'Oh fuck,' Alfie moaned. 'That's so fucking hot.'

I used my hands to press their cocks together as best I could, sliding my fingers up and down their shafts as I slid my wet, messy mouth over both of them, my tongue roving over the engorged heads.

'Such an eager thing. I bet your cunt's soaked, isn't it?' Logan said.

'Yes,' I moaned over them. 'I'm so wet.'

Alfie pulled me off of them and yanked me onto his lap so my back was against his thighs and I spread legs over the arm of the sofa. My head hung off of his lap.

'I'll give her a distraction and we can see if she can fit any more of that cock in her throat. I know she wants to.'

Alfie slipped two fingers into me as I cried out, but my cries were cut off as Logan knelt with one knee on the sofa and the other foot on the floor, his dick thrusting into my mouth as he held me by the throat.

Every nerve ending in my body screamed at me as I was awash with sensations. Alfie's fingers fucked me slowly, his thumb gliding over my clit as Logan worked his monster cock deeper into my mouth, his position giving him more leverage.

'Keep breathing, Valentina. You're going to take it all for me.'

I fought as the head of his cock pressed against my throat; it burning where he thrust. But as Alfie started fucking me harder with his fingers, I moaned, my throat relaxing and allowing Logan to force his way into it. Tears slipped as my chest heaved, Logan's groans delighting my ears as my body quaked.

'Such a fucking good girl,' Logan growled as he pumped his dick into my throat. His words sent me reeling, my thighs clenching around Alfie's arm as he curled his fingers inside me, keeping the pressure and pace as I fell apart around them.

The orgasm was blinding, my body tensing and clamping around them. Logan's fingers tensed on my throat as he pulled out, letting my cries fill the room.

'Should have filled her throat with cum,' Alfie said as he pinned my hips while continuing to thrust his fingers into me, eking out the last shudders of my orgasm.

'I'm going to fill her pretty ass with it instead.'

'It won't fit,' I gasped, my voice cracking with the burn from their cocks.

'You said that about your mouth.'

'Do you think you have room to fit us both in at once?' Alfie asked me as he pulled his fingers out of me and thrust them into my mouth.

I shook my head.

'Do you want to try?'

I nodded.

'Best get us some lube, then.'

CHAPTER THIRTY

LOGAN

'We'll take it slowly. Tell me if you need to stop.'

Valentina was all wide eyed as she nodded while straddling my lap. I caught her lips with mine, swallowing her moans as Alfie slid his lubed up fingers into her ass.

'He's going to get you nice and stretched out for me, sweet girl. You just focus on my lips.'

She whimpered into my mouth as Alfie worked her open, his lips on her neck and throat as I sucked on her tongue. Her mouth was eager as she opened deeper for me, her panting making me desperate for her.

She was everything I'd always wanted. Sweet, smart, funny and with a ravenous need for cock. All I wanted was to hole up in Rosenhall with her shackled to the end of my bed.

Seeing her stroking Alfie and me with her the metal cuffs sliding against her wrists had driven me mad with desire. It had taken every ounce of willpower not to fill her throat with my cum, but I knew if I could get my cock in her ass, she might not be able to take it for long, and I needed to fill her there before I let her go.

I needed to see her leaking, well fucked, before I sent her home.

Sharing her with Alfie was as much for me as it was for fulfilling the fantasies she had. It was the least I could do for her, really. She was giving so much to me, and I had a feeling I was going to leave her hurt after we went back to our real lives. But seeing her coming on his fingers or throat deep on his cock only made me all the harder. Seeing her take it for me was addictive.

Her breath caught as Alfie kept his fingers moving inside her while I pressed her chest to my face, capturing her small nipples with my teeth before licking the pain I inflicted away. Her fingers entwined in my hair as she trembled, her pussy so close to my hard cock.

I couldn't resist.

Pulling her hips down, I positioned my cock at her entrance, inching her down onto me as I nipped at her tits with my teeth.

I could feel Alfie's fingers through the thin wall that separated her cunt from her ass, the fluttering sensation adding to the intensity of her tightness.

'Such a dirty girl,' I growled in her ear as I pulled her right down onto me, her pussy clamping around my girth. 'My cock in your wet cunt while Alfie fingers your ass.'

Alfie captured her lips while I sucked on her neck, her moans getting louder by the minute.

'And all these people watching you. Seeing you being shared. They would love to join in, to fill you with their cocks, too. You've got room for another one once we're inside, but I want to hear you scream for me, sweet Cherry. I want them all to hear you cry out as we fuck you until you drip white.'

'Please... fuck,' Valentina mumbled against Alfie's lips. I slowly rocked inside her, feeling her relax around my cock as she craved more.

'When we're both inside you, we are going to keep fucking until we come. No matter how many times you come. I'm going to stretch that little asshole out and then fill it with my cum while Alfie fucks your pretty cunt until you cry.'

'Yes. Please.'

'You ready to take me?'

'No. Yes. Fuck. I don't know if I can.'

'You will, baby.'

'She's ready,' Alfie whispered against her cheek as I closed my eyes and gave a final few thrusts into her sweet pussy.

'Remember that this is mine. I'm only letting him borrow it,' I said into Valentina's hair as she writhed on my cock.

'All yours,' she whispered as I stood, picking her up while still inside her as Alfie sat on the couch.

Eyes followed our every move, playthings rapt while they worked at cocks or cunts around us.

Sliding out of Valentina, I positioned her over my friend's dick, kissing her neck as she slid down over his pierced shaft, shuddering with pleasure as he took my place.

'How does he feel?'

'So good. The piercings are... different,'

Alfie ground his dick into her as her eyes rolled back in her head. 'Such a good slut, you just want to be stuffed full of dick, don't you?'

She nodded as Alfie reached up and toyed with her nipples. I positioned myself between Alfie's thighs, tipping Valentina forward and grinning at the sight of his metal covered cock sinking deep inside my girl. Grabbing the lube, I covered my hand and stroked it onto my dick, using as much as possible. She'd need it.

Her asshole tightened as I placed my fingers against it, working in and out as Alfie fucked her slowly. When her resistance disappeared, I lined my cock up and pressed forward slowly but insistently.

So fucking tight.

'Ouch,' she said, squirming against my dick in a way that made me want to pin her all the more.

'Breathe, baby. Relax. Don't fight it.'

'It's not going to fit.'

'I'll make it fit, sweetheart. I'm going to come deep in your arse while you strangle my dick.'

I'd barely got half of the tip in when I felt her convulse around me.

'Fuck, Logan. Oh, my god!'

Valentina's body shook as Alfie increased his pace, his teeth gripping his bottom lip as her cunt milked at him.

I saw my chance, and forced my dick home, pushing past the tightening muscles as she came hard.

'Holy shit, ow, oh my god. Fuck. It's too much.'

'Shh,' I moaned into her ear as I let her get used to being stretched over my girth.

'The worst part's over, baby, and look at you stretched over two dicks like the best little cock-taker around.'

The feeling of being deep in her, while Alfie's dick nudged mine through the thin wall that separated us, was addictive. Every slight movement from either of us sent her quaking all over again, her breath coming in quick, harsh pants.

'Little demon, you're going to make me come if you keep that up,' Alfie said, his voice thick with lust.

Then she surprised me by moving, only a tiny bit at first, but within minutes she was sliding up and down on us like a pro.

'There it is. That's my girl. You take Daddy's cock right into your dirty little ass.'

I wasn't going to last. She was so fucking tight while stuffed with two big dicks. My balls tightened, and I nodded at Alfie, letting him know it was time to pick up the pace.

Reaching around her hips, I found her clit, running circles around it with my fingers as I pulled back before slamming into her, my cock sliding deep with the amount of lube and her body loose like a rag doll.

Alfie set his hands on her hips and met each of my thrusts with his own, his deep groans making me even harder, knowing he was enjoying my girl's pussy while I fucked her arse was such a turn on.

'Fuck,' she cried. 'I can't. Oh, my god. Daddy!'

Her ass clamped down on me as she dug her nails into Alfie's chest, another orgasm ripping through her.

I slammed to the balls as she cried out, all eyes on us as I roared my orgasm into her ear, jerking my hips as Alfie dumped a load into her.

'That's it, baby. Take it all. Such a good girl. You did it.'

'I did it,' she whispered, still humping our dicks as they softened inside her.

'Fuck, little demon. I think that's the best fucking orgasm I've ever had.' Alfie looked stoned, utterly blissed out as I lifted and turned her, kissing her hard, swallowing down her moans and tears.

'Time for bed. You coming up Alfie?'

'If I can bring wine and a cigar, then fuck yeah.'

Valentina stood on wobbly legs until I shook my head.

'You'll go out the way you came in, but this time everyone will see us dripping from you and hitting the floor.'

Her cheeks reddened as she dropped to her knees and turned. I walked behind her, not bothering with the leash so that Alfie and I got the perfect view of her round, well fucked ass seeping cum as she crawled.

'You're never going to get over her,' Alfie said as we exited the doors.

'I know.'

CHAPTER THIRTY ONE

VALENTINA

Birds chittered outside the window as I came to. I smiled as I found myself entangled in a sea of limbs. Between Alfie and Logan I was sticky and hot, and as nice as a man sandwich was, I needed a shower badly.

My ass was sore as I stood, a reminder of being stretched out to my max the previous evening.

Dried cum crusted my thighs as I found my linens and secured them around me. At least I'd peed before going to bed. A UTI would be the last thing I needed.

It was the last day at Rosenhall. My time with Logan had come to a close, and as much as I wanted to crawl back in beside him, it would just make it harder to leave.

It's not that I was in love with him.

Or obsessed with him.

Okay, maybe a little obsessed, but I had just never met a man who could hit my needs so precisely. Giving him up to my cousin, who didn't even want him, was torture.

Even if it was a torture I'd brought upon myself.

I slipped out the door after taking one last look at the two men

who had made my stay at Rosenhall one I'd never forget. Alfie's dark hair tangled on his pillow, his nipples glinting with yet more piercings. He'd been fun, and hot, but I wouldn't miss him when I went home.

But Logan, with his thick chest, salt and peppered hair and that magnificent cock? Oh, I'd miss him.

The halls were silent as I made my way back to my room. It must have been earlier than I thought.

I passed a few strung up playthings, fidgeting in discomfort as they waited for someone to let them down or wind them up.

A yawn stole over me as I neared my room, but my air was cut off as a hand slapped around my mouth.

I struggled against the grip before biting down hard and eliciting a yep from the person behind me. The tight hold over my mouth released momentarily, but only long enough to cuff me around the back of the head. The world spun as I lurched forward before someone shoved roughly me into the wall, a hand clawing at my linens and pulling them away from my ass.

'I may not have won you, but it doesn't mean I've forgotten you using me for your entertainment.'

I struggled, letting out a loud screech before he stuffed something in my mouth and used my linens to secure my hands behind my back.

I recognised the voice... it was the guy from the first night, Edwards, who I let touch me in his lap. He had bid for me too and almost won me before Logan stepped in.

'You owe me, missy.'

'No! Cease!' I yelled my safe word, my voice muffled behind the makeshift gag.

'Sorry, I can't hear you. I'm going to presume you said fuck me in the ass, please. I'll gladly oblige. It would be better if you hadn't already been stretched out, but Logan's sloppy seconds will have to do.'

I fought against him, refusing to let him take me as we both tumbled to the floor.

His dick pressed between my thighs as I thrashed, rug burns scoring my chest.

Then the pressure lifted from me entirely. I rolled over to see Logan pin the man forcefully to the wall. His eyes narrowed and his chest raising as though he'd run.

'What the fuck are you doing?' the man asked.

'She said the safe word.'

'I didn't hear her.'

'Bull-fucking-shit you didn't,' Logan roared before punching the man in the face. Hard.

Blood poured from his nose, dripping onto the floor with a solid dropping noise. The man tried to fight back, but Logan landed another thwack on his face, this time splitting his lip in two.

'Tell her you're sorry,' Logan said.

'Fuck off, she's just some slut.'

Logan hit him again, and again, until finally the man burst out with an apology. By that point, his face was a purple and red mess and a crowd had gathered, sleepily clutching clothes and blankets around them as they peered from their doors.

'Oh shit, Logan,' Alfie said, running into the corridor while trying to fasten some shirt buttons. 'What the fuck?'

'Edwards was trying to rape her, for fuck's sake.'

Alfie looked from me to Logan and then down at the man who'd collapsed at my feet.

'Everyone back in your rooms,' Alfie shouted as doors clicked shut left and right.

'You two get your arses out of here. Logan, drop her home. She lives near you. I don't know what the hell I'm going to do about this.'

Logan unties my hands and pulled the material from my mouth.

'Sorry,' I whispered, guilt washing over me.

'Hey, little demon, it's not your fault. Captain big balls over here didn't need to pulverise him. He shouldn't have touched you against your will, so I'm not going to say I'm mad. I pride my house on being a safe space. Now go get your shit and get out of here before some of his cronies find out. What I don't need is a war.'

Logan grabbed me by the hand as I made my way to my room to gather my stuff.

'Don't forget to pay Tony Valetti,' Logan said as we walked away from Alfie and the battered man.

'You gave me half a million quid. It's already done.'

CHAPTER THIRTY TWO
LOGAN

We'd made it out of the estate without being apprehended, Valentina having a quick shower while I got her clothes from Grieves and stuffed her things into a bag, before grabbing my belongings and throwing them and her into my car.

As I had washed Edward's blood from my hands, I'd tried to regret my decision to lay into his face. But I couldn't. Seeing him trying to force himself on Valentina had unleashed the side of me I tried to keep under control. Violence had always been a part of my life, with my job working for my father, and now controlling our syndicate. Usually, the violence was measured, and planned, to extract information or teach a lesson. Edwards was the first time I'd lost my temper and reacted with my fists since I'd been a teenager.

I wished I'd dragged my knife across his throat while he was down.

Valentina rested her arm against the window, her cheek pressed against it as her eyes focused on the trees whipping by as my car twisted through the highland roads. It would be a few hours before we reached Glasgow, and the atmosphere lay thick between us.

What the hell did you say to the woman you were bringing home to pretend she didn't exist, knowing she was taking a piece of your soul with her?

I should never have given in.

Never.

Silence bathed us for miles as Valentina scrolled on her phone and I focused on the road ahead, dodging the occasional red deer and hiker. Every so often, I'd feel her eyes on me as I stared ahead, trying to find something to say.

'Thank you,' she said in an almost whisper.

'For punching Edwards? My pleasure. He's always been an insufferable douche.'

'For standing up for me. For letting me in. For making things I'd only ever dreamed of happen. I know following you to Rosenhall was a bit unhinged, but I had to know what it would be like.'

Reaching over, I squeezed her thigh, finding it almost jarring for it to be covered in denim rather than the easy access linens. Fuck, I'd miss her thighs.

'I should thank you. You were everything I'd always dreamed about finding up at the castle, but I'd never quite found. You are going to make someone very happy one day.'

Her throat bobbed as she looked back out at the passing trees. I slid my hand back to the wheel.

'If you weren't you, who would you be?'

'What do you mean?' I asked.

'If you weren't a McGowan, who would you be? If your whole syndicate blew up overnight and it left you with nothing but enough money to start again, what would you do? Would you work to build your business back up?'

'For it to go that badly, I'd probably be dead.'

Valentina rolled her eyes at me before giving my arm a nudge. 'Come on, it's a long trip. Dream with me.'

When she smiled, I felt my walls crumble around me. Fine. I could play.

'I'd leave.'

'Leave Glasgow?'

'Leave everything. I'd find a little cottage in the highlands with a log burner and a bit of land. I'd spend the days chopping wood and feeding my animals, and my nights not worrying about deals going through or who I'd have to impress or placate to avoid a bullet through my head.'

'What kind of animals?'

'A couple of labs, maybe a cat to chase the mice from the wood store. Some goats. A donkey.'

Valentina laughed. 'What do you want a donkey for?'

'I love them. I'd have his field back on to the garden so I could go out and have a cup of tea with him in the morning and put the world to rights.'

'With a donkey?'

'Have you ever chatted with one?'

'Well, no.'

'Then you don't know what you're missing.'

Valentina turned her body toward me a little in her seat. 'Couldn't you have all those things where you live now? You've clearly got enough money to afford a donkey.'

'It doesn't fit my lifestyle. When I get married...' I swallowed down the words and glanced at Valentina.

'It's okay. I knew what I was getting into before following you.'

'When I marry Nicole, things will get even busier. I'll be going between homes when we have kids, trying to find a balance for our lives. And the union should open up whole new lines of business for me. It'll be good, but no time for a wee donkey pal.'

'It sounds miserable,' Valentina said.

'Life isn't always about fun. I used to think it was too. And then it came and swept my arse out from under me. I was never supposed to inherit. My eldest brother was killed a few years back. Even then, I hoped Dad would keep it going for years to come.'

'And he died too?'

'Hazard of the industry.'

'And you still want to bring children into it? To see them take it on as you have, whether or not it's what they want? Except it will be worse. My uncle is deep with the European mafia, and they make Scotland look like child's play.'

'It's what Dad would have wanted.'

'But it's not what you want.'

'What I want doesn't matter. It's what's expected. Loyalty lies with the family.'

'It's patriarchal bullshit. You have money, you have a family who cares about you. You have everything. You could spend the rest of your life living exactly as you pleased, having your children grow up happy and not worrying whether their dad will come home to them in a box of parts. People would kill for the opportunities you have.'

'Valentina...' I ground my teeth as she spoke, my jaw tightening as her words hit like poisoned little darts.

'You know it's true. It's one thing if you wanted it the way your dad did, but you're squandering your life for a dead man who couldn't care. Such a pity.'

I needed to turn the conversation around. There was no suitable answer to give her, and her prodding was making me sweat. For someone so young, she knew how to ask a question that left me squirming.

'What about you? What's your grand plan? You have half a million pounds to add to your pot.'

'I don't know. I'll pay off mum's mortgage so she doesn't need my uncle as much and put some in her bank account so she doesn't worry.'

'But what do you want?'

'What I want money can't give me.' Her hazel eyes darkened before she looked away and leaned fully back in her chair. 'I'll keep doing what I'm doing. I enjoy it. I don't have any other skills. There's nothing else I could do.'

'You could do anything you put your mind to. I've already seen how tenacious you can be when you want something.'

She gave me a devilish grin. 'I don't remember you minding my tenacity.'

'Behave yourself, brat. I don't want to pull this car over to give you an attitude adjustment.'

'Don't tempt me,' she muttered under her breath.

Hours later, after she'd plugged her address into my navigation system, we pulled up to a smart building near the city centre.

'So this is home?' I asked as I turned the car off.

'Yeah.'

'Nice and close to the bars and stuff.' My mouth felt like I'd eaten sand as I tried to converse to stop her from leaving. The drive had taken hours, but it still hadn't been long enough. I wasn't ready to let her go.

'I guess. I'm not huge on partying. The flat is big and old, with high ceilings and huge windows. Plus, the concierge is a saint. It's home. I bet you live in some fuck-off gigantic mansion.'

I laughed and shrugged. 'I do.'

'Just you?'

'No, my brother Ewen lives with me, and the staff.'

'Lucky. I wouldn't mind someone having to do all my washing. I bet you don't even know how to use a washing machine.'

She had me there.

'Anyway... I should probably...' Valentina tipped her head toward the front door and grabbed her bag from the floor.

'Yeah, I guess you should.'

We sat for a few breaths, neither ready for it to be over. Then the door clicked as she opened it and got out.

'I'll see you at the wedding,' I said, cringing.

She winced, and I cursed myself. What an idiot.

The door closed behind her as I watched her walk to the

building, her perfect ass leaving me for good. My breath hitched when she turned to look at me before looking around her and dashing back to the car. She ripped open my door and threw herself into my lap, her fingers sliding into my hair as her soft lips dragged at mine, her tongue slipping heat into my mouth as she moaned softly. The kiss was intense and slow, filled with longing and need as I poured everything into it.

Some people say that there is nothing like a first kiss, but knowing a kiss is the last one was a heady drug. I nipped at her lower lip as she ran her fingers down over my throat, pinning me back to the headrest with her want.

'I'll miss you, Daddy,' she said as she broke the kiss, leaning her forehead against mine.

'I'll miss you too, pretty girl. More than you know.'

'You know where I am... If you need me.'

With a final clash of our lips, she stole my heart right out of my mouth and took it with her as she left my world and went back to her own.

'I need you,' I whispered into the empty car as she dipped into the building and out of my view.

CHAPTER THIRTY THREE
VALENTINA

By the time the front door opened and Lara made her way noisily into the flat, I was curled up on the sofa watching reruns of American sitcoms with half of a greasy pizza on the table beside me.

'Hello,' she said, hanging up her coat and eyeing the half bottle of wine. 'All okay?'

'Not really.'

'Do I need to hurt someone?' The couch depressed as Lara sat next to me, helping herself to a slice of pizza.

'No. I'm just such a stupid bitch.'

'You fell for him, didn't you?'

'I don't know. It was only a few days together, and a few weeks of camming before that. That's not enough to fall for anyone.'

'My dad told my mum he would marry her on their first date. They are still going strong. Hearts don't come with minimum time limits. Come here.'

Lara slid an arm around my shoulder, pulling me into a cuddle before crossing her legs on the sofa and facing me. 'So he rocked your world, then?'

'Something like that.' I sniffed as I topped my wine up. 'It was the most intense few days of my life. He even let me sleep with his friend without being jealous. It was crazy.'

'You lucky bitch,' Lara said, taking a swing of wine from the few mouthfuls left in the bottle. 'He must be good if he fucked you so hard you fell in love with him.'

'It's not love. At least I don't think it is.'

'Are you feeling sick at the idea of not seeing him again? Trying to invent ways in your head to bump into him? Does the idea of him marrying your cousin make you want to stab her?'

I nodded through a smile, knowing that she was exaggerating.

'You've got it bad, kid. The good news is that there are a whole heap of guys out there who can rail you like a pro and not be involved with your family members.'

'But I don't want someone else.'

'You've just been dicknotized, Valentina. The best remedy for that is to find a superior dick and ride the ever-loving shit out of it. What about the friend?'

'He lives miles away. Having him involved was fun, but he doesn't make me feel like Logan does. His dick was pierced all the way up, though. Like a whole ladder's worth.'

'No fucking way? You're such a lucky bitch. Next time I should come with you.'

I didn't mention Edwards, as I didn't need her worrying about that.

'Do you think he'll go through with it? Marrying Nicole?'

'Did he give you any sign he wouldn't?'

'No. He was pretty clear that us sleeping together was a one occasion thing. She doesn't even want him. He could still come to me.'

'You deserve better than your cousin's seconds, babe. You'll find a man who worships you the way you deserve. You're beautiful, kind, sexy, and you bake like an absolute goddess. Any guy would be lucky to have you.'

'Thanks Lara,' I said as she grabbed another slice of pizza.

'Do you want to watch a movie?'

'I think I'm going to get some shuteye. I told mum I'd meet her early and I'm exhausted. It's been a long week.'

'No worries. Just let me know if you need anything.'

Curling up in my bed did little to bring on sleep. Every time I closed my eyes, I imagined being tangled up in Logan's arms, his lips kissing sweet words into my neck.

'I want to pay it,' I said, putting a heaped spoon of sugar into my coffee as my mum shook her head.

'You can't afford to do that.'

'I can.' I'd seen the six-figure amount in my account that morning, and stood staring at my phone for a good ten minutes before squealing with Lara over it. It seemed almost criminal to me I'd enjoyed myself so thoroughly and also made so much money from it.

'Love, I know you make okay money doing... what you do. But you need to keep it. It might not be a forever job.'

'I made a lot of money, Mum. And I want to do this for you. I want you to not owe anything to Uncle Tony. Please? You did so much for me growing up, and I can finally repay you.'

'You don't need to repay me. I'm your mother. I love you.'

'Please?'

My mum tore at her napkin as she stared down into her lap. 'It's too much.'

'It's not.'

She remained quiet for a few minutes before her shoulders dropped, and I smiled.

'On one condition; we put the house in your name. So that it's your house and your money goes into it.'

'I don't need your house.'

'But it'll go to you one day anyway, and this way you won't need to worry about inheritance tax. It's the only way I'll let you pay off the mortgage.'

She was so bloody stubborn.

'Fine. But you stay there until we are both old and grey and wrinkled.'

'And then you can always have it there as a backup.'

'Mum, I don't need a backup.'

'I don't need details. I just don't want to worry about you.'

Mum liked to keep any discussion of what I did to a minimum. While she never tried to dissuade me or put me down about it, she didn't want to talk about it either.

'Can I ask you something about Dad?'

'Of course you can, love.'

'How did you know he was the one? When did you know?'

Mum's smile was soft and sad as she met my eyes. 'I knew from the first moment he held my hand.'

'But how did you know?'

'It wasn't a concrete feeling. It was a wave, sometimes overwhelming and sometimes just lapping at my feet. No matter the size of the torrent, it always drew me to him. It was unavoidable. I needed to be near him, to hear his voice and feel his touch. It wasn't a knowing as much as it was an unavoidable need to be with him.'

'Oh, Mum,' I said, sliding a hand over the table and gripping her fingers.

'Have you met someone?'

I'd never been able to lie to my mum, and when she lifted a brow, I swore my ears even blushed.

'You have! Who is he?'

'It's not like that. I met a guy and I feel that pull to him, but he doesn't want a relationship.' I left out the fact it was her niece's fiancé.

'If he's right for you, he'll be back. He won't be able to resist it.'

God, however wrong it would be, I hoped she was right.

After donating another book to Muhammed and chatting through what he'd been up to since I'd been away, I headed for the lift, more than ready to take the rest of the day off. I was so ready to get back into the kitchen and whip up some treats, then scoff them in front of the TV as I caught up on some knitting. Life had been so crazy that I'd not done either of my chill activities in almost two weeks. I couldn't wait.

As the elevator doors opened, I jumped back. A figure blocked my path. I breathed a sigh of relief when he turned around and it was only Tim from next door.

'Oh, hey Tim,' I said as I stepped around him.

'Where have you been?'

'Excuse me?' Tim and I weren't exactly on the level of neighbourly acquaintance where we questioned each other's whereabouts.

'I noticed you haven't been around much for the past few days. I was worried.'

'That's... um... sweet of you. But I was just away visiting some friends.'

'A boyfriend?'

'I don't think that's any of your business, Tim.' I fiddled with my keys, trying to get the right one so I could escape my weird neighbour's interrogation.

'Sorry. No, of course it isn't. I just like to look out for you girls. On your own in the city and all.'

'We're okay. Thanks.'

My door swung open, and Tim fidgeted as he dropped his eyes to the floor. 'Okay. Sorry. Go safe, yeah?'

'So bloody weird,' I muttered to myself as I locked the door behind me.

CHAPTER THIRTY FOUR

LOGAN

Maeve topped up my glass with a rich red wine while Ewen slapped two boxes of pizza on the counter.

'It feels like forever since we've done this,' said Maeve as she perched on a barstool and grabbed a slice, the mozzarella making a long, stringy bridge between the box and her hand.

'That's because you are all boring marrieds now,' Ewen replied with a smirk.

'I'm not,' I added.

'As good as.'

'Ewen's just jealous because he's a single pringle,' Maeve said.

'Why would I be jealous? I'm single and own a sex club, I've got filth on tap. With whomever I fancy. You're stuck to one dick for life.'

Maeve grinned. 'It's a great dick, though.'

'Too much information,' Ewen said, 'speaking of too much information, we've not had nearly enough about what you got up to at Rosenhall. It's been forever since I've seen Alfie.'

'What makes you think I got up to anything?'

'Because you've been weird ever since you got back. Mopey. Even more of a grump than usual.'

As much as I'd tried to just get on with work and pretend like the Valentina situation hadn't happened, I was plagued with a mind full of her. Would talking about it help?

I looked from Ewen to Maeve, not used to letting people into my private thoughts.

'I met someone and I can't stop thinking about her.'

I'd leave out the details about her being too young for me and Nicole's cousin, I didn't need them to judge me any harder than I was judging myself.

'At Rosenhall?' Maeve asked, her eyes widening as she put her half-eaten slice of pizza down.

'Yeah. She's... fuck she's amazing. Pretty, sweet, and sexy as all hell. I wasn't prepared for it.'

'And what does your fiancée think about you dipping your wick in another pot of wax?' Ewen said.

'Nicole and I have an agreement.'

'Shit, Logan, what a mess.' Maeve said. 'What are you doing? What kind of marriage can you build on agreements to sleep with other people?'

'It's not the first marriage of convenience, nor will it be the last. It's what we need to expand. You married our enemy and figured it out.'

'Yeah, but I had no choice. You're choosing to walk into this like an idiot.' Pink spots appeared on my sister's cheeks as she got worked up.

'Dad would have approved.'

'That's exactly why we don't. Why not explore what you have with this other chick instead? Nicole is hot, and rich, and has some insane connections, but she won't make you happy.' Ewen grabbed the wine bottle and put another healthy glug of it into his glass.

'It's too late for that. It's all agreed. Tony would have my balls if I backed out.'

'He'd get over it,' Maeve shrugged. 'He didn't exactly want her to marry you.'

'I won him over. I don't want it to cost us any of our guys if I fuck it up.'

'So what, you just move into hers and listen as she rides her bodyguard every night?' Maeve raised a brow at me as Ewen took another slice of pizza and tucked in.

'I won't move in. I'll stay here.'

'And what about kids? When she has babies to continue this line you are so desperate to keep going, are you going to just never see them? Let her raise them? A nanny? Do you want your kids to have the same distant dad as we did?'

I rubbed my eyes and shook my head. 'No. I don't want that. I'll make it work. I'll keep the kids here.'

'While you run your mega crime syndicate throughout Europe? Tell me how that's going to work.'

'I don't fucking know Maeve. How do you make it work? You have kids, you are growing the Thompson syndicate from strength to strength. Why can't I?'

'You can, but something's going to have to give. The kids came to us as teens, that's a whole different thing than babies and toddlers. But I have something you won't have. Someone who will always be behind me, supporting me. Cam is my rock and we couldn't do it alone.'

'Tell me about the other chick,' Ewen said.

'Never mind. No point.'

I didn't think I could talk about Valentina without wanting to go over to her flat and snatch her up, taking her home and keeping her for good. I had to keep my mind on other things. Keep pushing forward with the business.

I'd been home almost a week when Tony would no longer take my excuses to avoid dinner. The dining room sat empty with only myself and the staff who loitered near the far wall as I waited for the Valettis to join me.

Hell, I didn't know if I'd even be able to look them in their faces after what I'd done to their cousin and niece.

Tony arrived first, walking past me and clapping me on the back with a loud thwack.

'Good to see you Logan. Fine job you did with Alfie and my money. Good to know I can count on you, son.'

Hearing son on his lips sent my stomach into a flip. I'd craved my father's approval so badly that it hit a part of me I'd been searching to fill. At the same time guilt roiled through me. Guilt because I wanted to ditch his daughter and try to convince his niece to give me a chance.

'No worries,' I said with a shrug as a young man poured me some wine.

'Have you thought about how you want to expand, drugs, laundering, hitmen?'

I coughed on my sip of wine as he spoke so openly. We rarely discussed business with guests in our home, but Tony clearly had no such qualms.

'You know we're big in the illegal pharmaceutical trade. I want to expand into more medical grade stuff throughout Europe.'

'Hmph,' Tony said as he took a mouthful of his own wine, holding up a finger to signal a moment, but before he spoke Hugh came into the room with his usual cocky grin plastered to his face.

'Ah, the prodigal son returns,' he said, taking the seat to the left of his father. His voice was full of ire as he said son, his dislike of me spilling into the word.

'Ah, Hugh. Have you been up to much since I last saw you? Or just nose deep in a pile of coke?'

Tony guffawed as Hugh reddened with fury.

'Where is Mother tonight?' Hugh asked, changing the subject while scowling at me like a sullen child.

'At a spa, I think. Or in Milan? I don't know.' Tony shrugged and looked at his watch.

'Where's Nicole? That girl would be late to her own funeral.'

We waited, conversation stilted and sparse between the three of us until Nicole entered ten minutes later, followed closely by her bodyguard.

Nicole wasn't her usual picture-perfect self, with hardly a speck of makeup and her hair pulled into a rushed ponytail. Creases marked her dress and the whites of her eyes faintly pink.

My brow creased as she gave me a brief smile before sitting beside me, barely glancing at the wine or the food that was swiftly placed before us.

'How was your trip?' she asked after clearing her throat. My chest tightened as I wondered whether she knew about Valentina. Had she found out and been crying about it before dinner? I glanced at Tony and decided that no. If she knew, he'd know. And if he knew, he'd have relieved me of my bollocks.

'It was fine. The midges were rife in the evenings. You know how it is up in the highlands.'

'I've never been to Rosenhall,' she said, not meeting my eyes before taking the tiniest forkful of the slivers of duck and sweet potato that made up our starter.

'I'll take you sometime.' I gave her a smile that I hoped came across as friendly. She looked like she could be done with a friend.

She glanced swiftly upward before her eyes sunk back to her plate. I looked across at Hugh and then back at her.

'I hear you two lovebirds have set a date,' Hugh said before spearing his food forcefully.

'We have?'

'Sorry, yeah. I meant to tell you. We got The Salvator on a cancellation. I hope that's okay?' Nicole's voice was smaller than I'd ever heard it, her usual confidence gone.

'Of course. When are you thinking?'

'It's four weeks on Saturday.'

My mouth opened and closed like a fish as I tried to find words.

A month.

Fuck.

It wasn't some obscure date where we would be married in the future, but a concrete one where I'd become her husband. Hers on paper and in business. Everything but a romantic husband. The room lurched as I took a breath.

'Why the rush?' I asked.

'Why wait?' She swallowed as she met my eyes. 'You still want this, don't you?'

No.

I wanted to scream it at her. But her expression held me back. There was a pleading look in her eyes that made me nod. Relief washed through her face as she glanced up at her brother, and then to her bodyguard, who stood at the wall behind him.

'We'll need to figure out the details, but it'll be good to have it done.'

Good to have it done.

What a way to describe marriage.

CHAPTER THIRTY FIVE

VALENTINA

Turning on the bed, I smiled sweetly at my laptop while toying with my hair. Names pinged in the chat, every one making my heart drop as it failed to be Logan.

Footguy messaged, begging me to join him in a private chat. I'd been avoiding him, knowing I couldn't see if Logan popped up when I wasn't in the open chat and Footguy had been losing himself with every excuse I gave.

With a sigh, I opened up his DM and started typing.

A ping had my eyes dashing to the edge of my screen, my heart all but stopping as ScotsDaddy38 popped up.

Crossing off the DM, I double-clicked on Logan. Maybe waiting would have been more ladylike, less desperate, but I didn't care. I'd waited for days on nothing but a hope and I wasn't going to let him go that easily.

> You're here.

There was a delay before he responded.

> I am. I couldn't stay away.

> I hoped you'd come back.

> I shouldn't be here.

> I'm glad you are.

> Me too.

> I heard about the wedding date.

I'd cried for a solid hour when I heard they'd moved the date forward. It seemed too quick.

> They informed me when I got back from Rosenhall. It's probably for the best.

It wasn't for the best. He was being a prize idiot.

> Can we talk?

> Baby girl, I think that's a bad idea.

> Just talking. As friends. I think that should be okay.

The dots bounced on my screen before his reply popped in.

> Fine. As friends. No naughty stuff.

I rang through with a private call to him, ignoring the numbers racking up on Footguy's DM box.

'Hey,' I said, smiling as his face popped up, no longer needing to keep me from seeing him. Dark circles ringed his eyes as he propped his phone up on his bedside table, resting his cheek on his arm and facing the camera.

'You're a sight for sore eyes,' he said.

'Tired eyes. You look exhausted.'

'I haven't slept well since... well, I just haven't been sleeping.' Logan's voice cracked as he broke into a yawn.

'Maybe take a long lie in the morning? You're your own boss, you can do that.'

'Mmm. Not tomorrow. I have to meet Ewen at his club at nine.'

I made a mental note of that little nugget before mimicking his stance, laying on my side facing the camera.

'You look so pretty, Valentina. You suit white.'

The white babydoll I wore was cute and flouncy, its delicate tulle body floating around my hips when I moved and giving flashes of the matching panties.

'The colour of innocence...' I said while winking.

'We all know that isn't true.' His face cracked into a grin that sent a warm wave through me. He always looked so much younger when he smiled. His eyes dipped closed for a moment too long before they opened back up, struggling to focus for a second.

'Tell me what you've been up to since you got home.'

'I tried baking a baklava yesterday, but something was a bit off. It felt too greasy, but still tasted pretty good. I've never tried making one before.' I kept chatting away, watching as his eyes eventually remained closed, his chest raising gently as he sunk into a much needed sleep.

'Night, Daddy,' I whispered, my heart aching to snuggle in beside him again. To feel his warmth as he pressed up against me and nuzzled into my hair.

I paused before closing the chat, typing my number into his box with a note to only take it if he wanted to.

Setting my alarm extra early, I went to sleep with a grin on my face and a plan in my head.

CHAPTER THIRTY SIX
LOGAN

My driver pulled up outside Ewen's club at nine twenty-five. I detested being late, but after hearing Valentina's voice, I'd slept like the dead.

I hoped Ewen had made it before me to let the suppliers in.

Storming to the rear entry door, I pulled up short. Valentina sat neatly on the low wall by the door, a short red dress peeking out from under a knee length camel coloured coat. She wore knee high brown boots and a swatch of tanned thigh was visible. An oversized, knitted scarf in a whole gamut of autumnal colours took up her entire neck and chest while her hands gripped a floral cake tin. My insides tightened at the sight of her, all dark hair and rosy cheeks in the cold nip of the morning.

'What are you doing here?' I asked her.

'Stalking you. As a friend, obviously.'

Well, shit.

'You're late,' she said with a pout as she stood up.

'And you aren't supposed to be here at all.'

'I made something for you. I bet you haven't had breakfast.' The way she bit at her lower lip had me wanting to bend her over the fucking wall and make her scream.

'That was kind. But we can't do this.'

She walked toward me, pushing the flower covered tin into my hands. 'It's just some cinnamon buns, Logan. I'm sure that I know you can take some sweet buns.'

Fucking hell. Alfie was right. She was a little demon.

I took the tin as she blinked up at me, her thumb grazing over the back of my hand before she removed her hands from mine. My skin blazed in the small area where she'd touched me.

'I'll be needing the tin back. Apartment twenty. I've put you on our approved list with my doorman.'

'You can take it back now--'

'No. I want you to sink your teeth into... them. Think of me when you have something sweet in your mouth.'

'Valentina.' I warned, my voice sounding gruff.

'What are you going to do? Spank me, Daddy?'

Shit. I'd thought I'd be the one to ruin her, but she already had me by the balls. Seeing her there in the flesh made the intense desire for her flood back to the surface.

She turned and walked away, leaving me there, dumfounded, with a tin of buns and a hard dick in my trousers.

It was almost ten by the time I'd convinced my dick to deflate enough to be able to walk into the building without a red face.

'Took long enough to get here,' Ewen said as I placed the tin on the bar and took a seat.

'Sorry, got waylaid.'

'Not just laid this time?'

'No.'

'What have you got there? Have you been baking?' Ewen prised the tin lid off before I had a chance to speak. 'Sweet! You brought breakfast.'

He'd hauled out a sticky, icing covered bun, biting into it before his eyes rolled into his head.

'Holy shit,' he said through a mumble.

I watched as he swallowed before immediately taking another bite.

I had to admit, the swirled buns looked pretty appetising. Reaching in, I pulled one out before taking a bite. They were pillowy soft and still slightly warm, the icing melting over my fingers. I licked the icing from them between bites.

Ewen was right. The buns were a holy shit level of good. Baby girl could bake.

As I finished up my bun, I noticed something stuck to the underside of the tin lid. A folded piece of lined paper.

Unfolding it, I read the brief message before having to hide my crotch beneath the bar for another ten minutes.

My dirty girl had left a note.

Daddy, I hope you licked your fingers like I want to lick my cream from your big dick.

CHAPTER THIRTY SEVEN

VALENTINA

Saturday inched by, every minute seeming to take five as I waited to see if Logan would show up.

I'd cleaned the flat to within an inch of its life, baked about a million cupcakes and changed my outfit four times. It had been one thing to meet him at Rosenhall in a neutral zone for us, but he was going to see my home. Assuming he came, and that he didn't just drop the tin in my hands and go.

I wanted him to see me as an equal. Not too young or too immature for him. To see that I looked after myself, had a well-paid job and a proper grown up life. Maybe then he'd see me as an option rather than a poor decision. He'd marry Nicole in four weeks, and I wanted to make him change his mind. Even if he didn't end up with me, he shouldn't be marrying a woman because of what his business would gain. He should be happy.

And even if he didn't want me like that, I absolutely needed more of his hot mouth and big dick before he took himself off of the market.

Good decisions be damned, I was out to get as much of him as I could.

Smoothing my dark hair down around my shoulders, the light

curl in the ends holding perfectly, I took another look in the mirror, making sure my makeup sat just right. I'd redone my eyeliner three times to try to get both eyes to match with a sultry cat-eyed look. My short, chequered sweater dress rode high on my thighs and I wore slouchy over the knee socks to compliment it.

When a loud knock sounded, I jumped and took a slow breath.

'You've got this, Valentina. Make him sweat.'

His muscular frame filled the doorway as I pulled open the door. Logan stood awkwardly, holding my floral cake tin and swallowing hard as his eyes roved up my figure.

'Good evening,' I said. 'Come in.'

I walked into the kitchen without giving him a chance to deny my offer.

'A little wine?'

'Valentina. I'm just here to return your tin,' he said, but he'd walked inside and closed the door behind him.

'Sure. I'm just having a glass and it's rude not to offer.' I topped up two glasses anyway, walking toward him and swapping the tin for the wine. 'What's the worst that could happen?'

Hopefully him bending me over the sofa and stuffing his fat cock into me...

'One glass. Then I'm going.'

I smiled at him and took his coat, skimming my fingers down his arm as I did.

'There are cupcakes too, if you're hungry.'

'I'm not.'

He sat on a barstool and took a large sip from his glass. Shit, he'd finish it too quickly if he kept that up. I took the stool next to him and crossed my legs, my foot grazing his calf as I angled myself toward him. His fingers clenched the stem of his wineglass as his eyes fell to my tanned thighs.

'Busy week?' I asked, wracking my brain for a way to make him give in to the electricity that I could feel sparking between us.

'Yeah. All go back at work after being away. One of the shipments went AWOL, so we had to track that down and deal with the people who lost it.'

'Sounds stressful.'

'It was.'

'Maybe you need a little something to help you relax?'

'I need... to get home soon.' He'd almost said something else before changing his mind.

With red wine staining my lips, I stood and moved toward him, lifting a hand to brush through the hair behind his ear. His body shuddered at my touch and I let my hand follow a path down his neck and over his chest.

'I've missed you, Daddy. I need you to take care of me.'

'Fuck, Valentina. I can't.'

'It's okay. I can take care of you instead.'

I pressed between his open thighs and captured his mouth with a small kiss. He didn't respond, and I swallowed hard, his rejection hitting me painfully.

'Baby girl, I want you so fucking badly. I can't sleep because my dreams are full of you and then I wake up with an empty bed and remember that you aren't mine.' His words were hot against my lips as I closed my eyes.

'I'm all yours, Logan.'

His fingers grazed my throat as he tipped my chin upward, heat washing through me.

'You're the biggest temptation I've ever had. If I was a better man, I'd be able to resist you.'

'Then be a terrible man, Daddy, because I want you so fucking bad.'

He let out a growl before pulling me onto his mouth, his tongue sweeping between my lips as I moaned. Sliding my arms around his shoulder, I pulled my body flush to his, lost in his mouth as he deepened our kiss. Emotion bubbled up as I finally got what I wanted, Logan in my arms again.

'We can't,' he gasped against my lips as he broke our kiss.

'Are you saying that I'm forbidden?'

'Fuck, yes.'

'That just makes it even hotter.'

'I get married in four weeks.' His words were pants between nips and kissed down my throat.

'Just until the wedding. Please?'

His fingers slid between my thighs, and I grinned when his eyes widened.

'No knickers?'

'I wanted to be ready for my daddy.'

'Fucking hell, Valentina.'

Sliding his fingers over my wetness made me gasp, and I saw the moment he caved entirely. His eyes darkened with lust as I ground myself against his fingers, not caring how desperate I looked.

In one swift motion, he pulled my dress up over my head, leaving me in nothing but my long socks.

'Look at you, baby. Perfection. Come here. I want to taste that delicious little cunt of yours.'

I giggled as he hoisted me up on the breakfast bar and spread my legs wide, gazing down at me as I blushed.

He watched my face as he slid two fingers inside of me, curling them upward as he fucked me slowly with them.

'God, I've missed you,' I moaned as I arched my back.

'You've missed having this greedy pussy filled, haven't you?'

'Yes, Daddy.'

'You can take more for me though, can't you? You took Alfie's cock and my dick all at the same time. I think you can manage some more fingers.'

I writhed as he worked his third finger into me, before having his fourth finger join in, too. My pussy lips spread wide over his thick fingers and the vulgar image made me quiver with need. The slight pain from being stretched wide only made me all the wetter.

'That's it sweet girl, ride my fingers until you come all over them.'

Logan stood as I pulsated around his fingers and pushed me back onto the counter by the throat, pinning me there between one solid hand while the other fucked me furiously, making my insides turn to jelly.

'Oh, my god. Fuck.' I breathed a chorus of curse words as he made me come hard, my whole body shaking as he refused to let up his pace.

'Such a greedy, needy little slut. You'll take more, baby. As much as I give you.'

'I'll take anything you give me,' I panted as his fingers tightened on my throat. As my orgasm subsided, I expected him to remove his fingers, but if anything he increased the pressure inside me, fucking at my spent pussy until he made me writhe again.

'That's it, baby girl. You're going to be Daddy's good little slut, aren't you?'

'Yes, I promise.'

'Do you want my tongue, Valentina?'

'More than anything.'

I missed the pressure on my neck when he removed his hand, but cried out when his mouth fit over my pussy, his tongue working at my clit as I gripped the edge of the counter.

'You taste so fucking good.' He growled into my pussy before biting my thigh as I rocked against him.

His tongue slid into me as he removed his fingers, fucking my hole as I wrapped my thighs about his ears and moved my hips. His hair was soft under my fingers as I pulled his mouth back to my clit and rode his face. A laugh flitted over my heat as he grasped me by the ass and devoured my cunt. 'I love seeing you this desperate for me.'

When he pushed his fingers back into me with one hand while his tongue lashed from side to side, I almost blacked out with pleasure. My lower body lifted entirely off of the counter as I cried out, my hands clawing desperately at him as I came again, this time against his face.

Logan kept licking and sucking at me as I rode through wave after wave of pleasure, my chest rising rapidly as I panted.

I'd barely finished coming when he shoved me to my knees on the floor and unzipped his trousers.

'I need to see you crying all over my dick, baby girl. Open up for Daddy.'

His cock was fully engorged and a dark red as he slid the tip into my mouth.

'Lick it, sweetheart. Make me nice and wet so I can fuck that pretty pussy of yours.'

I worked at his cock with my tongue, moaning as he gripped his fingers into my hair and guided me onto his cock. He didn't take his time or give me time to adjust to him this time. He pushed straight into my throat as I heaved and pushed my hands against his thighs.

'You can fight it, baby, but you're going to take my dick in your throat. You made me do this, and you're going to deal with the consequences of your actions.'

Fuck. He had me wet all over again. His rough actions and dirty words had me grinding against his leg as he speared my mouth.

I tried to take him like a good girl, but every time his cock nudged at the back of my throat, my stomach would heave and I'd pull back.

'No baby, you're going to let me in. I need to feel that hot throat wrapped around me.'

Logan held my gaze as he tipped my head roughly with his grip in my hair, thrusting his dick deep in my mouth as I fought against the invasion. He was just too big. His eyes rolled as he fucked my mouth, saliva, tears and snot coming out of me uncontrollably.

'My messy little slut. Swallow me down, sweetheart, and I'll put my big dick inside your desperate little pussy.'

He pulled back and let me gulp down air before filling my mouth again, this time forcing himself past my point of resistance. My eyes widened as he groaned, my chest and stomach fighting for air as my throat burned.

'Fuck, yes. Good girl. You did it. Holy shit, baby, your throat feels almost as good as your tight arse does.'

When he pulled out, I coughed violently, my breaths ragged as I smiled. I'd done it. I'd taken him all the way into my throat.

Logan picked me up and slammed my back against a nearby wall.

'I'm too heavy,' I whispered against his throat as his dick split my pussy lips, pausing at my entrance.

'You're perfect. I'm going to fuck you hard, Valentina. Hold on.'

I wrapped my arms around his neck as he slid his cock into me. Fuck, he felt so fucking good as I stretched around him.

I arched my back as he retreated before slamming into me, my back scraping against the wall with every thrust.

My mouth found his neck, licking and biting at him as he groaned, his fingers digging bruises into my ass as he spread me wide for him.

'I've missed you so fucking much,' he said into my ear.

'I've missed you more,' I gasped as he tilted his hips making my eyes roll.

'Impossible.'

Then we were lost in a sea of pleasure, of hard dick and soft flesh and gasps and whimpers and moans. Mid-fuck, he put me down and pulled out of me before dropping us both to the floor and filling me from behind. His dick felt even bigger from behind and each hard thrust made me yelp with a mix of pain and pleasure.

'Such a good fucking girl. You'll take it all for me, won't you, baby?'

'Anything, Daddy. Anything to please you.'

When his fingers found my clit, I was gone. Crying out as I dropped to the floor, his body following and pressing me into the hardwood as he thrust fast, riding my orgasm relentlessly.

'My god Valentina, you feel fucking amazing.'

His teeth found the back of my shoulder and he bit down as he came hard, my hips grazing against the wood flooring as he fucked his cum deep into me.

We lay there panting for a long time, his body over mine as we both caught our breath.

'Thank you, Logan,' I whispered as his lips grazed my ear.

'Thank you for not taking no as an answer. I needed you so badly.'

When he slid out of me, he pulled me up to my knees and wrapped his arms around my bare chest, tipping me to kiss me slowly.

His cum dripped out of me onto the floor below us, and I blushed when we both looked down at the puddle.

'Nothing hotter than seeing my cum leaking out of you.'

I turned to face him before grinning, bending on all fours and running my tongue through the sticky mess.

'Fucking hell,' Logan groaned before pulling me to his mouth and kissing me with his cum all over my tongue.

'You dirty wee slut. Keep that up and I'm going to have to fuck you all over again.'

I bit my lip before sweeping my fingers through the cum and licking it from my fingers.

I laughed when he groaned and pulled me to the floor again.

CHAPTER THIRTY EIGHT
LOGAN

Waking up tangled with Valentina was like a balm to my soul.

Her hair smelled like coconut and sex and I was halfway to hard before I'd even opened my eyes.

Going to her house had been the best, stupid decision I'd made. Every night since getting back from Rosehall had felt like torture. My body craved her next to me and refused to cooperate properly when she wasn't. I'd barely slept, my workouts had been half-arsed, and I hadn't been eating properly. My whole being was consumed with thoughts of Valentina.

I was in too deep.

Pulling my arm out from under her, I smiled as she rolled over and pressed her round ass against me. Her breaths were still settled into a regular pattern as she slept on.

I found my trousers and pulled them on, running a hand through my hair. My bladder was about bursting, I'd use the toilet and then bring my sweet girl a coffee in bed.

After washing my hands and face, I walked out to the kitchen area, my torso still bare.

'Oh, my god!' A shrill voice met me as I rounded the

corner and I saw a pretty blonde woman holding a spatula up in the air like it was a weapon. It had to be her roommate, Lara.

'Uh, shit. Hi. Sorry, I didn't realise anyone else was home.' I held my hands up in mock surrender as she narrowed her eyes at me before lowering the spatula.

'You must be the dirty old guy with the massive cock and the fiancée.' She crossed her arms over her chest and glared at me.

'I'm not really sure what to say to that.'

'Good. You're fucking with my bestie and I'll rip your balls off when you hurt her.'

'Don't you mean if?'

'No. When. She cried her eyes out when your wedding was moved up. She thought you were mad at her, or disappointed with her, or some shit. Valentina is a ray of fucking sunshine and I'm pissed that you are fucking with her.'

'Whoa. She came after me.'

'She did, because she's twenty-two and has dick on the brain. You're practically forty and should know better.'

I walked over to the kettle and flicked it on, my head thumping. 'I know. I can't help it. She's wormed her way in and I can't stay away. I keep trying.'

'Maybe you should try getting yourself unengaged then,' Lara said, pushing me out of the way as she loaded the coffee machine instead.

'I can't.'

'You can. You're just too weak to do it. You can't have it both ways, and the longer you string her along, the more you're going to devastate her. I don't know what you think's happening, whether it's just a fling to you, but it's not just sex for her, no matter what she says. She likes you a lot.'

Guilt ate at me as she finished making two coffees and thrust them into my hand. 'I don't want to hurt her.'

'Lots of people have done horrible things without meaning to, but your intentions don't override the pain your actions cause. Be a better human.'

Walking back into Valentina's room left me warring with emotion. Placing the coffees down on the bedside table, I sat down beside her and watched as she slept peacefully. Her hair was silky soft between my fingers as I tucked a strand behind her ear. Lara was right. She deserved better than what I was giving her. I wanted to do better for her. But how? I'd made my bed with one of the biggest crime families in western Europe, and pissing them off would leave me destitute or dead.

I gathered up my t-shirt, pulling it on and finding my belongings. I'd leave her a note and go before hurting her any more.

I opened her nightstand to look for a pen when I spotted an envelope inside, photographs spilling out. Not photographs; screenshots. Taking one out, I saw Valentina splayed wide on the screen, her fingers between her thighs and a look of ecstasy on her face. Over the printed screenshot the word WHORE had been scrawled. Rage filled my blood as I pulled out shot after shot of similar scenes with other similar words written on them. Inspecting the envelope left me with no more clues. It had an address and stamp, which meant whoever sent the images to her both knew her screen persona and where she lived.

'What are you doing?' came a small voice behind me.

'Who sent these?'

'I don't know.'

'You should have told me. I can help. What do you need? Security?'

Valentina sat up and pulled the blanket around her chest. 'It came while I was at Rosenhall. I'm sure someone is just fucking with me.'

'How many people know your screen name and website as well as your address?'

'Just Lara, and you. Well, as far as I know. I guess anyone I know could have found the site. I'm sure it's nothing. Just some jerk messing with me.'

Pushing the pictures back into the envelope, I put it back in the drawer before pulling Valentina into my lap and kissing her softly.

'I want to help, baby. I'll have someone hack in and see if they can track the user who might have sent these.'

'I'm sure lots of people screenshot.'

'Yeah, but it's postmarked to Glasgow. It's someone local.'

Her eyes widened as I ran my fingers up and down her back. 'I need to go, sweet Cherry, but I'll come back in a few days. Would Wednesday work for you? I'll see if my guys can track down anything about the pictures before then.'

'There were flowers too, before. I think we kept the card. I'll get it for you.'

I pulled a card out of my wallet and handed it to her. 'That's my driver's details. If you need to go anywhere, you can call him anytime and he'll escort you.'

'I'm sure it's nothing,' Valentina said.

'Being involved with me means I can't just let it go. It might be someone I've pissed off. I just need you to be safe, okay?'

'Yes.' Her lips grazed my neck as she nuzzled in. 'I will, I promise.'

'Good girl.'

CHAPTER THIRTY NINE

VALENTINA

'Oh god, yes,' I said, shifting my hips so that my ass faced the camera, my panties riding high as I wiggled. 'I love it when you tell me what to do.'

I glanced at the clock on the screen as I touched myself through the thin piece of material stretched over my pussy. Turning to stifle a yawn away from the camera, I continued to arch my back and move my hips.

One more private chat would mean I'd hit my goal and could log off for the night to get ready for Logan arriving. After paying off Mum's mortgage, I still had a bit of money in the bank, but I wanted to keep adding to it rather than seeing it deplete.

My door clicked open, and I didn't even look toward it, expecting it to be Lara sneaking in to grab something as she often did. The screen didn't face the door, so no-one knew as long as I didn't react.

Sliding a bra strap down my shoulder, I looked back at the screen and blew a kiss. When my door clicked shut a few moments later, I glanced over to be surprised with Logan leaning against the wall, his cock in hand as he stroked it while watching me perform.

Heat flushed my cheeks, and chest as he smiled wickedly at me.

I turned toward the camera and knelt facing it, Logan off to my left as I kept stealing glances at his big dick.

'Keep it on,' he growled when I went to close my laptop. Messages flew up from the chat screen.

Who is that?

Are you going to have a guest?

I'd love to see you get railed babe.

'They can hear you,' I said.

'Good. They should know you're mine. That they can watch and stroke their dicks while looking at my baby girl, but that I'm the one who gets to fuck your pretty cunt.'

His voice was feral as he spoke, my laptop pinging with message after message and the possession in it made me swoon.

'Do you want to show them, Daddy?'

'Show them what?'

'That I belong to you?'

'Do you want them to see Daddy make you cry, baby?'

I nodded, holding my breath as his eyes glittered. 'Dirty girl.'

The messages were going feral.

'I'm going to an open private chat. You can join Daddy and I in a minute on the pay per minute channel.'

I muted my mic for a moment before springing off the bed and into Logan's arms.

'Do you really want to fuck on camera, Valentina?'

My head bobbed as I kissed him hard, already raring to go.

'Do you?'

'I want to make you happy. Plus, I enjoy people watching you on my cock, as well you know. Do you have any masks? Just in case our screen-shotter is about?'

I went to my cupboard and rooted through the Halloween outfits. 'I have a Scream one? And a venetian one?'

'Perfect. I'm going to make it quick and rough, because I want you all to myself as soon as possible.'

I kissed him once more before he stripped off his clothes and pulled on his mask. The tattoos that wrapped his arms and torso would be an instant giveaway to anyone who knew him.

'The mask is kind of doing it for me,' I admitted as I put on mine and climbed back on my bed. 'There's something hot about not being able to see your expression. Creepy, but hot.'

'I'll show you creepy, my little slut.'

I opened up the paid chat, amazed to see person after person join in. Their comments were ravenous, but I blocked them out as I sat on the bed and watched Logan off screen, stroking his big dick. Looking at the mask on top of his thick muscles made me squirm.

He came to the edge of the bed and fisted my hair roughly, pulling my face toward the camera.

'Look at them, baby. Look at all those names waiting to see you ride my dick.'

I winced as he held my hair tight. 'Open your mouth and let them see that tight throat. My dick feels fucking amazing when I shove it in there.'

'Do you want them to see you choke on me, baby?'

'Yes, please.'

His thumb grazed my jaw as he climbed on the bed and pressed his dick against my tongue, the ridges making my mouth water. 'Suck me, Cherry.'

I worked his cock with my lips and tongue, running them over the tip of his erect dick again and again as I lost myself in worshipping him.

'Such a good girl.'

He slid deeper into my mouth, and I coughed on his dick, a stream of saliva dripping down my chest.

'Still learning to take it all like a good girl.'

I nodded as he fucked my mouth with sure strokes, occasionally thrusting deeper and holding my face on him as he pierced my throat.

Logan snatched my face up to his masked one, pulling my panties off with the other.

'Show them your wet cunt, baby. Let them see how horny you are for your daddy.'

I spread myself for them, my face burning as tears slid down my cheeks from the rough face fucking.

'That's it. She's such a good girl. They'd all love to taste your sweet pussy. But it's all mine, isn't it? But I don't want your pussy today baby, I want to fuck that tight little ass again.'

My stomach clenched with the memory of him deep inside me there. The pain. The pleasure.

'Will you let me fuck your ass for them, love?'

I melted as he ran his fingers lightly over my clit, nodding.

'Say it.'

'Fuck my ass, Daddy. Please?'

He grabbed some lube from my dresser before kneeling behind me and spreading my thighs wide over his legs. Everything was on display and I buried my face into his neck as the cold lube dripped all over me. He started with my pussy, rubbing his hand over my swollen clit again and again as I writhed in his lap.

'You want me to finger her pretty cunt?' Logan said to the viewers, and a whole load of messages pinged back. I cried out as he forced three fingers into me, clamping around him almost instantly.

'That's it, ride them sweet girl,' Logan whispered into my neck, his words only for me, as they couldn't see his lips move beneath his mask.

His other hand circled my nose and mouth, pressing firmly as I whimpered.

'You don't get to breathe until you come, baby girl. Come for Daddy and all his new friends.'

His hand cut off my breath entirely as his fingers worked me to the edge. My chest battled for air as I struggled against his hand. My head grew fuzzy as my body fought for air, all the while the intensity between my thighs grew to a new height. Then he won out as I came hard on his fingers, his other hand sliding off my face as I gasped in a breath, my whole body throbbing with pleasure.

He didn't give me any quarter, his fingers sliding into my ass and stretching me over them. Then his cock was there, pushing into me.

'Just the tip, baby, you can take the tip.'

I winced as he stretched me around him, my body tightening.

'No baby, don't fight it. Let Daddy fill you up.'

'I can't.'

'You have to. You've got me all worked up, and I need to fuck your arse. You'll like it. You did last time.'

My breath caught as he gripped me by the hips and forced me down on him, my asshole stretching around him.

'It's too big.'

'It's the perfect fit. God, you feel so good.'

I could see us in the picture on the screen, his big dick in my ass and his muscled arms wrapped around me, the creepy mask by my head as he rocked his hips back and forth.

'You need to relax for it to feel good. To take it like my little anal princess.'

'You're so big.'

'I know. You'll grow to crave my enormous dick in your ass. I'm not going to be gentle for long. I need to fuck you properly. I'm burning for you.'

Tears slid down my cheeks as the intensity overwhelmed me.

'Do you want me to stop?' he whispered.

'No. I need more Daddy.'

'Yes, you do.'

His fingers fluttered over my clit as he started to increase his strokes. Between his touch and the visuals of him pistoning in and out of me, he had me on the edge in minutes.

'Wait for me,' he gasped into my ear as he thrust hard.

'I can't.'

'I'll punish this pussy if you don't.'

My back was slick with sweat where our bodies connected. I fought off my orgasm, trying my best to be a good girl and wait for him.

But I couldn't do it.

My body quaked as he growled, pinning me roughly to him as he fucked me hard, my ass flaring and clamping around him as a deeper, different kind of orgasm ripped through me.

'Fucking... hell...' he swore as my body turned to mush in his arms. I saw his balls tighten on the screen as he panted into my neck, pushing me down onto him as he unloaded his hot cum into my ass.

Holding my thighs wide, he pulled his dick out, letting our viewers see my ass gaping as his cum dripped out of me.

'Shows over,' he said. Leaning over me to close the app down before ditching his mask and gathering me up against him.

'You okay, Valentina?'

'I think I might be in heaven.'

It didn't feel like I was even in my room. I was floating somewhere outside myself as tears rolled down my cheeks.

'Did I hurt you, love?'

'No. I think you've fucked me stupid.'

'I'll go run a bath if I can get through there without Lara chewing me out. I thought she'd slap me when I showed up early.'

'I'm glad you did,' I said, before pulling Logan down onto my mouth and offering him a slow, sweet kiss.

'God, you're something else, just perfection.'

Later, after he'd bathed me back to my senses and filled my tummy with takeout, we snuggled in bed.

'I made you something,' I said, feeling silly, but wanting to give him the gift I'd made.

'You made something for me?' His handsome face crinkled at the eyes as he smiled. 'No-one's ever made me a gift.'

I handed over the wrapped gift, feeling a little sheepish. 'It's nothing major. You might hate it. It's okay if you hate it. I won't be offended.'

Logan took the small package and ripped into it with glee. I held my breath as the knitted socks fell out onto his lap.

'I got the softest wool, and I wanted to make you something. I know you probably have like the most expensive socks in the world and don't need--'

Logan cut me off by scooping me up against him and kissing me.

'I love them. I've never had a homemade present. Ever. They are amazing. You're amazing.'

He flopped me down onto the bed as I laughed while he pulled on the socks, moving around the room wearing only them to give me a modelling show.

'They fit perfectly,' he said.

'You know what they say. Big cock, big socks.' I grinned as he pounced on me and pulled me against him.

'Thank you, I love them.'

I love you.

I kept the words caged behind my teeth, but I meant them with every fibre of my being.

I had fallen for Logan McGowan.

I couldn't let Nicole have him.

He was mine.

'I don't deserve you,' he murmured against my lips as he alternated between kissing my jaw and my mouth.

'You do. You deserve the world, Logan. You deserve to be happy.'

'I've never been happier than with you in my arms, baby girl.'

CHAPTER FORTY
LOGAN

My phone buzzed as my driver pulled up outside the Valetti residence.

'James,' I said as I answered it.

'I've traced the line back as far as I can, but it's not someone who doesn't know what they are doing. It's VPNed to the max. There's just not enough information to follow the trail.'

'No worries, hopefully the florist will have a lead.'

'Sorry. Just a dead end. Whoever it is has covered their arse.'

I hung up with a frown. It would have been much easier if whoever sent the pictures to Valentina had been some idiot fan. I'd have taken pleasure in breaking every bone in his hands as a warning.

The butler let me into the mansion and led me to the morning room for my meeting with my wife-to-be. Scheduled in her diary like any other appointment.

She looked far more put together than the last time I'd seen her, her hair and face immaculate as usual.

'Logan,' she said, standing to kiss both of my cheeks before offering me a seat on the sofa that faced her with a hand gesture.

'How are you? You look well.'

Nicole lifted a perfectly neat brow. 'Are you saying I'm fat?'

'God, no. You looked upset last time I saw you, that's all.'

'Ah. Yes. A lover's tiff, one might say. Water under the bridge. What did you want to meet for?' She crossed her long legs one over the other while we paused for a staff member to serve us tea.

'I want to call off the wedding. I think we've made a mistake rushing into everything.'

Nicole cleared her throat and met my eyes. 'No.'

'No?'

'No. I won't cancel our arrangement.'

'Why? You don't even want me.'

'Correct, but we have a deal that we are both counting on. You approached me and convinced me that this would be good for us both. Now you want to bail? The answer is no.'

Anger flared in my chest and I worked to temper it.

'It takes two people to make a wedding happen. You can't make me go through with it.'

'As you know, Logan, my family's reach is extensive. Hence why you wanted to use me for your gain. That reach can just as easily be used against you.'

'What are you going to do? Bump me off?'

'Nothing so basic. But you should know that I have people throughout Europe. It would be a shame if a car were to hit that sweet little niece of yours in Spain.'

I was on my feet, her throat in my grip as her men rushed toward us, guns drawn. She laughed, her throat moving against my hand.

'Simmer down before they blow your brains all over my expensive carpet. I'd rather not have that mess in my home.'

I loosened my fingers before clenching them into a fist beside my thigh.

'You are much more useful to me alive than dead, Logan, but if you try to ruin this for me, then you'll be bringing a war to your family's doorstep. Is that what you want?'

Fuck.

'You don't need me, Nicole. There are a thousand other syndicate guys who would happily fill my boots.'

'Indeed. But you're a good man, and those are rare in this world. I may not want to climb into bed with you, but I'd be an idiot to fail to see your worth by my side in business and in rearing a family.'

'I've met someone else, Nicole. I love her.'

'Love is messy Logan, I'd recommend you avoid it at all costs. It makes no difference to me where you place your heart, but you belong to me now. Know your place.'

My hand went to my hip, my fingers grazing over the knife in my pocket. I needed to end it to be with Valentina, but attacking Nicole wouldn't solve the issue. It would only leave me and the people I loved at risk.

Nicole smiled before walking up to me and repeating the kisses to my cheeks as I stood rigid, fighting every urge to stab her in the gut.

'Your stag do is next week - make sure you, and anyone important to you, are there. My brother and father will join you all, along with their men.'

She turned as she reached the door.

'Don't do anything stupid, Logan. I actually like you and I'd really rather not have a war with you.'

Fire burned in my stomach as they left me alone.

It had been for nothing.

CHAPTER FORTY ONE

VALENTINA

Logan was quiet as I curled up in his lap on my sofa, his fingers gliding through my hair as we watched a movie. My stomach knotted as I toyed with the sleeve of my hoody and tried to focus on the film. I couldn't. He was too quiet and hadn't even tried to hit on me the past two times we'd met.

I rolled over and looked up at him, his hand resting on my stomach as he kept his eyes on the TV.

'Are you not into me anymore?'

He blinked slowly before looking down at me, his expression unreadable.

'I am.'

'Why are you being so distant?'

Logan sighed before pulling me up into his lap and circling his arm about my waist.

'I'm sorry. There's just a lot going on.'

'With your wedding?'

'That and other things.'

'Is it because we agreed to keep this going until the wedding and then calling it quits? I'd prefer to have you all in until then rather than being here but not being present.' I brushed my lips over his neck as he pulled me against it.

'I'm struggling. Ever since you came bursting into my life, you've made me realise a lot of the things I wanted so badly don't matter at all. I want to be with you, Valentina, but I can't. I can't back out of my agreement without people getting hurt. I can't go through with it without hurting you.'

'We can keep doing what we are doing. I don't need your name and your ring to be with you.'

Logan closed his eyes tightly before tipping my face up and kissing me tenderly, his tongue sweeping into my mouth. He tasted like whisky, and the smell mingled with his aftershave in a heady male scent.

'You deserve to be someone's whole world, Valentina, not a dirty little secret. You need a man who can put you on his arm and tell the world that he's proud to call you his. I can't do that, no matter how much I want to.'

His words hit me in the chest as I sniffed in his arms, fighting back tears at the emotion packed into his words.

'I would prefer to be your secret than not be yours at all.'

'I know, baby.' Logan pulled me down onto the sofa, his body caging me in as he kissed the tears from my cheeks. 'I love you Valentina. So fucking much that it's tearing me apart.'

'I love you, too. We can make it work.'

His mouth closed over mine, swallowing down my words as he poured his love into his kisses. Kissing me like he'd never get to kiss me again.

'Please, Logan,' I begged as goosebumps prickled my arms. 'Please don't leave me.'

'I'm drowning.' His voice was pained as he spread my thighs.

'Pull me under with you.'

CHAPTER FORTY TWO
LOGAN

Come on guys, we'll go to my place,' Ewen said as he walked out of the pub down the street from his club. 'No-one's too pissed are they?'

Our awkward group of guys ambled after him. My brothers and me, my brothers-in-law Cam and Alec, Tony and Hugh Valetti, and an assortment of our close syndicate guys. The night had been strained from the beginning. I wasn't sure a sex club would increase the mood at all.

'The girls are going to your club,' Hugh said, smirking at Ewen.

Would Valentina be there? Fuck, I'd have to go.

All but Tony and his men followed Ewen as he waved us in, and we met Nicole and her group, including my sisters, Maeve and Esther, and Nicole's mum and aunt. There was a whole host of pretty women with her too, attracting attention from all corners of the club.

'Ah here's my lover,' Nicole said, drunk and happy as she slung an arm around my waist.

I clenched my jaw as she draped herself around me, her tight white dress complete with a short veil. I'd have expected her to opt for a classier celebration with her usual level of perfection.

Hugh stormed up to her, his face red. 'Are you drunk?'

'Lighten up, Hughy. It's my hen do, I'm supposed to be drunk.'

Hugh stared at his step-sister, looking as though he wanted to pull her aside. I watched them both with interest.

'I'll talk to you about this later,' he said before stalking off in the directions of the toilet.

'Why is he so angry with you?'

Nicole sighed and leaned heavily against me.

'He's always angry about something. I can't remember him ever being happy. He thinks Daddy should have let him take over. He's older than me, and a man. He thinks he deserves it more. But I'm going to be like your sister and kill it when I take over.'

'I don't doubt that you will.' My anger with her dissipated a little in her drunken state. Clearly Nicole was going through some shit too. I still wanted out of our marriage, but I wanted to kill her a bit less.

'Where's your cousin?' I asked, unable to resist when I couldn't see her anywhere.

'She's flaky as they come. Pulled out at the last minute. Not that I really care. Hugh says that she's just jealous of me. I'm older, wealthier, have a Daddy who loves me.'

So does she. I wanted to say.

'She was so sweet when she was little, I used to dress her up and she'd follow me everywhere.'

'What changed?' I asked.

'I can't remember. I think she must have. I need to pee. You'll have to excuse me.'

Nicole tottered off toward the ladies' room as Ewen passed me a beer.

'Man, she's smashed. I've never seen her like that,' I said.

'What's got into her?' he asked.

Maeve sidled up next to us, her arm around Esther's waist. 'Probably guy problems.'

I pulled Esther toward me and gave her a hug, glad to see her after months going by since the last time she visited with her little family. 'Missed you kid.'

'You too. I really didn't think I'd be back for your wedding. Would have thought you'd have seen sense before now.'

'He did meet someone,' Maeve said, dropping me in the shit.

'Who?' Esther said with a squeal.

'No-one, it doesn't matter. I can't back out of the Valetti deal. They've made that perfectly clear.'

'Are they threatening you?' Ewen asked, pulling himself up to his full height.

'Calm down. It'll be fine.' I hadn't forgotten Nicole's threats toward Esther's elder daughter.

'Where's Mac and Katie?' My youngest brother had disappeared the moment we hit the club.

'Need you ask?' Maeve said with a roll of her eyes. 'He'll be balls deep somewhere. They still can't keep their hands off of one another. Like a pair of rabid teenagers.'

Nicole hadn't come back from the bathrooms, and with the state she was in, I was worried she'd either be passed out somewhere or taken advantage of. Maybe both.

'Back in a few, guys,' I said, dropping my beer into Ewen's hands as I made my way through dark corridors and writhing bodies.

The glass windowed playrooms held multiple groupings of people in them, in a multitude of different scenarios.

I caught a flash of Katie pressed up against a wall with whom I assumed to be Mac between her thighs, his face masked as he pinned her by the throat.

Shit, I didn't need to watch my brother and his missus at it.

I turned a corner and heard soft sobs up ahead.

'I'm sorry. Stop. Not here. Ow. Hugh!'

I picked up my pace, Nicole's desperate pleas filling me with concern.

'You are fucking mine, and I'm not going to let you forget it.' Hugh's voice carried to me before I rounded the corner and almost tripped over my jaw at the scene unfolding before me.

Nicole's dress was round her waist, her panties on the floor as her step-brother thrust deep inside her. She sobbed as he slapped her hard.

'What the fuck?' I said, staring at them and waiting for the scene to make sense.

'Logan. Oh, my god. Hugh get off of me.'

Hugh thrust twice more before groaning deeply, emptying his balls into his younger sister. Fresh tears fell on her face as she looked at me, her head shaking as I walked forward and pulled Hugh off of her, tossing him to the ground and levelling a hard kick to his stomach.

He laughed. Nicole righted her skirt, her mascara running down her cheeks as her breath came in shudders.

'I'll call the police,' I said, pulling out my phone.

'No. Please don't.' Nicole grabbed my wrist while Hugh laughed louder while gripping his stomach.

'You think I was raping her?' Hugh asked, pulling himself to his knees as he pushed his dick back into the pants. 'She wants me. You all think she's been fucking her bodyguard, but it's me. It's always been me.'

My eyes went to my fiancée, waiting for her to deny it. Her eyes dropped to the floor as her shoulder shook.

'You're both sick fucks. You have until tomorrow to tell your dad, or I'll do it.'

I left them there, feeling vomit rise in my throat and making for the nearest fire exit, gulping in fresh air as I made it outside.

Pulling out my phone, I text my siblings' group chat and told them to get to our mansion as soon as possible.

It was time to call the fucking wedding off and get my girl for good.

Even Tony Valetti wouldn't expect me to marry his daughter when she was in a relationship with her step-brother.

Back at the house, we gathered in the formal sitting room.

'The wedding's off,' I said as jaws dropped around me.

Maeve clapped her hands and threw herself into my chest. 'About time, Logan.'

'Why the change of mind?' Mac asked.

'I found her brother up to the balls inside her at the club.'

Ewen choked on his drink while Alec laughed. 'Always knew Hugh was a slimy little fucker. How on earth did he convince Nicole to fuck him? I'll never know.'

'What if it wasn't a choice?' Katie asked. Her voice was soft as she leaned back against Mac's chest. 'She's a good few years younger than him, and their parent's married when he was a teen and she was only a kid. What if he groomed her?'

After everything Katie had been through, I didn't doubt her perception.

'Maybe it's been his game plan all along. Make her belong to him, be the little bird in her ear to get her to convince her dad to do his bidding.' Maeve paced as Cam watched her.

'But why agree to Logan's proposal? He would have been active in the family and Tony would get the son he never saw Hugh as,' Cam added.

'Because he needed her locked down with someone who wouldn't take her from him. He knew we didn't have a connection, so he'd still be able to exert control over her.'

'What if he planned to get rid of us all after we wed and had children? He'd be seen as the natural choice to run things until any children were of age.' I rubbed a hand over the back of my neck as I spoke.

'Whatever the reason, you can't go through with it. They won't be able to hold the agreement over you.' Maeve smiled at me.

'Will you all back me up if shit goes south?' I asked.

'Always. Yes. You know it.' Their replies came in a flurry that warmed my heart. Valentina had been right. I didn't need to do it alone.

CHAPTER FORTY THREE
VALENTINA

The bin bag was heavy as I pulled it out of the lift and toward the rear door of the building.

'I can do that for you, love,' Muhammed said, standing up and putting his book down.

'No, no. I'm fine, go back to your book.'

'It's not a problem, Miss Valetti.'

I smiled at the kindly older man before hoisting the bag up into my arms. 'I've got it.'

'At least let me open the door for you.'

Shimmying past him, I said, 'Thanks, Muhammed.'

'Do you want me to hold it for you?'

'No it's fine, I need to swing to the corner shop and grab some more flour.'

Muhammed's eyes widened. 'What sort of treats are you making today?'

'Just some scones. I'll drop a few down for you and your missus, promise.' I laughed as Muhammed patted his tummy before closing the fire escape door behind me.

The bag was heavy, but I knew Muhammed suffered with a dodgy knee and I didn't need him hurting himself on my behalf.

I was panting by the time I shoved the bag into the skip. They could be done with making them shorter, what kind of giants were able to just drop a bag in there?

'Valentina,' a voice startled me from behind.

When I turned a figure stepped out from the shadows. Tim pushed his phone into his pocket before stepping close to me as I backed up against the bin.

'I've been waiting for you. You shouldn't have ignored me.'

Fear crept up my spine as I was sandwiched between him and the skip.

'When did I ignore you?'

'When you started being a slut with the tattooed guy.'

Logan. He was jealous of Logan? I wasn't even aware he knew Logan existed.

'You used to be there for me every night. I wasn't asking for much. I let you ignore me and knit or read. I just wanted to be there.'

My mind raced as I worked to make his words make sense.

'Footguy? Tim, are you Footguy?'

'Yes.' His face was pained as he reached out and stroked a shaky hand over my cheek. 'I just wanted to see them. But he took you away.'

'Did you send me the screenshots? The roses?'

'I sent you the flowers, but you gave them away. That hurt.'

'I'm sorry,' I said, my voice quavering.

'But he sent you the screenshots. The other guy.'

'What other guy?'

'He paid me to make a hole in our wall, my bedroom backs onto yours, and he made me install a camera so he could see you.'

'When?'

'When you came back from your trip. When you let the man fuck you on camera. He said he needed evidence that wasn't from the cam site. And I was so mad at you. I did it.'

My hand shook as I reached into my pocket, but my phone wasn't there. I'd left it inside.

Shoving past Tim, I made a run for it, pleased when his footsteps didn't follow me. Looking back over my shoulder, he just looked crestfallen. With a thump I ran straight into someone, but before I could see their face, a strong smelling cloth pressed against my face. Flailing, I fought against the arm around me, kicking and punching as my vision blurred. I slumped in my attackers arms as the world dipped to black, Tim's sad face the last thing I saw.

CHAPTER FORTY FOUR
LOGAN

An incessant buzzing woke me up. Shit, I'd slept in late.

Sitting up, I grabbed my phone and smiled when Valentina's name popped up, a little cherry emoji beside it.

'Hey, baby girl,' I said into the receiver.

'Logan?'

My brown furrowed as the voice met my ear.

'Who's this?'

'It's Lara. I need your help. Valentina is gone.'

The world slowed as I tried to grasp her words. 'Gone?'

'She went to take the bin out and get some flour a few hours ago and she never came back. I tried calling the police but they say she needs to be missing for a whole day before they can get involved. But she left her phone, her keys, even her purse, she just grabbed some change from the bowl for the flour. She's not with her mum, she's not with you and she's not with me. There's nowhere else she would have gone without saying something.'

Lara's voice shook with the same panic that I felt rising in my chest as I leapt out of bed and dressed.

'I'll be there as soon as I can. Is there no way she's just stopped for a coffee somewhere?'

'Logan, I know her. She always tells me where she's going. Especially since the pictures. She would have come back in to grab her stuff.'

'Right, hold tight, be with you soon.'

My chest burned as worry fled through me. Was it whoever sent her the images? Shit, had we angered them by being together on camera? I'd had my guys tracing everyone who had logged in to watch us, hoping that the instigator would send more images to prove he'd watched. But nothing had arrived.

My sweet girl.

If someone hurt her, I'd strip them to the bones while they watched for as long as I could keep them alive.

'Is there anyone who would have taken her?' I asked as I paced the sitting room to the kitchen.

The pictures were strewn on the table along with Valentina's laptop and phone. We couldn't find anything.

I went back into her room, searching for something, anything, that would lead to finding her. On the carpet near the far wall of her bedroom, a small pile of white dust gathered in one spot next to her wardrobe. It was only a tiny amount, but significant enough to be odd.

Following the wall in a straight line up the edge of the furniture, I found a tiny hole with a smooth glass fitting inside.

'Who lives on the other side of this wall?'

'Our neighbour, Tim. But he's been home all morning. Muhammed said he got home just after Valentina left. He wasn't with her.'

'Tim's been spying on her.'

Lara's eyes widened before her face pulled into a frown. 'I'll kill him. He's always had a thing for her, but I didn't think he was an actual creep.'

She tore from the room and I ran to catch up with her as her knuckles rapped hard on the neighbour's door.

'Hey,' he said as he opened the door. Confusion turned to fear when he saw me, trying to slam the door closed. Pushing my foot in the gap, I blocked the door from closing fully before forcing my way into the apartment and holding the scrawny little loser up by the throat.

'Where the fuck is she?' I growled as Lara went into his bedroom, coming back with a pin-hole camera in her hand.

'You sick fuck!' she yelled. 'You've been watching her room non-stop, haven't you?'

'Only after the guy asked me to. He said that I needed to get him proof so he could make Logan go away and I could have her back on the site. I'm Footguy. I'd never hurt her. I love her.'

I punched him in the face, his nose bursting a red torrent down his shirt.

'What fucking guy?'

'He's her brother or something?'

'She doesn't have a brother,' Lara said.

Hugh. It had to be Hugh. But there was no way he knew about us. Unless he'd been watching Valentina for a while. Fuck.

I pulled out my phone and dropped the snivelling creep to the floor. Nicole's Instagram did the trick.

'Is this him?'

'Yeah,' Tim nodded while wiping at his nose. 'That's him.'

'Fuck.' I put my fist through Tim's plasterboard wall as he squealed. Storming to his room, I smashed anything electronic I could find. Hard drives, his laptop, even his phone.

'Stop!' he shouted.

'Get out of this flat and stay away from Valentina and Lara for good. If you ever set foot in this building or within a mile of them again, I'm going to split your ballsack open and feed you your nuts.'

'Lara, go home and lock the door. I'll send some of my guys round to make sure Tim here listens to me.'

'I'll call the police,' he said.

'You think we don't have them in our pockets? That they'd give a shit about a peeping-fucking-tom?' I rounded on Tim and laid a boot into his ribcage. 'You're lucky I haven't suspended you out of your window by your guts. If I didn't need to go get my girl, I would.'

Sending a text to my tech guys, I had them destroy any trace of Tim's online backups while I got into my car and headed straight for the Valetti mansion.

CHAPTER FORTY FIVE

VALENTINA

My head throbbed as I blinked awake, taking in the dimly lit space around me. Large metal pipes and old machinery surrounded me. My mouth was dry as I licked my lips.

'Where am I?' I groaned, my voice crackling.

'Ah Valentina, you've joined us at last.'

The hairs on the back of my neck stood up as my cousin's voice came from behind me. I tried to turn, but my arms wouldn't cooperate. Looking down, I found myself tied to a metal pipe that disappeared into the floor.

'What the fuck, Hugh?' I said, trying to crane my neck round to spot him.

Two of his men loitered near a doorway, but I couldn't see Hugh.

'Untie me!'

Hugh laughed, and footsteps approached directly behind me.

'Why'd you have to be such a little whore? Hmm, Sweet Cherry? You tried to ruin all my plans.'

'What plans?' Confusion swept through me as I tried to make sense of what he was saying through my thumping headache.

'My plans to have Nicole marry Logan to take the heat off of us.

So I can continue to have her, but please Uncle Tony and his need for her to wed a decent mafia guy. To fill her with my babies and pretend they were Logan's. To see my sons claim both the Valetti and the McGowan lines and steal them right out from under their noses.'

'You... and Nicole?' Nothing he was saying made any sense. 'You want to get your sister pregnant?'

'Not want to, Valentina, I already have.'

My stomach lurched as he walked around me and crouched beside me. 'But you've bewitched Logan with that slutty cunt of yours, haven't you? He tried to call off the deal for you. But we couldn't let that happen.'

'That's why you've taken me?'

'No. We had enough to keep him playing the game like a good boy. I've taken you because he caught Nicole and I together last night, and I need to keep his mouth shut until the wedding goes ahead.'

'He's not going to sit back and let you hurt me.'

'He will. He has no idea where you are. If he doesn't play, then you'll die.'

'You're a sick fuck.'

'I'm taking what is mine. I am the eldest child and the only son, and Tony has forced me to take what belongs to me.' Hugh's face broke into an unhinged smile as he leaned forward and stroked a finger along my collarbone. 'It was never her I wanted. It was always you. I used to watch you sucking on those cherry lollipops and imagine it was my dick. You were always such a tease.'

My chest seized as I tried to move away from his touch. 'I was just a kid.'

'Age isn't a barrier when you know what you want. I'm younger than Logan.'

'Yes, but I wasn't a kid when he met me.'

'You call him Daddy, though, don't you? I'd have been your daddy, Valentina. I still could be. Once the baby is here, I can get rid of Tony, Logan and Nicole and become it's guardian, taking over

until the child reaches majority. I'd intended on killing you and
Logan soon after the wedding. But I could be persuaded to let you
live.'

I pulled at the ties on my wrists while Hugh reached down into
my top and pinched my nipple hard. Crying out, I jerked back from
his hand.

'Don't pretend you don't like it. I've watched you every day for
years on that filthy site. I saw you take his dick in your ass like a little
whore. I know you like it forbidden. You'll grow to beg for my cock
just like you beg for his. I got so fucking hard watching him fuck your
ass that I went back and fucked Nicole there while she cried. From
behind, I can almost pretend she's you. But she hates it in the ass,
whereas you're the little slut who takes whatever dick she's given.'

His eyes were glassy as he spoke, his fingers still groping at my
chest. 'I love him.'

'That's a shame. Still, it won't matter when he's dead, will it?'

'Don't you love Nicole?'

'No. She's a spoiled little daddy's girl. I've spent years pretending
to care for her, twisting truths so that she needed me more and more.
But she's a means to an end.'

'You're such a fucking creep,' I said, wincing as he dug his nails
into my nipple.

'I am. And I can't wait to play with you. If you don't decide to
come around, our games might even get to have a bloody conclusion.
I've never fucked a woman while watching the light leave her eyes
permanently.'

Vomit surged from my throat at his words, splattering over his
shoes as he jumped back, standing and looking at me with disgust.

'Logan will kill you,' I gasped as he stopped and wiped vomit
splashes from his shoes with a handkerchief.

'I doubt that very much. If he kills me, you'll rot in this building,
dying a slow, painful death of starvation. He wouldn't dare.'

'Uncle Tony will help him.'

'Uncle Tony isn't going to help you if he finds out Logan's been screwing his niece while engaged to his daughter. She's his universe. Fuck, he might do me a favour and kill Logan himself if I let it slip after the wedding.'

'Please, let me go.'

'I can't, Valentina.' Hugh bent down and ran a thumb up my chin, gathering the vomit left there on his fingers and shoving them into my mouth as I heaved. 'You're the carrot to make the donkey behave.'

'Gag her,' Hugh said to his minions as he walked toward the door. 'And don't fuck her until after I have.'

Tears fell as one of the men stuffed material into my mouth, ignoring my pleas for help.

Logan was my only hope.

CHAPTER FORTY SIX
LOGAN

I didn't wait for the butler to fetch Nicole as I entered the mansion, pushing past two of Tony's men with a glare.

'Nicole?' I roared as I took the stairs two at a time, looking for her.

She poked her head out of a doorway, her eyes wide as I stormed past her.

'Logan, you can't just burst in here...'

'Where is she?'

'Who?'

'You know who. Where the fuck has he taken Valentina?'

Nicole's face crossed with genuine confusion as she tried to make connections meet in her head.

'Who has Valentina? And why do you care?' Her voice trembled as I closed the space between us, shoving her up against the door and reaching round her to lock it as I heard hurried footsteps on the stairs.

'Because I'm in love with her and your shit-for-brains brother has kidnapped her.'

'You love Valentina?'

'Yes. And I need to get her back. Now.'

Nicole shoved lightly on my chest before sitting down heavily on the end of her bed, her head dropping into her hands as she took a breath.

'You're in love with my cousin. How the fuck?'

'You're screwing your step-brother, so let's hold off the pointing fingers, shall we?'

Her eyes were wet when she looked back up at me, her face paler than usual. 'I thought he loved me, but it's all gone wrong.'

I needed answers, but with her crumbling, I'd need to tread a little more carefully. My fists and blades would only end with both of us dead. My body itched for answers to get my girl, but I forced myself to sit on the bed beside her.

A loud banging sounded on the outside of her bedroom door while our eyes met, and I gave a small shake of my head.

'I'm fine. We're fine. Leave us to talk.' She shouted, wiping at her eyes.

'When did it start?' I asked, seeing her need to talk. Getting her onside would serve me better than forcing details from her.

'I don't know.'

'How can you not know?' Shagging your step-brother wasn't exactly a forgettable experience.

'It's been going on as long as I can remember.'

My throat ached as realisation swam over me. Hugh was older than Nicole, almost ten years older than her, and their parents had married when she was just a little kid...

'Fuck, Nicole. I'm sorry.' I wrapped an arm around her shoulder and pulled her into my side as her tears flowed. 'He's a piece of shit.'

'He told me I was special, and that he loved me more than anyone. Even more than my dad, and then he'd make sure we'd be together forever. When I got a little older, it started to feel good, and I told myself that it must be okay if my body reacted to him like that. He would get me to ask for things he wanted, or sway Daddy's decisions. I thought I couldn't live without him. When you asked to marry me, but weren't looking for an intimate relationship, I thought it was the best of both worlds. He could have me behind closed doors while the world thought I belonged to you.'

I screwed my eyes shut at the memory of hearing her and him after our engagement party, bile rising in my throat. He'd groomed her and turned her into his puppet when he realised that his step-father had no interest in letting him take over. He'd stolen her childhood and her twenties, all for his own sick self interest.

'I'm pregnant,' she whispered. 'He messed with my birth control pills. He told me afterward that he wanted to stick a kid in me before you did and pass it off as yours. It was then that I realised how wrong it all was. That he'd been using me. His kid would take it all, my syndicate and yours, and he'd find a way to be the one guiding the child as a twisted voice in its ear.'

'You don't have to do it, Nicole,' I said, squeezing my arm around her. 'You've never known a life without him, but you can have one. With or without the baby. You are strong, smart and beautiful, and you have your father's endless support.'

'I love him.'

'Hugh's made you believe that, but it's not love. Love should never leave you strapped down with fear. The only person Hugh loves is himself. And power. He's used you as a means of control, but everything he's told you is a lie. He's a slimy, deceptive little prick.'

A sob caught in her throat as she looked up at me.

'Keep the baby, or get rid of it. But Hugh's got to go. I won't sit by and watch him abuse anyone else.'

I gave her a few moments, my leg twitching as I ached to find my girl.

'Please tell me where she is,' I said, brushing the tears from her cheek, aching for her but needing to help my girl more.

'I didn't know he even had her. I didn't realise you two knew one another.'

'I found her on the cam site before I knew who she was, and then one thing led to another. I didn't want to hurt you or go back on our deal, but I didn't expect to fall so hard, so fast, either.'

Nicole gave a small smile. 'Valentina's always been a wee tornado. I miss her. Hugh always made problems between us. I didn't see it then, but looking back, it's so obvious now.'

'He would have wanted to keep you isolated. Control is easier if you don't have anyone on your side.'

'When we were younger, he used to take me to a pump house deep in the woods on the south side of our estate. It's where he would... well, you know. He said it was best that way so no-one would hear me crying.'

Anger blistered in my veins. I was on my feet in seconds.

'You won't hurt him, will you?'

I looked back at Nicole with her pale face and broken spirit.

'The first chance I get.'

CHAPTER FORTY SEVEN
VALENTINA

Blood dribbled down my chin as Hugh punched me again, my head ringing.

'Smile for the camera, Valentina. Your fans will love the video when I upload it.'

'Stop,' I cried, my resolve to not let him see my tears had long since waned.

'I was going to fuck you first, but I might let Dean and Steve fuck your whore-cunt until you bleed and then I'll use your blood as lube while I rape your ass.' Hugh put his phone back in his pocket after shutting off the camera.

'No. Hugh, no.'

'Would you prefer to choke on my blood-soaked dick? I can give you a choice if you prefer.'

A slap to the face had me reeling as he tore open my top, exposing my chest to him and his men.

'I tried to tell myself I'd be able to keep you until later. Keep you as my little pet to keep Logan in line, but as long as he thinks you're alive, that'll do. Which means I can finally fuck you until you're nothing but a bag of meat. The last thing you'll ever see is my blood covered dick as you choke around it.'

'I'll bite it off if you put it anywhere near my mouth.'

Hugh grasped my chin painfully and smiled. 'Oh darling, I'll remove your teeth one by one before I dare stick it in there.'

My stomach lurched as pleasure seeped into his eyes from my fear.

'Please, just let me go.'

'In a few days you'll be dead and Logan will be wed. It's a shame none of you are due for a happy ever after. Only me.'

A gurgle to the left had me dart my eyes behind Hugh, relief washing over me as Logan dropped Dean to the floor, blood spilling from the great gaping wound in his neck.

'Logan,' I cried as Hugh let out a frustrated growl.

Steve pulled out a gun, but he was too slow as Logan went flying into him, shoulder first, sending them both to the floor as they grappled for Steve's gun. Hugh stepped back and calmly took a gun from his waistband, aiming it at the tangle of men.

I kicked out at Hugh's legs, but with my arms restrained to the pipe, he barely paid me a glance.

A shot went off from beneath Logan and I froze, sending out a prayer that it wasn't Logan who'd been struck.

Logan rolled off of Steve, his stomach bloody as I sobbed. But the gun was in his hand. He stood as a puddle of dark crimson spread out beneath Steve.

Cold metal pressed against my temple as Hugh ducked behind me. 'Drop it big man, or I'll take her down with me.'

'Get your fucking hands off of her,' Logan said, his eyes taking in my bruised, bloody face and exposed chest.

'Tsk, tsk. Sounds like he's up for risking your pretty head, Valentina. Do you really prefer that to me?'

'Just shoot him Logan.'

He couldn't though. The moment he tried, Hugh would send a

bullet through my skull. Assuming Logan's bullet wouldn't hit me first.

'Put your gun down and get to your knees if you want to keep your sweet Cherry breathing.'

Logan's face warred as he looked for something, anything to help. Hugh kept his gun trained on Logan as he walked toward him, kicking Steve's gun to the far side of the room and under some machinery. Grabbing a set of handcuffs, Hugh threw them to Logan.

'Be a good man and fasten yourself to that pipe behind you. Nice and tight.'

He watched as Logan followed his commands, his eyes holding mine throughout.

When he was safely restrained, Hugh turned back to me and grinned. 'Well, my sweet cousin, it seems you'll have an audience to watch you die. I'm mighty pissed that my plans have all gone to shit, but forcing Logan to watch you die with my dick in you will appease me a little.'

Hugh was fully focused on me as Logan reached into his pocket and pulled out his phone, typing quickly with his one free hand before sliding it away. Hope bloomed as I made Hugh keep his attention on me.

'You don't have to kill me. I could be useful. You could keep me here for whenever you need someone to play with.'

Hugh's eyes glittered as he reached down and stroked his fingers over my nipples. 'You'd like that. You pretend not to want these things, but I heard about what you were up to at Rosenhall, being paraded on a leash like a slut.'

His hand circled my throat, cutting off my air as he put his gun back into his waistband. I tried not to sob as he pushed his hand into my trousers and forced them inside me.

'I've always wanted you, Valentina. Ever since you were little. Every time I fucked Nicole, I imagined your pretty pink lips beneath me. I knew you wanted me too.'

Logan's face burned with fury as he pulled his knife from his pocket, the one he'd used to inflict pleasure on me, and threw it hard. Hugh's eyes widened as it embedded in his lower back. With a hiss, he tore his fingers from me and rounded on Logan.

'Keep your hands off my girl,' Logan said with a growl.

Hugh laughed maniacally as he reached for his gun, ignoring the blood seeping around the blade in his torso.

'Looks like you'll have to watch me fuck her while you bleed out.'

'No,' I screamed as Hugh pointed his gun at Logan's thigh and pulled the trigger. A deafening bang made my ears ache as Logan writhed on the floor, pressing one hand against the wound, the other pulling hard at the pipe he was attached to.

'Is it true?' A female voice said with a tremble.

Nicole stood by the door, watching the scene unfold. I pulled at my bonds as I tried to get to Logan. Hugh still stood above his panting body as Nicole walked toward him.

'Shit, baby, you shouldn't be seeing this. It'll be bad for our little one.'

'It is true?' Nicole asked again, her voice firmer even as tears pricked her eyes. 'Is it true that you always wanted her? That you never loved me?'

Hugh looked from me to Nicole before shaking his head and lowering his gun. 'Hey, no, baby. You know I love you. I'm the only one who loves you. I've always looked after you, haven't I?'

'I looked at your computer after Logan left, and it was just folder after folder of pictures and videos of Valentina. There was only one folder about me and all it was just things you needed me to get from Daddy for you. You used me.'

'It's not like that.'

'You're a liar.'

'We love you,' I said to Nicole. 'We all do. He's poisoned us against each other since we were little, but we can all see exactly who he is now.'

Hugh strode toward me, his gun pointed right between my eyes. 'Shut up, you little slut.'

My chest tightened as my bladder loosened when I saw Hugh's finger twitch against the trigger. Logan roared as he pulled hard against the pipe, the metalwork groaning with the sheer force he exerted, then wavered, his body slumping from blood loss.

The world slowed as I closed my eyes, waiting for the bullet to tear through me, every minute nerve in my body thrumming to escape, but unable to do so.

When the gunshot tore through the room, I waited for the pain, but instead I felt a heavy weight slump against me. Metallic blood dripped over my face as I opened my eyes and looked at Hugh. Half of his head was gone. A mushy, red pulp with splintered bone greeted me.

I vomited at the sight.

Nicole's hands shook as her arms remained extended from her body.

'Fuck,' she whispered, shaking her head. 'Oh, fuck.'

'Nicole, it's okay. It'll be okay,' I said, feeling like everything was so far from okay. 'I need you to get help. Logan's hurt. Please help me?'

For a moment, I thought she would bolt, her face draining.

Then she pulled out her phone and pressed the screen.

'Daddy,' she sniffed. 'I need you.'

CHAPTER FORTY EIGHT
LOGAN

My crutch caught on the doorframe as I hopped inside.

'God, it's good to be home,' I said as Valentina held the door for me.

'Are you sure it's okay for me to be here? I don't want to crash your sibling thing.'

I pulled her to me with my free arm and kissed her softly. 'Baby girl, it's always okay for you to be by my side.'

I'd woken up in hospital two days after Hugh shot me, multiple transfusions and a surgery later. The first thing I'd done was try to leave, off of my tits on pain meds and screaming for Valentina.

The next time I awoke, she was by my side and had barely left since. I'd come so close to losing her I needed to keep her close.

'Love you, Daddy,' she whispered against my lips as I slid my hand down to cup her full arse.

'They're here!' A shout echoed from the main sitting room as noise filtered through our gargantuan home.

'Ready?' I asked.

'As I'll ever be.' Valentina smoothed down her dress and bit her bottom lip as a torrent of my loved ones emerged.

My niece Grace threw herself at me, nearly knocking me over as my crutch slid out.

'Sorry Uncle Logan,' she said. 'I'm so glad you're okay.'

Elais, my other teenaged nibling, awkwardly shook my hand before I pulled him against me. The two of them just kept growing, both standing almost as tall as the surrounding adults.

They were all there, Mac and Katie, Esther and Alec with their two toddlers, Maeve and Cam, and my brother Ewen.

'Happy non-wedding day, bro,' Mac said, passing me a glass of whisky as I took up residence in the armchair closest to the fire.

'Thanks. Everyone, it's about time you met my girl. This is Valentina.' I took her by the hand and pulled her onto my good thigh, trying not to wince as she touched my healing one.

'Welcome to the madhouse,' Ewen said as she smiled at him, her hand gripping mine tightly.

'Thank you,' she said. 'It's nice to properly meet you all.'

'What a way to come into the family,' Ewen said with a grin.

'Oh, we do like a dramatic entrance, a rite of passage,' Maeve said with a laugh. 'You'll fit right in.'

Valentina raised a brow at me and I kissed her cheek softly while whispering, 'I'll tell you all about it later. You're not the only one who's arrived in a blaze of bullets. Nor the only one who went a little stalkerish.'

'I didn't stalk you,' Valentina said, giving me a pretty little pout.

'You totally did. Not that I would have it any other way. I only wish I'd given in sooner.'

The bubble of my family around me warmed me as I held my girl in my arms. I'd still need to talk to Nicole after everything that had happened, and likely her father too, but they'd agreed to cancel the wedding with nothing more to be said about it.

'Have you spoken to your mum yet?' I asked Valentina.

'I did. She's pretty mad at me but understands that you and Nicole were never meant to be. She's also pissed that she doesn't get to wear her fancy frock to the wedding.' Valentina smiled, making light of the situation, but I knew hurting her mother had hurt her too.

'She can wear it to our wedding instead,' I said.

'You're so sure I'd say yes, are you?'

'I'd tie you down and edge you until you've got no other choice.' Pleasure filtered through me at the blush that rose in her cheeks.

'Logan! Behave. Your family is here.'

'They'll be your family too, baby girl.' I pulled her lips onto mine and swallowed her light moan as she let me taste her.

'Doctor's orders. You can't exert your leg for three more weeks. Don't rile me up with a promise you can't keep, Mr. McGowan.'

'Takes no exertion at all from my leg to make you ride my face, sweet Cherry.'

Her face was crimson when Maeve called us through for dinner.

The following day was quieter in my home as my siblings ventured out together, catching up and entertaining the young ones. Valentina had gone back to her flat to spend some time with Lara, with two of my men in tow.

Nicole sat on the sofa opposite me, fidgeting with the hem of her dress and tears running down her cheeks.

'Come here,' I said, holding out an arm and waiting for her.

'I'm okay. You don't have too--'

'Get your ass over here and let me hug you.'

She sat awkwardly beside me as I wrapped an arm around her shoulder, letting her cry while I waited. Eventually, her tears dried and only a few sniffles remained.

'I may not be your husband, but I can still be your friend.'

'You don't have to do that.'

'I want to. All that shit, none of it was your fault. You were just a kid,' I said as she pulled herself a little away from me and turned to look at my face.

'I know he was wrong, and that he hurt me, but I feel horrible for shooting him.'

'The first kill is always the hardest, even more so if it's someone you loved. Feel the feelings, and when you're ready, let them go. You'll get past this. You'll find someone who truly deserves you and can love you without an ulterior motive.'

'Like you love Valentina?'

'Yes. And I'm sorry for falling for her behind your back. She swept me off my feet.'

'And you don't care about the camming?' Nicole dabbed at her face with a tissue that she pulled from her pocket.

'I don't. I want her to be happy, and she enjoys it. Plus, I find other men wanting her kind of hot.'

'You two really are made for each other.' A small smile crossed her face before her eyes dropped back into her lap. 'I got rid of the baby. I had to. I couldn't bring up a child knowing it would always be his, and that I would have been the person who killed their father.'

'I get it.'

'It was still really early.'

'It doesn't mean it hurts any less. You can mourn if you need to.' She reached for my hand and squeezed it as I spoke.

'Your sister, Maeve, has actually been an enormous help. She's helping me restructure my dad's business to my liking now, so I don't meet resistance later. It's been a rollercoaster.'

'You're going to be great, Nicole. You are strong, and fierce and will be a great leader. Don't let anyone, or anything, make you doubt it. You did what needed to be done, and you'll be stronger for it one day.'

'Valentina's a lucky girl. I didn't want you like that, but I meant it when I said that I saw your potential. My father was more annoyed about losing you than Hugh.'

'I think that may have had more to do with Hugh than with me.'

I couldn't help but wonder if Tony had treated Hugh more like a son than a burden, whether he would have turned out so selfish and mixed-up.

'Stay in touch,' I said when Nicole stood to leave a few minutes later. 'You're always welcome here.'

'Valentina might not like that.'

'She'd love to see you more. Now that the thorn is gone, the sharpness between you both will dissipate, too. If you guys want it to. Now get your butt out of here. I need to get my dressing changed and you'll see a whole lot of ass if you don't go.'

Nicole pulled a face before laughing and covering her eyes. 'God no, keep your trousers on until I'm well clear of the threshold.'

Relief flooded me as I realised that she'd be okay, and didn't harbour any ire toward Valentina.

We could all move forward.

CHAPTER FORTY NINE
VALENTINA

The car bumped beneath me as rain splattered at the windows. I turned my head and listened for any clues.

'Where are we going? Can I take this off yet?' I fingered the blindfold that covered my eyes.

'Not yet, nearly there. Have some patience.'

Patience wasn't my forte.

Our relationship had gone from strength to strength in the weeks following Hugh's attack. I'd worried that after the forbidden aspect of our lust driven relationship was gone, Logan would grow tired of me. But his obsession with me grew with each passing day. He was almost as obsessed with me as I was with him.

Logan hummed softly as we continued down the bumpy road until at last he stopped the car.

'Don't touch that blindfold yet,' he said, opening his door and coming round to open mine.

'I was kind of hoping you'd make me keep it on...' I joked as he held my hand and walked me over some uneven ground. Rain spots hit my cheeks as fresh, cold air swept over me. Pine and rain, that's what it smelled like.

'We can keep the blindfold for later,' Logan said, nipping at my neck before he undid the material. His voice in my ear sent electricity through me.

I opened my eyes and took in the scene in front of me. A picturesque chocolate box cottage sat nestled in the woods with Glencoe's mountains rising behind it and a babbling river running alongside it.

The cottage looked a little worn, but the cherry red doors and ivy-covered walls made me melt.

'Is it an Airbnb? I love it. It's so cute.'

'No baby, I bought it.'

With a gasp, I rounded on Logan. 'No, you didn't?'

'I did.'

I pulled him toward it, my eyes like saucers, not caring in the slightest that the rain was making my hair stick to my face.

'It even has your little wood stack,' I said, brushing my fingers over the pile of firewood that leaned against one wall.

'I love it.'

'I love you,' he said, pulling me up against him and licking the rain from my lips before sliding his tongue into my mouth. 'I thought I could never have this. You showed me I can have anything if I try hard enough.'

'What about work?' I asked, wrapping my arms around his shoulders.

'I'm taking a back seat and handing the reins over to Maeve. We're going to formally join the Thompson and McGowan syndicates, with her and Cam leading both. I'll still be involved, but mostly, I'm all yours.'

'I like the sound of that,' I said, running my fingers through his wet hair and tugging lightly.

'I've ordered super internet for you too, so you can keep camming if you want too.'

I loved camming and loved being seen, but between Hugh and Tim, it had left me feeling unsafe.

'I don't know if I want to. Maybe if I can find a way to do it anonymously, and with you.'

'You know you'll never have to work if you don't want to. Or you can stay here and make and sell socks and cakes, or whatever your pretty little head dreams up.'

'I do like to be watched,' I said, trying to broach a subject I'd been unsure of. We'd done some kinky things together, but now that we were in a real relationship, I didn't know where I stood.

'Baby girl, I'll make all of your dreams come true. Right down to the absolute filth you crave. If you want to be watched, or fucked, or anything else, just let me know. I'm more than happy to share, as long as I'm the one who gets to keep you for good.'

'You wouldn't be jealous?'

'Of seeing you writhing in pleasure? Never. As long as it's agreed before it happens, I'm down for whatever sick little fantasies you want to explore.'

He led me into the cottage before stoking the log burner and getting the fire crackling and popping.

'Will you help me decorate it?' he asked. 'Or we can pay someone to come in and do it all.'

'I'd love to. Do I get my own drawer?'

'No, Valentina. You get the whole damn house. If you want to. Move in with me?'

'Really?'

'I don't want to go between my place and yours any more. I want to have you all to myself. You can keep the apartment with Lara if you want to, for when we visit the city.'

'What about your flipping massive mansion?'

'Ewen's going to keep living there, and it's going to always be kept for our family get-togethers, where any of us can stay when we want to. This can be our country digs.'

He sat down on the rug in front of the fire, his leg still stiff when he tried to fully bend it.

I straddled his lap and stole a kiss, melting against him as the heat from the fire licked at the side of my face.

"Is that a yes?' he asked.

'It's a yes, Daddy.'

'Now be a good girl and get out of your wet clothes so Daddy can christen his new rug.'

'The doctor said—'

He pulled my hair back harshly and bit at my neck while I whimpered. 'Fuck the doctor. If I don't fuck you, I might explode.'

Logan stretched me out around him by the fire, filling me until the day darkened into night and we both lay in an exhausted, sweaty heap in our new home.

CHAPTER FIFTY

LOGAN

Spring gave way to early summer as flowers bloomed to their fullest along the edge of the cottage. I'd left Valentina sleeping in our bed as I made a coffee, inhaling its deep scent, before heading out to the garden and grabbing an apple on route.

The early morning sun flooded the hills to the rear of our property, sending golden hues bouncing through the valley.

'Morning,' I said as my donkey, Rosie, came trotting toward the edge of his field, nudging at my pockets as I reached out to scratch her behind the ears. 'Alright, alright. Calm down. You know I've got it in my pocket.'

She stomped a hoof as I pulled out the apple and broke it in half, giving the first half to her as I sipped my coffee.

'Such a greedy girl.'

Breathing in the damp morning air, I closed my eyes and sighed happily. The months I'd spent in our cottage with Valentina were the best I'd ever had. I hadn't realised how heavy the responsibility of taking on my father's business had weighed on me. In stark contrast, Maeve thrived under it, working alongside her husband, Cam, as well as Tony and Nicole. She was truly creating a crime empire that rivalled those in Europe.

By the time I finished drinking my coffee while chatting to Rosie, chopped enough wood to power our extra large wood-fired hot tub, and made it back to the cottage, Valentina was up and the kitchen looked like it had been hit by a flour bomb.

'Jeez, what happened?' I asked as I washed out my cup and cleaned my hands.

'I turned the mixer power up too high before the eggs had incorporated enough and it sprayed the flour everywhere.'

Valentina was in a flap, cursing as she wiped at the counters.

'Hey, baby girl, slow down.'

'I don't have time to slow down. Everyone will be here in three hours and I still have a load to do.'

I slid behind her and pulled her back against me, nipping the spot on her neck which always made her melt. 'Let me help. I'll clean up while you finish making the cake. I can set out the sandwiches and pastries and such on the table while you have a shower. It'll all be okay.'

She took a breath and let her head rest back against my shoulder.

'Thank you. You always know how to take the stress off.'

'That I do.' Reaching under her apron, I slid my hand into her pyjama bottoms and cupped her in my palm. 'You don't do well when Daddy hasn't paid your cunt any attention, do you?'

'No, Daddy.'

'Do you need to come all over my fingers before we worry about the kitchen?'

'I don't know if we have time.'

Twirling my fingers over her clit made her gasp.

'There is always time for your pleasure, my love. You've been such a good girl getting everything ready. I think you deserve a treat. Now open your legs like a good slut and let me in.

Hooking one of her knees over my arm, I pulled her thighs

roughly apart and slipped my fingers inside her already wet pussy, fucking her with slow, deep strokes.

'That's it, sweetheart, grind on my fingers. Take what you need.'

'You feel so good, Daddy.' Her chest rose quickly as I worked her into a state.

'Always so fucking wet for me. I should give you my cock for being such a good girl.'

'Yes. Please?'

I laughed as I kissed her throat roughly. 'No time for that today. You'll have to beg me later.'

Her pussy clenched at my fingers as she neared her orgasm, writhing so prettily on my hand.

'So fucking needy. I love how desperate you are, Valentina. Can't go a day without my dick inside of you.'

Her breath hitched as I added a third finger and swept my thumb over her clit. 'Come for me, baby, fill Daddy's hand with your wetness.'

My fingers quickened inside her, her body jerking as I got rougher with her. She always came harder when I was rough.

'Daddy!' she yelped as I continued until she came hard around my fingers, moaning and clawing at my arms with her nails. I didn't let up until she sagged in my arms, the orgasm fading.

'There's my girl.' I turned her head and sought her lips, wiping my wet hand over them as she licked at my fingers.

'God, I fucking love the shit out of you,' I said as she grinned.

'Love you more,' she replied.

A few hours later and our open plan kitchen and sitting room were stuffed full of people. Lara, Valentina's mother, Lucille and Nicole were all squashed into the room amongst my siblings and their families for our official housewarming.

Nerves bit at my stomach as I watched Valentina playing the perfect hostess, adoring the chance to show off her baking skills and our cute little house.

The short little sundress she wore did ungodly things to me. Even as the months had passed, my desire for her hadn't waned, and with each passing day, my love for her grew more fierce.

'Lucille,' I said, as she passed me. 'Could I have a word?'

Her eyes narrowed for a moment before she nodded and followed me out the back door to our struggling vegetable patch.

'You know I love your daughter with every inch of my soul?'

'Mmm.' Valentina's mother had not fallen in love with me as fast as her daughter had.

'I'm going to ask her to marry me. Today. This isn't a request for permission, as there is no way I am willing to go on without proposing to her, but I hope that you'll give us your blessing. I know how much it would mean to her.'

Her shoulders dropped as she sighed before reaching up and patting my cheek. 'Logan, despite the age gap and the wholly wrong way you came into her life, I don't doubt for a moment that you adore her. But if you so much as hurt her, I'll skin you alive myself.'

I grinned and pulled her into a hug as she cleared her throat.

'Thank you. I promise I'll let no harm ever come to her again.'

'Go in and get your girl,' she said, folding her arms and leading the way back inside.

With her mother's blessing, I couldn't wait a single moment longer.

Pulling a single rose from where I had hidden it, I crept behind her and dropped to one knee. She continued to chat until she noticed the silence that had fallen around us. Following everyone's stares, she turned around before covering her mouth.

Holding out the rose, I licked my dry lips and spoke. 'Valentina Valetti, you came into my world like a hurricane, wrapping me up in you and holding me close. You are fierce, and sweet, and clever and you make me want to be a better man. A happier man. No dream is too big or too small with you in my life. This rose is from the place where you stole my heart. Back then it would have been frostbitten and decayed, cold and shrivelled, but now it blooms with a bright red fury like you do. You've transformed every part of my life, and brought me colour, fun, and beauty, replacing my loneliness and bitterness with nothing but good.'

Valentina sniffed as she lowered her tear covered hand and stroked my cheek tenderly.

'I love you Valentina, and I don't want another day to go by without the world knowing it. Baby, will you marry me?'

Her face broke out into a grin as she nodded. 'Fuck yeah I will.'

She flew into my arms as our loved ones clapped and cheered around us.

'I love you so much, Logan,' Valentina whispered into my ear.

Then we were swept up into the arms of our family as we celebrated long into the night.

EPILOGUE
VALENTINA

The summer sun warmed my naked body as I writhed. With my hands tied up above me to an overhead branch, I couldn't do much other than pant and wriggle as Logan dragged the cut roses across my skin.

'Isn't it amazing how roses can be so delicate, so soft, but also have such a nasty bite?' Logan said as he rounded my body and scratched my skin with the sharp thorns before flipping the flower and using the soft petals to tease my nipples.

'Please, Daddy, I need you so bad,' I whimpered as Logan leaned in while taking the thorns to my nipple and swallowing down my cries with a sweep of his mouth over mine.

'Not yet, my love. I told you I had a special treat for you? Didn't I?'

'You did.'

I'd been so excited to be back at Rosenhall for the beginning portion of our honeymoon that I hadn't imagined there was a further surprise.

'I've brought some friends to play with you. I hope you'll be a good girl and show them how much you like cock.'

My eyes went to the hedges that made up the central square of the rose garden, where Logan had me restrained. Three masked men approached, wearing only trousers and half face masks that concealed the upper portion of their faces. One figure I recognised instantly, while the other two were a complete mystery.

Alfie was back to play.

'What do you say, princess? Ready for Daddy to share you with my friends? I've told them all about what a sweet little cunt you have. They're eager for a taste.'

A jolt of electricity shot straight to my core at the sight of the three of them flanking me. 'I'm ready.'

Logan lifted one of my legs and spread my thighs wide for the men. 'Look how wet she is at the sight of you all. My delicious little whore wants to take you all.'

He moved behind me, reaching up to loosen my hands as he whispered into my ear. 'Enjoy yourself my love, remember you can use your safe word and I'll make it all stop.'

Logan pushed me to my knees on the grass, using his foot to spread my thighs wide. 'Touch yourself for them, Valentina. Show them what you'll do for their attention.'

Swallowing hard, I slid my hand between my legs as I arched back, rubbing myself for them. Logan continued to use the rose to torture me, alternating between soft caresses and sharp thorny bites. As I touched myself faster, feeling the building pressure, Logan crouched behind me and fisted my hair.

'Look at them. They know exactly what a dirty little girl you are. You're going to take all of them for me, love. In your mouth, your fists, your pussy and your ass. You'll be so full when you're pleasing all my friends. They're going to fill you up with cum until you've drained us all dry.'

'Fuck,' I moaned. 'Daddy, I'm going to come.'

Logan snatched my hand up away from my pussy as I trembled in his arms, arching myself against nothing but air as my pending orgasm dissipated.

'Sorry, baby girl, but I need you desperate for them.'

'I am,' I whimpered as he nodded at his friends.

Tilting my head as they circled me, Logan gripped my hair. 'Open up, sweetheart.'

The masked men dropped their trousers and reached out to me, their fingers stroking my jaw and pinching my nipples as Alfie slipped his pierced dick into my mouth. With a moan I sucked him eagerly, Logan whispering sweet nothings into my ear.

The three men standing before me pressed the tips of their dicks together as I slid my tongue and mouth from one to another, stopping to take one into my throat whenever they pressed against my lips.

Logan pushed my ass up as he slid his cock along my soaked pussy, lining himself up and filling me as Alfie pressed his cock deep into my throat. One of the other men dropped to the floor and licked at my clit as Logan slowly pumped himself in and out of me. The sensations were heady, as so many body parts connected with me. When the last man knelt beside me and reached to kiss Logan, I lost myself, coming hard in their arms as I watched Logan kiss another man. It was too fucking hot.

'You got any lube?' someone asked as my mind blurred, my body quaking at their continued touches.

'Over by the tree,' Logan said, picking me up and placing me on Alfie's cock, kissing me as I slid over the impressively pierced dick and moaned. I wrapped my arms around Alfie's neck as Logan let me go, grinding myself on him.

"Congratulations, little demon, all wifed up,' Alfie said into my hair as his fingers dug into my hips. 'Fuck, I forgot how good you felt.'

'God,' I groaned as Alfie thrust into me while someone fingered my ass from behind.

'Not God, but I'll be your devil,' Alfie said, kissing my neck as I tensed. 'Relax. They're going to fuck your arse. You liked it last time, remember?'

I held my breath as one of the men lined his dick up with my ass, stretching my tight hole over the tip before thrusting in fully. His groan in my ear set me alight. I had a stranger's cock in my ass while Alfie filled my pussy. A hot mouth closed over one of my nipples, sucking and nipping at it while I writhed between the men.

Logan stood beside us, stroking his dick as he watched me. 'Look at you, baby girl, so nearly airtight. Just need to take Daddy's big dick in your throat.'

His tip slid against my mouth, and I moaned as I felt Alfie's tongue slide against mine as we both licked along Logan's length. My body jerked as the man fucking my ass found his pace, his cock grinding against Alfie's inside me as I stretched around them.

'Look at you two,' Logan growled as we continued to lick and suck at his dick, our mouths meeting in a kiss around his thick tip. 'Dirty little whores.'

Alfie's fingers tightened on my hips as he took Logan into his throat before pulling back as I took a turn.

'Yes, baby girl,' Logan moaned as he forced his way deep into my mouth. I'd gotten better at swallowing him down over the months, but it still made my eyes water as he pushed his way into my throat. 'Fuck, your hot little throat always feels so damn good.'

Logan gripped my hair as he fed his cock into my throat again and again, biting his lip as Alfie tongued his balls.

I'd never been so fucking turned on in my life. Every hole stuffed at my husband's demand.

The man behind me groaned as he fucked harder, a punishing pace on my ass that sent me hurtling back into another orgasm. Coming hard around so many dicks increased the intensity to a new level as I bucked and squirmed against them.

'Fuck, little demon.' Alfie said as Logan pulled out of my mouth, and let Alfie claim my lips with a lust filled kiss as he unloaded into my pussy. With Alfie pumping me full of cum as I quaked around the men, I went to jelly.

'You're not done yet, baby girl,' Logan said as the man removed himself from my ass, only to be replaced seconds later with another dick. Logan shifted us around so that the man filling my ass lay under me while Alfie slipped out of my pussy, his cum seeping out of me with each thrust of the dick in my ass.

Logan knelt between me and licked up the hot cum leaking out of me, sucking and teasing me until I was needy again. Seeing another man's cum on his tongue made me almost pass out with want.

'Matt and I will work to fit both of our dicks in your pretty little pussy while James stretches out your asshole for me. You're going to take us all, Valentina.'

I nodded as James reached around me and pulled my hands up over our heads while Matt and Logan positioned themselves between my thighs, rubbing the heads of their dicks up and down my slit. Taking turns, they dipped into me again and again until I was begging for them to fill me up.

'Please Daddy, please fuck me. Please force me open with your dicks,' I panted the words as Alfie laid beside me, propping himself up as he toyed with my nipples.

'Look at you, little demon, a perfect fucktoy for all these men. Spreading your thighs and taking all of them like a good cum slut.'

'We're so proud of you,' Logan said as they worked both of their cocks into my pussy at the same time.

I couldn't breathe. The pressure was intense as I burned, the stretch almost too painful.

Alfie placed his mouth over mine, kissing me deeply as he muffled my cries with his tongue. His fingers found my clit, making circles over it as his tongue invaded my mouth.

'Look down,' Alfie said as both Logan and Matt moved in tandem, their groans making me hot. 'Look at how hot it is when they fill you.'

I glanced down between my thighs to see my lips spread wide as their cocks filled me. It was a filthy, erotic image I knew I'd never forget. The way their cocks rubbed against one another made me pant.

Alfie pulled my mouth back on his as he touched me until I fell into an orgasm that seemed endless. Fire shot through my veins as I shook in their arms, my body jerking involuntarily as Alfie gulped down my cries. The man in my arse came first, his hands sliding down my body and pinching my nipples viciously as he did. When my pussy clamped down on Logan and Matt, Alfie slide down my body and took my clit in his mouth, sucking it relentlessly as I squealed and bucked against him.

'Fuck, baby girl. You're going to make Daddy fill you up,' Logan said as he thrust quicker and harder, Matt's eyes rolling back as Logan's dick stroked him to orgasm inside of me. As Logan thrust into my over stuffed cunt, he leaned down and grasped me to him, squishing Alfie's face into my clit as he kissed me.

'I. Fucking. Love. You,' he said as his body tensed, filling me.

'Take all my cum, my dirty little whore.'

My body thrummed as we lay in a pile, spent as we caught our breath.

Eventually, they all slipped their cocks from my well-fucked body as torrents of cum leaked from me and onto the grass. Matt and James slipped away without me caring as Logan lifted me into his arms while Alfie pet my hair.

'Welcome to married life, you two,' he said with a devilish grin. 'Never thought I'd see the day a woman could tame him.'

I didn't have any words to offer, my mind on another dimension.

'I'm the luckiest man alive,' Logan said as he carried me back to the manor house, pressing sweet kisses into my neck.

'I'm the luckiest woman alive,' I murmured into ear as we crossed the threshold. 'There's nowhere I'd rather be.'

'I'll never let you be anywhere but here, sweet Cherry. You're mine.'

THE MCGOWAN SERIES

Ewen and Anna

ALSO BY EFFIE

Alfie, Darling

Heart of Wrath

Theirs for Christmas

A NOTE FROM THE AUTHOR

Thank you for reading Logan and Valentina's story, the fourth book in my Scots mafia series. I really enjoyed writing Valentina's unwavering relentlessness in her pursuit of Logan, and his struggle to be loyal to his father's dream.

Just Ewen to go! And our pal Alfie might be back to visit too...

A huge thank you to my wonderful family. My husband who doesn't sulk too much when I ignore him for days on end to meet a deadline and my lovely children who support me even though there's no way they'll ever be allowed to read Mummy's books.

Thank you to you, for reading this book, and to all my readers and supporters. It's thanks to all of you that my writing dream is becoming a reality, and I am endlessly grateful.

Love, Effie

If you'd like to keep up with my books and me, you can find me on TikTok and Instagram (@effiecampbellauthor), Facebook (effiecampbellauthor) and Amazon.

If you enjoyed Dark Desires, I'd love a review on Amazon or Goodreads, or wherever you enjoy reviewing books.

Subscribe to my mailing list for new releases and news or join my reader group to chat to like minded smut readers.

Made in United States
North Haven, CT
09 January 2024

47217218R00153